Praise for *When In Doubt, Add Butter*

"Harbison dazzles in her latest, a perfect blend of chick lit and women's fiction. . . . Absolutely first-rate."
—*Publishers Weekly* (starred review)

"A lovable heroine and an engaging cast of eccentrics make for a cheerful summer read."
—*Kirkus Reviews*

"Harbison's airy prose, likable heroine, colorful characters, and engaging story are sure to appeal to fans of Jennifer Weiner, Jane Green, and Emily Giffin. Think of *When in Doubt, Add Butter* as a soufflé. It's a tasty dish. . . ."
—Examiner.com

"Harbison's cast of characters is delightful."
—*SheKnows* Book Lounge

"Delicious, just like dessert."
—*People*

Praise for *Always Something There to Remind Me*

"Harbison serves up a deliciously light blend of 1980s nostalgia and women's fiction. She packs the teenage flashbacks with age-appropriate miscommunications and emotional indecision, and cleverly uses [a] present-day story line to bring Erin to a point of understanding.

Harbison raises the emotional stakes and gives this story a little more bite without losing her fun, breezy style."

—*Publishers Weekly*

"*Always Something There to Remind Me* is a riveting look at the tender agony of first love. Full of self-awareness and scathing wit, Beth Harbison deftly contrasts teenage romantic idealism with the reality of growing up. Touching, truthful, and profoundly satisfying, Harbison delivers her finest work yet."   —Jen Lancaster, *New York Times* bestselling author of *If You Were Here*

More Praise for Beth Harbison

"A fast and fun read . . . sure to appeal to anyone who came of age in the late 1980s."

—*Library Journal* on *Thin, Rich, Pretty*

"Told with Beth Harbison's knack for thirty- and forty-something nostalgia and heartwarming humor, *Thin, Rich, Pretty* will strike a chord with any woman who has ever looked in the mirror, or the bank account, and said, 'If only . . .'"   —*The Province* (Vancouver)

"Fun nostalgia for those of us who loved Bonne Bell Lip Smackers & Sun-In."

—*Fort Worth Star-Telegram* on *Hope in a Jar*

"Harbison continues to wow readers with particular chick-lit charm and genuine characters."

—*Booklist* on *Hope in a Jar*

"Harbison's writing is zingy and funny, and her light touch allows her to get away with the ridiculous situations in this nutty beach read."

—*Publishers Weekly* on *Secrets of a Shoe Addict*

"Kick off your Keds (unless you're driving) and meet a motley group of D.C. women who bond over designer shoes. It's chick lit with heart *and* sole."

—*People* on *Shoe Addicts Anonymous*

"I would happily recommend *Shoe Addicts Anonymous* to anyone who loves shoes . . . or to smart, funny, realistic women."

—Jennifer Weiner

"Readers will root for these four plucky women. Like the designer shoes that pepper its pages, this book is pleasing and stylish. This frothy confection is sure to fly off the shelves this summer."

—*Booklist* on *Shoe Addicts Anonymous*

Also by Beth Harbison

Secrets of a Shoe Addict

Shoe Addicts Anonymous

Hope in a Jar

Thin, Rich, Pretty

Always Something There to Remind Me

When in Doubt, Add Butter

Beth Harbison

ST. MARTIN'S GRIFFIN

New York

WHEN IN DOUBT, ADD BUTTER. Copyright © 2012 by Beth Harbison. All rights reserved. Printed in the United States of America. For information, address St. Martin's Press, 175 Fifth Avenue, New York, N.Y. 10010.

www.stmartins.com

THE LIBRARY OF CONGRESS
HAS CATALOGED THE HARDCOVER EDITION AS FOLLOWS:

Harbison, Elizabeth M.
    When in doubt, add butter / Beth Harbison. — 1st ed.
        p. cm.
    ISBN 978-0-312-59909-6 (hardcover)
    ISBN 978-1-250-01502-0 (e-book)
    1. Cooks—Fiction.   I. Title.
    PS3558.A564W47 2012
    813'.54—dc23

                                        2012007423

        ISBN 978-0-312-59908-9 (trade paperback)

St. Martin's Griffin books may be purchased for educational, business, or promotional use. For information on bulk purchases, please contact Macmillan Corporate and Premium Sales Department at 1-800-221-7945 extension 5442 or write specialmarkets@macmillan.com.

First St. Martin's Griffin Edition: June 2013

10 9 8 7 6 5 4 3 2 1

To Jami Nasi, Melody Winnig, and Jill Jacobs Stilwell, who kept me sane(ish) during the writing of this book in a way bigger than they will ever know. I honestly don't know how to thank you enough.

Jamie Taylor, what can I even say? And what *could* I say that wouldn't make you say, "Shut up, Mouthy"? You're the best!

Finally, Mr. Bigosi . . . you're the bomb. Like it or not, I love you. And you don't know it but you saved me.

Acknowledgments

The past couple of years have brought a lot of good and some not-so-good, but the greatest blessing of all was having the support of my friends no matter what. There were nights when I would write to you guys and send my thoughts out into the darkness hoping you wouldn't think I was nuts, and, wow, you stepped up so much I am humbled. So, in no particular order, thank you: Annelise Robey, Cinda O'Brien, Jen Enderlin, Al Dobrenchuk, Meg Ruley, Connie Jo Gernhofer, Sara Poska, Carolyn Clemens, John Obrien, Steffi Alexander, Mimi Elias, Shannon Perry, Sean Osborn, Pips Harbison, Chandler Schwede, Stef Moreno, Nicki Singer, Lucinda Denton, Helen Carrese, Annie Sacasa, Martina Chaconas, Russell Nuce, Robyn Dunlap, Maureen Quinn, Kristin Reakoff, Patrice Luneski, Chris McLean, Kate Genovese, Jenna Novotni, Kristin

Murphy, Brian Hazel, Mary Kay McComas, Anita Arnold, Basia K. Atkins, Jacquelyn Taylor, Elaine Fox, and Connie Atkins. Wow, that's a big list. How lucky I am to have such friends and family!

Ideally, life is made of moments, not speculation about the possibilities of the future or memories of a past that can't be changed. Thank you all for the wonderful moments. I will always be grateful.

When in Doubt, Add Butter

Chapter 1

When I was twelve, a fortune-teller at the Herbert Hoover Junior High School carnival said to me: "Gemma Craig, you listen to me. Do *not* get married. Ever. If you do, you'll end up cooking for a man who'd rather eat at McDonald's; doing laundry for a man who sweats like a rabid pig, then criticizes you for not turning his T-shirts right side out; and cleaning the bathroom floor after a man whose aim is so bad, he can't hit a hole the size of a watermelon—"

This man sounded disgusting.

"—make your own money and be independent. Having kids is fine, but get married and you will be miserable for the rest of your life. I promise you, *the rest of your life.*"

This chilling prediction stayed with me long after I realized that the fortune-teller was, in fact, Mrs. Rooks, the

PTA president and neighbor who always gave out full-sized 3 Musketeers bars on Halloween, and that her husband had left her that very morning for a cliché: a young, vapid, blond bombshell. Mrs. Rooks had four kids, and at the time, I thought of her as really old, and I didn't quite get why she cared so much if she was married anymore or not.

She was thirty-seven.

I was thirty-seven last year.

But for the most part, I have followed that sage wisdom she imparted, whether it came from a place of deep inspiration or, maybe, from a place of bitter day drunkenness. It had an impact on me either way.

Dating was fine. I love men. I love sex. I love having someone to banter with, flirt with, play romantic tag with, and finally yield to. Many, many times I have thought, in the beginning of a relationship, that *maybe* this guy could be different and the relationship might last against the odds my young brain had laid out.

But inevitably things soured for me, usually in the form of boredom, and *always* within two months. Seriously. This was consistent enough for my friends to refer to it as *two months too long.*

The good thing about a breakup at two months is that there usually isn't a lot of acrimony or anguish involved. The bad thing is that it gets tiresome after a while. Honestly, I'm a normal woman, I'd *love* to be in love. I'd love to have a family to take care of and to surround me as I navigate the years.

But once I hit thirty-seven, I had to wonder if that was really in the cards for me.

And if that was the case, I was okay with it because I had a career I loved that allowed me some of the better parts of June Cleaver–dom, along with the ability to hang up the apron at the end of the day and be my own, single self.

I am a private chef.

Being hired to cook for people is really different from standing around a kitchen with friends, drinking wine and making snacks. It's different from making a whole Thanksgiving dinner for family. It's vastly different, even, from cooking for strangers at the soup kitchen, where the pride of creating something delicious is just as compelling but somehow . . . easier. Less judgmental.

Cooking for people in their homes *can* be like cooking for friends, but more often than that, it's like cooking for the meanest teacher in elementary school: someone you want to shrink away from, hide from. Someone you hope to God won't call on you or make you speak in front of everyone else. Someone you're pretty sure will yell and scream at you if you do one little thing wrong.

The many scenarios include—but are not limited to—taking the fall for a failed party ("the food wasn't good enough"), taking the blame for a neglected hostess ("you shouldn't speak with the guests even if they talk to you first"), shouldering the blame for the burden of unused ingredients ("I have to do something with the rest of these onions now, thanks a lot"), and other failures of life in general ("my husband doesn't want to come home on time for dinner, but if you made something he couldn't resist, then he would!").

Fortunately, most of the time I'm treated as if I'm invisible. Which is okay with me, except the dodging out of the way of people and not making eye contact can sometimes be challenging.

Still, I prefer that to being faced with accusations.

At first, I didn't see this coming. I always loved to cook, and got pretty good at it early on—though a few major mishaps come to mind (root beer extract in cupcakes was . . . a mistake)—but it never occurred to me that I could make a living this way. I guess that seemed too domestic for me at the time.

When I was working in Manhattan right after college, my mother tried to convince me, time and again, to meet a nice man and settle down. She wanted me to open a retirement account, and my legs, and start a future and family.

Not me. After what I'd been through, I think I was seeking some form of anonymity. What I would have said at the time was that I simply wanted to be free to go wherever the wind blew me. Like I was just a whimsical spirit, blowing through life and open to everything.

The problem was, the wind wasn't a reliable headhunter, so I moved from one go-nowhere job to another, proving my mother's fears more correct every day. Every time I found a job I liked, something happened to ruin it: like when I temped in the props department for a local morning show in the city, and I mistakenly got a Cat in the Hat costume out for a celebrity guest who was supposed to be Uncle Sam for a special Fourth of July segment, but in my defense, the electricity was out and it was very hard to see in the storeroom. (And who would have thought they'd have a Cat in the Hat costume at all? Seriously, how often could that have come in handy?)

When I hit twenty-six, I started to question if I was being irresponsible and immature by continuing my "free-spirited" ways. To my mother's delight, I settled into some good corporate jobs with excellent benefits. Three years in the research department at the local CBS affiliate led to two years at the Discovery Channel—and a routine rut that would have bored even the most patient yogi in Tibet.

But as I settled into a routine life and watched the years fly by like the calendar pages in a movie, I started to feel *old*. That was all. Not pious, correct, responsible, or anything else, just *old*. Suddenly I realized that actors and actresses and singers and even pro football players were *younger* than me.

Ten years ago, my life was *I have plenty of time to figure out what I want to do.*

Five years ago, I reached *Hmmmmm*.

Two years ago, I found myself teetering on the edge of *Uh-oh*, and looking straight down the barrel of *Oh, shit.*

I quit my tedious job, got myself a place that was tiny and modest but it was *my own*, and I followed my passion into a cooking career. I loved it. I *love* it. I'm my own boss, I meet interesting people all the time, I'm never bored, and whatever small part of me has a maternal instinct to take care of people is satisfied by nourishing them.

Then leaving.

Monday nights, I cooked for the Van Houghtens. The pluses included: the location (Chevy Chase), beautiful kitchen (the marble counters, stainless steel *everything,* and one of those fridges that blend into the cabinetry), and the stability of the job. I'd been doing it for a year now. Minuses included Angela's attitude, and the fact that they had the ugliest pantry you've ever seen in your life.

Not cosmetically; it was the stuff inside it. Angela had very specific and spare tastes. Think of the fussiest eater you've ever known, and Angela made them look like a glutton. Honestly. There was so much she *couldn't*—or, more appropriately, *wouldn't*—eat that it was astonishing that the woman even had functional bones, much less any flesh on them. And really, there was very little of that.

No dairy. In fact, no "moo food" of any sort: no steaks, milk, sour cream, cheese, and check every package of bread for signs of whey, casein, and so forth.

No onions. Not dried, not powdered, not within three feet of anything she eats because "the essence will permeate it" and it will have to be thrown away.

No soy. Including soy lecithin, mono-diglyceride, guar gum, even citric acid.

No nuts. No nut derivatives. Nothing that was processed in a plant anywhere near nuts, even if the plant was in Georgia and Jimmy Carter lived five hundred miles away.

No honey. Nothing even vaguely connected with bees,

including certain plants. So, yes, it was easy to avoid honey, less so to avoid anything Angela considered "honey related," but I did it.

No cinnamon or "warm" spice.

No garlic.

No fun.

Every time I looked at Peter and Stephen, her unfortunate and emaciated husband and son, I just felt an overwhelming urge to make them a pot roast with caramelized onions and a big ol' coconut cream pie.

"Peter," Angela would coo, narrowing her eyes and scrunching up her nose at him as he reached for another meager portion of romaine lettuce (beets were too sugary, radishes too "hot on the stomach," whatever that meant, and onions already established to be out of the question), "do you *really* think you need more?"

It was as if she were talking to her son and not her husband. Yet it didn't hold any maternal kindness. Just bossiness.

Once in a while he'd say yes, and eat it anyway, but for the most part, he'd set the bowl down with a dull thud and level a burning look at her once she looked back down at the bowl she was slowly working her way through. I like to think that was only when he had a witness—me—and that normally he'd tell her exactly where to stuff it. It's hard to understand why a smart, hot, successful man would spend his life being whipped by a switch like her.

Perhaps it was because of Stephen. How he had gestated in Angela's slight body, I cannot imagine. Maybe that was before she adopted her radical diet. But at six years old now, he'd never known any other diet, I'm pretty sure.

In fact, maybe the post-pregnancy weight was the *reason* she adopted her radical diet. I don't know. All I know is that in their pantry, where any normal American kid might find Oreos (or Newman-O's—I can be flexible about hydrogenated oils and organic ingredients), there was some kind of faux melba toast, made from spelt, and unseasoned almond butter. That was his after-school snack.

You just know if that kid ever went to a birthday party and got a bite of the manna that is sheet cake from Costco, he'd never want to come home. I can picture him there, in a wild-eyed eating frenzy, face smeared in icing, wondering why on earth his parents never told him of this bliss before.

It's like those people who grow up without TV. Move them into the real world and plop them in front of *Wheel of Fortune,* and they're not getting up until the national anthem is playing. If it's on cable, the only hope of having them move is if nature calls.

Believe me, I had a roommate like that once. I don't know how he managed to avoid TV into his thirties, but when I was watching *The O.C.,* I'd feel him creeping up behind me, and he'd just stand there, eyes glued to the set, like he was a caveman wondering at the magic box with the tiny people in it.

"Want to sit down, Darryl?" I'd ask, because there's nothing creepier than someone standing behind you, rasping their breath through their perennially stuffy nose. Especially if you're eating a bowl of popcorn, as I usually was.

"No, no," he'd say vaguely, eyes dilating like something out of a 1950s alien movie.

And there he'd stay.

"Seriously, Darryl. Since you're gonna watch, anyway, why don't you just sit?" Elsewhere. Anywhere. Not there.

"I'm on my way to the kitchen."

And forty-five minutes later, he'd finally make it the other three yards to the kitchen, where he would prepare some vile midnight snack along the lines of a bologna and onion sandwich. I'd like to think his distraction by the show was what caused this revolting food choice, but alas, it was just one more slightly off thing about him.

Anyway, Mondays at the Van Houghtens' were challenging. To say the least.

But Angela Van Houghten was also the events coordinator for the country club where my most profitable work was—usually one banquet every other week, though sometimes it was more—and that made the pressure of working for Angela that much greater. I needed to keep her happy so she'd keep recommending me to people who were having parties.

Tuesday was a lot more pleasant.

Tuesday was Paul McMann, a lawyer I never, ever even caught a glimpse of, but for a long time I imagined him to look a lot like Fred Flintstone, based on his culinary tastes.

Paul—or Mr. Tuesday, as I like to think of him—is a big

fan of June Cleaver–style comfort food. Pure back-of-the-box stuff: noodleburger casserole, onion soup mix meat loaf, beef pot pie, chicken 'n' biscuits, Philadelphia cheesecake, and so on. He probably would have been perfectly happy if I made him Hamburger Helper every week.

Butter, sour cream, white flour, cheddar cheese, canned Campbell's tomato soup, macaroni noodles . . . all that stuff that was missing on Mondays, I got to make up for with Mr. Tuesday. Even iceberg lettuce, which is nutritionally dull, but culinarily fun to slice and embellish, was A-OK with him.

I *loved* cooking for Mr. Tuesday.

He worked late *all the time*, it seemed. I never saw him, though I did arrive between five and six, and I suppose it was possible his workday started at noon. Nevertheless, he was a mystery to me.

For example, he was clearly a man's man: no frills, no fuss. It showed in his food tastes, his books, and especially in his choice of very spare décor. It works for me. I really kind of enjoy the clean wood and leather feel of his apartment. Decidedly masculine, but for some reason I find it reassuring. It's like sitting in an executive office, waiting for a big inheritance check from an elderly and unknown relative to be cut and cashed.

So, whereas I usually do most of the prep work for my people at home and take the food to their places to heat and serve it (no, this isn't strictly legal, since I don't have a commercially licensed kitchen, but no one really cares), I usually take all the raw ingredients to Mr. Tuesday's place in Friendship Heights and spend hours relishing in the glorious peace of it. Sometimes I'd take the remote from its usual spot and blast some Wham! through his mounted Bose speakers, and sometimes I'd just crack open a window and listen to the nothing outside.

Always—*always*—I would look forward to the notes he'd leave for me.

After I'd noted my disdain for peas, which I regard as fake vegetables since they are green but almost as starchy and sugary as Skittles, he wrote:

All I'm saying is give peas a chance.

His response to the appetizers I'd left for a party he was having for his office staff:

Everything was great, but I especially loved the things that I know weren't Snausages but looked just like them. Is it unreasonable to ask for them with dinner sometime?

They were chicken and sage sausagettes that I got from a local butcher and wrapped in homemade pretzel dough, minus the salt but painted with butter. They are incredible, so I gave him points for good taste *and* I gave him Chickens in Throws, as he later jokingly referred to them, in a freezer bag the next week so he could have them whenever he wanted them.

And on one memorable occasion, he taped a hundred-dollar bill to a broken Corningware casserole dish I'd left with him and wrote on a Post-it:

I hope this wasn't your grandmother's or some other sentimental antique. I also hope you're wearing shoes because the vacuum cleaner hasn't worked the same since I accidentally sucked up a toupee. Not mine. I'll explain over a beer if we ever meet.

My guess was that he probably had a lot of stories I'd enjoy over a beer if we ever met.

Other than that, though, the guy was a mystery. I had a pretty good handle on most of the people I worked for—if nothing else, you can tell a lot about people by the things they surround themselves with in their homes—but Mr. Tuesday had very few clues to his personality in the main part of his apartment, and I'd never been into his bedroom or anything. Essentially, it was like trying to figure out something about the last person who'd been in your hotel room.

Wednesday was a different story. Wednesday was Lex Prather, who was usually there for at least part of the time I was. Personality-wise, he seemed to be the exact opposite of Mr. Tuesday, flamboyant where Tuesday was understated. Social, where Tuesday seemed to just be working all the time. But Lex was almost as much fun to cook for, though his tastes were far more highfalutin.

Until a year and a half ago, he lived with his mother in this two-bedroom flat in the old Westchester, off Mass

Avenue. She was like Perle Mesta, and he was Felix Unger—they must have been quite a pair. Anyway, when she passed away, he hired me to cook all his old favorites, which consisted of the kind of fussy white tablecloth dishes one might have found on the menu of the *Titanic*. Shrimp Louis, oysters Rockefeller, Waldorf salad; even the occasional molded Jell-O dish incongruously made it onto the menu. He apparently had no problem drawing the line at mint jelly, however.

Lex is tall and thin, and always impeccably dressed, which is appropriate, since he owns the venerable old Simon's Department Store downtown. It outlived both Woodward & Lothrop and Garfinckel's department stores, though I believe its reputation might be wobbling a bit now in the shadow of Nordstrom and everything you can find in Tysons Corner and the Galleria.

Anyway, the movie version of Lex could be perfectly played by Tony Randall. He is of completely indeterminate sexual orientation—though by "indeterminate" I mean that I don't know if he's gay or completely asexual; straight does not appear to be an option, although it's *possible* I'm wrong about that, I suppose.

A social butterfly, Lex often had me cooking for his mystery book group or his annual Christmas, New Year's, May Day, Fourth of July, Labor Day, and Halloween parties.

The upshot is that Lex had champagne tastes and a champagne budget. This made him pretty fun to cook for in and of itself, but he was also just a really great guy and I enjoyed seeing him every time. That's a luxury I don't always have with my clients, and it's particularly nice since work is basically the only social contact I have at all.

Which takes us to Thursday.

Thursday nights were with the Oleksei family, which was sheer chaos. Not really *bad* chaos, necessarily, just *crazy* chaos. The Oleksei family consisted of a grandfather, Vlad, who was clearly the patriarch of the family, often holding court in a mysterious back room I never saw but from which people would come and go at all hours, often leaving looking fearful or even in tears.

I half suspected that they were part of the Russian Mafia.

Seriously.

They made me a little nervous sometimes.

Vlad Oleksei's wife had died years earlier, leaving him with three strapping sons—now in their thirties and forties—and a handwritten recipe book I could not read because it was in Russian. Fortunately, my sister's boyfriend worked in the Russian department at American University and was translating the recipes as best he could, though the metric translation was still a bit of a challenge for me.

The Oleksei sons—Borya, Serge, and Viktor—were all nice enough to me, and always politely appreciative of the food I prepared, but there was something . . . *off* about them, too. They owned a dry cleaning and tailoring store, which I knew from *The Jeffersons* could be profitable, but it was just hard to picture the three of them going into one little dry cleaner every day and whistling as they busily worked out a stain in the collar of a shirt.

Nevertheless, assuming that wasn't a cover for their actual work with the Russian mob, that was what they did.

Viktor was the only one who was married. His wife was American and stood out in that family like a sore thumb—blond, big-lipped, brash, and boisterous. It was hard to imagine how she lived in such a traditional old-world atmosphere. I could picture her much more easily in a football jersey, tailgating with a bunch of burly blond lumberjack types, than with this dark, moody family.

Fridays I had the Lemurras in Georgetown.

What can I say about Marie Lemurra?

For one thing, she was a social climber to the nth degree. In the three short months I'd worked for her, I'd watched her try to get in with politicians, a few former B-list movie stars who now lived in or outside D.C., and most recently, local famewhores on the D.C. *True Wife Stories* reality show.

For another thing, she seemed to hate me, though that *had* to be impossible, given that she knew me *only* in a professional context and even that involved me doing her bidding and not arguing. Nevertheless, she was a woman who didn't seem satisfied with acquiescence of any sort; she wanted it to include at least a small measure of pain. I think Marie Lemurra needed other people to be wrong so that she, herself, could feel right.

It wasn't an ideal work situation, believe me, but I don't

think very many people among us would say their work is always 100 percent awesome.

Marie Lemurra, and those like her, was the price I had to pay for having a job I otherwise loved.

So that was my week right now: the Van Houghtens, Mr. Tuesday, Lex, the Olekseis, and the Lemurras. They ran the gamut, in every way.

With the banquet work added on the weekends, my life felt full and secure.

Famous last words, huh?

Chapter 2

This time, it wasn't my fault.

I mean, seriously, who the hell owns a peacock in *Georgetown*?

I had worked for the Lemurras for three months, every Friday night, and had *never* encountered anything living on their property, though their premium lot in the middle of the city certainly had room for undetected livestock. I was surprised once by what I still contend was some kind of werewolf there.

But that was ages ago, and when I pulled up to cater their biggest party of autumn, no one warned me to *keep an eye out for the fucking peacock*.

I mean if you had just acquired an exotic pet that no one in their right mind would expect to see someplace so incongruous, wouldn't you think to give everyone a heads-up? I'm sure the place that sold the peacock *must* have had some sort of PEACOCK AT PLAY signs to put by the driveway, like those green turtle things that warn drivers to slow down because of children running in the streets.

On top of that, if the exotic pet in question had a tendency to be sexually attracted to blue cars, and you knew your private chef was going to show up, as she had every week for three months, in her blue Toyota, wouldn't that be another thing you'd take into immediate consideration? *Hey, let's tell Gemma to watch out for the peacock.*

I would have.

But there was not a word of warning. Just like that time they had a guest who was deathly allergic to onion and they didn't mention it until her husband was frantically searching for the EpiPen as she turned red and struggled to breathe.

All I know is that one minute I was maneuvering my car toward the kitchen door so I could carry the thirty Cornish game hens—and accoutrements—into the house, and the next thing I knew, there was a little scraping sound on the bumper that I took to be a bit of the bramble that littered the wooded property.

Because frankly, you don't immediately think, *Wait a minute . . . I know that sound. That's the sound of a peacock trying to mount and sexually dominate my bumper.* Or even that a peacock might be territorially jealous of said car, viewing it as a romantic rival, which is something, I kid you not, I have since learned in my extensive research on peacocks.

Of course, I prefer to think Pepe died happy. I mean, at least he thought he was getting laid. That's good, right?

Especially since, as soon as the feathers began to fly, I knew I'd just lost my job.

After the thrashing and hysteria ended—Marie Lemurra's, not Pepe's; you will be relieved to know that he went quickly and quietly after his few scratchy advances toward my car— I had to go into the house and prepare the meal anyway.

Fortunately, Marie was very aware of all eyes being on her, so she didn't allow her anger toward me to continue bursting forth. The tension was unmistakable, however. I would be amazed if anyone there didn't feel it.

Then again, there was always an edge to Marie, so anyone around her would have been hard-pressed to determine exactly what her problem was at any given time.

Mishaps like this were rare, thank goodness, but they *did* happen. People were usually very happy with my work. I can't remember the last time I had a complaint. (I mean one that didn't involve running over exotic pets, anaphylactic shock I had no way of preventing, or on one unfortunate occasion, a drunken spouse making a pass at me . . . and no, it wasn't the husband.)

If the night had not involved a dinner party, I have no doubt that I would have taken a bath on this one. The way I worked was to buy the ingredients myself, then get reimbursement for them, along with my pay, at the end of the night.

In this case, it was a party for thirty, including Marie and two cast members from *The Real Famewhores of D.C.* or whatever the show was called. Marie had been fervently hoping the whole event would be filmed and included on the show in order to increase her screen time. Last year, she'd already made several appearances, backstabbing one person or another—at the time, she'd been tagged on-screen only as MARIE L—but then one of the cast members had grown popular enough to get her own show and there was room for one more in the regular cast, and Marie got the gig.

The camera crew had been to her house several times, including tonight, but filming never guaranteed the scene would actually be aired. This, of course, made Marie the number one most attentive fan, intently watching for any sign of herself, even if it was just her overbleached hair dipping out of the corner of the shot at Columbia Country Club's banquet hall.

Once, when I'd arrived at her house for a small dinner party, I noticed she had the DVR strategically on hold for more than an hour until her first guest arrived so she could press PLAY and then pretend it just *happened* to be on when a close-up of her filled the screen.

"That was dramatic," Lynn Bowes, my pal who worked as a waitress at most of these events, whispered to me as I chopped a Vidalia onion.

We'd become friends after we worked together a few times at the Chase Country Club, where my most lucrative work came in the form of special events several times a month, and we'd hung out a few times over the past couple of years on the rare occasion we both had a weekend night off.

"I'll say." I kept my voice low, but I was frustrated. "I don't know what her problem is."

"You don't?"

I looked at Lynn. "What do you mean?"

"I mean a perfectly catered party for her friends going off without a hitch is about as interesting on-screen as paint drying." She raised an eyebrow. "But histrionics, a catering catastrophe, and a dead peacock might just be enough to tip her over the edge into a leading role on that stupid show if the rumors of cast changes are true."

It made total sense. *"Are* there rumors of cast changes?"

Lynn snorted. "Oh my God yes, this is the most boring bunch since the Bradys!"

I had always liked *The Brady Bunch,* but I took her meaning and gave a laugh. "Then Marie must be salivating at the prospect of getting a full-time gig here."

"Ho yeah!"

My cell phone rang and I glanced at it. It was Penny, my cousin. She was heavily pregnant, on bed rest, and bored out of her mind. She called about three times a day lately. Fortunately, she was always entertaining.

"Excuse me a minute," I said, and Lynn gave the *Ok* signal and walked away. "Hey."

"Are you alone?" Penny asked.

"Ish."

She laughed. "I'm calling to remind you not to hide

from the cameras. I know you hate having your picture taken and yada yada yada, but someday, trust me, you'll be glad you did this. In fact, I was thinking if you got on camera, this might even be like the first step toward getting on *Top Chef* or maybe even getting your own cooking show on the Food Network or something. This could be like your audition tape—"

"I'm not going to be on the show."

"*Gemma!* You have got to *stop* this bullshit of being so shy about publicity."

"I don't *want* publicity."

"You *need* it! You make frozen dinners for five people a week—that's not going to get you a retirement plan."

"No, but the country club will."

She sighed. "Okay, but still—if you could make buckets of money being on TV and becoming a celebrity chef while that's hot, why wouldn't you?"

I sighed. We'd had this conversation so many times. Her confidence in me was touching but a little overly optimistic, I thought. "So many reasons."

She made a sound of irritation. "I can't believe you are so bullheaded about this."

I laughed. "Why don't *you* do it?"

"I swear, if I could so much as boil water, I'd be all over it!"

"I'll teach you. I think I'll have time on Fridays from now on, since I'm about to get fired."

"*What?*" Everything was always big to Penny. Two years older than me, but about a hundred times more energetic and bubbly, for her life was one huge party and she wanted to taste every single piece of cake and lick ice cream, good or bad. I could almost hear her adjusting herself into the most comfortable listening position.

"Oh, the usual, you know"—I peeled another onion—"dead peacock."

"You tried to serve dead peacock to someone?"

"No!" I laughed at the thought. "Although that might be what they're left with. No, the Lemurras bought a peacock as a pet or decoration or something equally ridiculous, and I ran over it."

"How do you run over a peacock?"

"I didn't see it."

There was a pause on the other end of the line. "Aren't they kind of . . . obvious?"

I already knew I was going to get this question a lot. "Well, *maybe,* if you know to look for them! Otherwise, believe me, they're fucking invisible. You can back right over one and not know it until you hear the screaming."

"It *screamed?*"

"No, *she* did. Marie." I frowned. Had there been cameras running at the time? I sincerely hoped not, though they couldn't put me on the show without me signing a release, could they?

"You are totally making this up!"

"Really? *This* is the story you think I'd come up with on the spot? That I ran over a peacock?"

"Well, why would they even *have* a peacock there?"

"The eternal question. Look, I have to get back to work. Are you at home?"

"Very funny." She was so sick of being homebound, it was starting to make her crazy.

"Sorry, I keep forgetting."

"Would that I could!" I heard the bed creak as she obviously moved with some effort. "I can't stand being pregnant for one more second. I think it's time to start taking cold showers, running, doing all the things they say you shouldn't do, in case it sends you into premature labor."

"Don't you dare! I can't stay on the phone and babysit you right now, but if you take any chances that land you in the hospital for anything other than labor, you'll be really sorry."

"I know, I know."

"I *mean* it."

She laughed. "Okay, okay, got it. But promise you'll call me if you want to talk."

"I promise."

I took out the asparagus and started to chop off the woody ends. I was about halfway through five pounds of them when Lynn came back, wearing a tight expression.

"She's on the warpath," she warned. "I don't know if she's really pissed or if she's just playing it up for the cameras, but I get the feeling this is the real thing."

I nodded. "That's the impression I had."

"I mean, she's at a boiling point *right now*. You might want to gather your knives."

"Oh, no, really?" My nerves jangled.

"She's probably afraid PETA is going to come after her publicly and ruin her image or something."

That would make the papers, albeit the small papers and probably just a corner thereof. "Good point. Jeez, do you think they will?" I paused in the midst of searing the game hens in a large pan. "Would they come after *me*?"

"Nah. That was an accident. The crime here is having a peacock on a property like this at all! It's like keeping a pony in Times Square. Well, almost. Anyway, she's the one who's wrong here, not you."

Dread knotted my stomach. "I hope you're right."

"I'm always right." She glanced around and took a slice of Vidalia and popped it in her mouth. "I love these things. I could eat them like apples."

"And never get another date because you perpetually smell like onions."

"Who are you kidding? I'm never gonna have another date anyway. And I hate to break it to you, but neither are you. Our jobs are to cater to *other people's* dates!"

"We need to get out now and then."

"Damn right! We're not going to be spinsters forever!"

I am *not* a beautiful girl. I am prettyish in the right light, I guess. Average height, average straight brown hair, murky green eyes that have been called everything from "exotic" to "expressive" to "creepy" (thanks, Mark Hutchinson in third grade) but are the one feature that keeps me from blending into the wallpaper.

I *used* to have a great figure—this was what fooled guys into thinking I was something I was not in high school,

I think—but thanks to life and my vocation, I had to give up on the idea of maintaining a supermodel physique a long time ago. Where once I was tight, I am now best described as voluptuous, and really, I'm okay with that.

It beats the hell out of the obsessive dieting and exercising that characterized those thin years.

Look, I'm just being honest, not self-pitying. Because I also happen to know I'm quite charming to the right type of person. And a lot of men have called me beautiful. Even if that always feels like an exaggeration and almost always like a ploy of some kind. Don't get me wrong, it's a compliment I will absolutely relish, but deep down I know it's not something construction workers see when I walk past them on the street. Those wolf calls they're supposedly famous for? It has rarely been a problem for me.

So there you go. It was actually Lynn's use of the word *spinster* that made more of an impact on me.

I was fine being alone.

I just didn't like feeling like I was *stuck* being alone.

"Women aren't spinsters anymore." I carefully set three more hens onto the large screaming-hot pan. They sizzled as soon as they touched the scorching steel. "Plenty of women choose to be single because the alternative is too appalling."

"What, *marriage?*"

"Yes, for one thing." That idea had *never* appealed to me, though I'd been semi-engaged once. Back when getting engaged and married and so on seemed like the Right Thing to Do. "Relationships in general. Show me a good one."

"Don't look at me! I've been married twice, and look what I have to show for it!"

I was so shocked, I burned my arm on the side of the pan when I turned to look at her. "Ouch! Shit!" I felt my face go hot, as well as my sleeve. "You've been married *twice*?"

"I never mentioned that?"

"No!"

She shrugged. "Then I guess you know everything there is to know about my marriages."

"Wow." I shook my head and looked at the baking sheets full of seared brown hens. "I'm amazed you're even willing to date, given that every hookup could lead to something—"

"Don't say it!" She held up her hand and laughed. "Don't. Say. It. I fall in love easier than a toddler falls down. From now on, it's just sex or nothing."

"Good luck with that."

She smirked. "Thanks."

"So, chickie, what are you going to do for work on Friday nights now if this gig is up?"

"I'm going to have to find another client," I said, feeling a twinge of panic in my stomach. It was like looking at a steep, slippery hill and knowing I'd have to climb it. Money was tight. Really tight. I couldn't afford to luxuriate in a few Fridays off; I needed to get someone new quick. I had a small list of people I'd had to turn down in the past, but experience had taught me that when you call someone after the mood has passed, usually they're no longer interested in your services.

So it would be another costly *Washingtonian* ad for me.

My clients were not Craigslist kind of people. Craigslist was for bargain hunters, and I couldn't afford to be a bargain.

"Want me to spread the word?" she asked.

"If you know anyone who wants a private chef"—I nodded—"absolutely."

The conversation was interrupted then by Marie Lemurra herself, marching in to ensure that her servants didn't waste a moment of her hired time chatting amongst themselves or having what could, in any way, be perceived as an enjoyable time on her dime.

"Work, work!" she trilled, but there was an unmistakable edge to her voice. "There's no time for chitchatting. Not right now, anyway." Her eye caught mine, and in that split second, I knew exactly what she was saying.

I was definitely fired.

So now I had Friday to contend with. Or, more specifically, the *lack* of Friday.

The Lemurras hadn't been exactly what you'd call a *pleasure* to work for, but mostly they stayed out of the kitchen, which made them comparatively easy. There were always moments of exception, of course. Like that one time I had to tell her I was unable to come devein and grill five pounds of shrimp on a Sunday for an impromptu soiree Marie was holding, and her response was to close her eyes and whisper, "I *hate* you."

All you can do in a situation like that is rationalize that that was probably just her *thing*, something she said to people without really realizing how ridiculously harsh it sounded.

She probably said it all the time, to the dogs, to the neighbors, to her friends. Even Pepe the Peacock probably heard it more than once in his short but glorious tenure at her house.

I'm almost sure that was what she was shouting behind me as I drove away that last evening after she grudgingly handed me my check and told me she no longer needed my services. Ever. Although then, it has to be said, she was expressing herself with a good deal more feeling and verve than most people would ever feel, much less reveal.

There was no question of whether I would ever be back.

I was never very good with the whole . . . like . . . "savings" thing. I hadn't put money aside for a rainy day or a dead peacock, so if I didn't get a new Friday soon, I might really be screwed.

And I couldn't ever let that happen.

But it was times like these that I looked back at my choices and felt a certain peace that, no matter how hard it had been to give up that baby, it had been the right decision. Because look at me: looking ahead at forty and still worried about my financial security in a very real, immediate way.

You know that old rule of thumb that you should have at least six months' worth of expense money in the bank "just in case"? Yeah, I was not even close.

It made for a lot of stress about day-to-day living, but to look at the bright side, it was a hell of a motivator to find more work.

Chapter 3

No one promised life would be easy or that the game wouldn't change without warning. There you are, all ready to pass Go and collect two hundred dollars, and suddenly Colonel Mustard is trapped in the conservatory, ranting and raving and waving a wrench, and no one knows what exactly a conservatory is or why anyone thought a *wrench*—of all things—would be a good murder weapon, or what branch of the military Colonel Mustard even served in! Has anyone *seen* his credentials?

Well, you get my point: You've got one life with zero guarantees, so you do your best, adapt if possible, and keep on breathing. I recommend striving for happiness, but many opt for duty and responsibility. Mileage varies.

Your life, your game, your rules.

Here's the only thing I know for sure: Chopped pineapple is *incredible* on hot dogs. Honest to God, I *love* pineapple on *everything*—I would probably even eat it off a cadaver's hand—but toss it with a little chopped red onion and put it on a hot dog, and it's bliss. There's not a lot you can count on in this world, but pineapple? It's solid.

Once upon a time, I thought I had bypassed the entire issue of dating into my dotage. Of course, thirty-seven is not dotage, but when I was a teenager, it sure seemed like it was, and given that I had a boyfriend who I thought was my Forever and Ever at the time, I was pretty smug—as only a seventeen-year-old can be—in the knowledge that I'd never have to deal with the dating world again.

That all changed the day I realized that I'd been happily cavorting in the pool in my swimsuit for two months straight without ever having my period. One EPT three-pack later— BUY TWO, GET ONE FREE!—I was a different person. Right up to that moment of confirmation, I had been myself, even though, of course, the confirmation was just that, and the fact existed with or without it.

But I will never forget the feeling of standing there in front of the beige counter of my bathroom in my mother's house—a counter that had, over the years, held everything from plastic tub toys to muddy summer science experiments to Tampax Juniors to my first Maybelline eye shadows— looking at three positive pregnancy tests that confirmed, without any room for doubt, that I would never be the same person again. I would never be the same person I'd been *that very morning* again. Amazing how your perspective can change your reality, huh?

I know it seems stupid; to this day, I hear stories about people going months and months without knowing they were pregnant, and I think, *Just how stupid are you?* for a moment before I realize I know just *exactly* how stupid someone can be in that situation. It's a very easy thing to be going along in your life, doing all the things you always do, feeling the way you always have, and not realizing that something—either within you or outside you—has shifted.

His name was Cal, by the way. This boyfriend I thought I would be with forever. The father of my child.

Cal Isaakson.

As I worked through the shock over the next few days, I wrote that name down a million times, like the child I was myself instead of the woman I should have been in order to handle this situation responsibly.

Cal and Gemma Isaakson.

Gemma Isaakson.

Mr. and Mrs. C. Isaakson.

And so on.

There was never a point of relief for me. Never a point at which I thought to myself, *Phew, now I really have him.* Whether that was because I believed so thoroughly that I *did* have him or because I knew deep down that I *didn't*, I can't say.

All I know is that telling him was harder than I expected it would be, and that, right there, was my first clue. He was, immediately, a person I didn't recognize.

This is going to fuck up my whole life!

How could you let this happen?

I'm not missing college to get married and raise a kid.

Find a place to get this taken care of.

Don't. Tell. Anyone.

The guy I had believed was the love of my life—a guy I'd been with for a year, through all four seasons and one of every holiday and birthday—suddenly viewed me as his enemy. Not even a person anymore. He dehumanized me thoroughly. I was just something trying to block his way to happiness and success.

Obviously, I realize that we were young, I had no idea what "the rest of my life" would look like, or how long that really stretches (if you're lucky), but even now, I am shocked at the vehemence of his response. The cruelty of it.

And yet I guess I'm glad it was handled that way, rather than in a more mediocre fashion, because if he'd hidden his coldness, or if he'd grudgingly agreed to marry me, I would have ended up in what I have no doubt would have been an epically terrible marriage.

As it was, I told him I'd take care of it.

He didn't even ask how. Or if I needed help. Or even if it was done.

That was the beginning of August. We spent about three more awkward weeks together, pretending nothing had happened, and when he left for Rutgers at the end of the month, I'm not even sure we went through the pantomime of kissing good-bye.

And that was it.

He was gone.

In those days before e-mail, it required more effort to

stay in touch. Not a lot of effort, of course, just some paper, an envelope, a stamp, and a few minutes to jot down a few words. But he didn't even bother to do that.

Neither did I, of course.

But I was busy floundering in the previously uncharted territory of teenage pregnancy. Wild hormones, terrible mood swings, depression that felt like something separate from me, yet something I'd never be free of. I had real problems, to be sure, but hormones can take whatever you're feeling and make it a million times worse. PMS was nothing compared to pregnancy.

And PMS was bad enough.

To say nothing of getting bigger by the day, despite the inability to keep down anything I ate. "Morning sickness" was a great fallacy for me, since it lasted all day and well into the fourth month.

Finally I was able to eat macaroni and cheese, as long as it was made with Velveeta and topped with Frank's hot sauce. Lots of it. I don't think a vegetable crossed my mind, much less my lips, during those nine months.

What did cross my mind was lots of thoughts of baby names and tiny clothes and locks of wispy soft hair and an increasing determination not only to keep the baby but also devote my life to being the best mother I could possibly be.

I didn't see marriage in my future. Not only did Mrs. Rooks's warning ring hollowly back in my subconscious, but Cal's turnaround made me feel like I could never trust another man again.

Time has set me straight on that, fortunately, though I

never came back around to the marriage idea. For a few years, I didn't think I could ever trust anyone again. I didn't even think I could trust *myself* to have reasonable judgment about anyone else. After all, I'd been sure I could trust Cal forever, and until he was put to the test, I had no idea that wasn't the case.

What if he *hadn't* been put to the test? What if I hadn't gotten pregnant, and our relationship had limped along until eventually we did what might have been expected of us and got married? I might have learned what was already a very hard lesson in a much, much harder way.

In fact, I could even still be learning it today if it weren't for his showing his true colors when he did.

So I guess I had to be grateful for that. Still, it was a very hard time for me, as well as for my family.

I worked as many hours as I could get at the Roy Rogers Restaurant where I'd been working since I was sixteen, saving my pennies and living in my mom's house with the idea of staying at home with the baby as long as I could.

I gestated.

Ate macaroni and cheese. With Frank's hot sauce.

And gradually, I came to view the baby as my own and let go of the fear that some resemblance to Cal would forever haunt me and keep me from giving as fully to the child as I wanted to. This was a human being, a person—boy or girl, eventually man or woman—that I was being granted temporary custody over, to guide in life toward whatever he or she would be. Sure, genetics mattered. They *existed* and potentially had implications for health and heredity, but that was just the physical. That had nothing to do with the *soul*, or with the true essence of the person who was being formed.

This baby was no more Cal than I was.

This baby was . . . Well, I didn't know who the baby was. But I wanted to find out. To take that emotional journey for the next sixty or seventy years together.

I was ready.

Or so I thought.

Then, in the blink of an eye, it all changed. Things went wrong: I lost my job over something stupid and found it difficult to find another because I was pregnant. My mom was as supportive as she could be, but her anxiety problems were increasing and I felt her detachment as clearly as if she were encased in ice. My memories of the time involve a lot of her sitting on the couch, smoking cigarette after cigarette, shaking her head. I knew I couldn't live a suspended childhood in her house myself and raise another baby. This wasn't a crazy TV movie where Baby Tender Love came to life and I had to step up until the spell could be reversed; I had to get it right from the beginning. Losing my meager income made me realize that if it was that difficult to get a job while pregnant, how was it going to be trying to get work when I had a child to take care of?

How much did day care cost versus the minimum wage I was earning? How could I get a job that would pay enough for me to cover day care?

And what about *college*? I had always planned on going to college. A college degree was as expected in my family as a high school diploma. I was an only child, and thanks to my father's life insurance policy, my mother had saved enough for me to go to, and live at, a Maryland state school, and she offered me the option of using that money toward another school if I preferred, with the understanding that the responsibility for the rest—whether grants, loans, scholarships, or whatever—was my own. I was expected to succeed, not just exist. I *wanted* to succeed, not just exist.

So when I had a child, I wanted to be a great example for him or her to do the same. With my lack of experience and job marketability, it was easy to imagine being the clichéd single mother—exactly like my own—working to death at a low-paying job, too tired to play, too spent to contribute meaningfully to my child's development.

As much as I wanted it, there was no way to truly make this work.

The veil was lifted, so to speak, and I realized with deadly clarity that I had been living in a fantasy world. I was a seventeen-year-old kid playing house like a six-year-old, with an imagined baby and no husband or father around. That idea had its place as the game of a child, but in reality, I was barreling forward, fully intending to raise another human being in a life that would inevitably be defined by struggle from day one.

For months, my future visions had involved rocking a baby and playing Santa Claus and other idealized Disney Channel movie moments, but very little reality.

Reality was grim.

So with the kind of certainty people usually describe as

"a religious moment," I decided that if I really loved this baby, I had to give him or her up for adoption to a family that could provide everything I would want to provide myself but never could.

My heart was broken. The decision itself gnawed a hollow inside me that I didn't think would ever be filled. Knowing I was doing the right thing, the best thing, was some comfort, but it didn't do squat toward helping me imagine a future in which I would ever have peace of mind.

I was just going to have to wait that out and hope for the best. Hope that time would heal, the way so many songs and poems promised it would.

The adoption process was easy, though it's a blur in my memory. I worked with a private agency and got to be involved in the choice every step of the way.

My only stipulation—and to this day, I don't think I regret it—was that I didn't want the child ever to find out who I was. Not because I didn't want to be "bothered," but because I knew myself well enough to know that, for the rest of my life, every time I saw a kid who looked about the right age and who resembled either Cal or myself in any way, I would wonder, and it would be painful. The idea of adding a cocktail of hope and potential disappointment to every day from the eighteenth birthday on just felt like torture.

Time passed.

Labor started in the movie theater, where I was seeing the second run of an old Tom Cruise movie.

It hurt more than I was prepared for. At two centimeters

dilated, I was in agony, but part of me didn't feel I deserved comfort or relief. Or maybe I felt other people didn't think I deserved it. At any rate, it was an excruciating physical experience compounded in countless ways by the myriad emotions that swam around it.

I was not the smartest teenager ever. Obviously. I made a lot of mistakes and a lot of poor judgments, but one thing I think to this day that I did right was I did not look at the baby or let them tell me if it was a boy or a girl.

To some, that sounds callous, but for me, it was the only way to survive. I could not spend my life remembering and potentially magnifying a moment of perceived eye contact with the baby. I could not spend my life wondering if that boy was my son or that girl was my daughter. I could not second-guess my decision ever, much less *forever*, and details would only have fueled my imagination.

Thirty-six hours after I went into labor, I was back home in the bedroom I'd grown up in with nothing to show for the past nine months except a stomach that felt like jelly and a hole in my heart.

But it was the right decision. I know, to this day, it was the right decision. And I try to keep the wondering from becoming obsessive, because I set the conditions and I know I will never *know*.

Not hard to figure out how I ended up in the business of nurturing people I would never be closer to than an employee, is it?

Romantic relationships are unreliable at best. A smart woman had to find satisfaction in other things, and then, if some great guy came along and added quality to her life, it was reasonable to consider the question of commitment.

I think Mrs. Rooks would agree.

So far, for me, that guy had not come along. Every serious relationship I'd had contained some element that made me lonelier *with* the guy than without. Casual dating was fine; even that first promising glow of excitement worked for me, kept the idea of possibility going in my mind.

But nothing ever went beyond that for me. Something always threw a roadblock in the way. And, I know, many people would say that was a personal psychology issue that had more to do with my past than my present or future, but honestly, I sincerely disagree. Okay, I will admit that when I'm not feeling bitter and being called a spinster, I've seen plenty of evidence of good relationships out there. I know they can work; I'm not against them on principle at all. But I think the right fit is more rare than people think, and though hope might spring eternal, eventually skepticism does find its way in.

And it's not that I'm some fiercely independent woman who doesn't like intimacy. I *love* intimacy. I love sex. Granted, it took a long time to get over Cal's betrayal, and perhaps *over* isn't even the right word. *Around* might be better—it took a while to get *around* Cal's betrayal.

But I did. Eventually. I really did.

It didn't make me bitter for life. The prospect of truly being *in love* and having a life partner to nurture and take care of—and be taken care of by—has held strong appeal for me ever since I was a kid and first saw Maria and Captain von Trapp dance the ländler on the patio. That's probably what led me so neatly down Cal's garden path in the first place. Obviously, he wasn't the perfect boyfriend. When it comes down to it, he didn't even really love me. And maybe I didn't really even love him. I don't know.

But I wanted to.

And there are times when I want that kind of love still. When I want someone to watch TV *with* in my ugly pajamas, and who offers to order the Chinese food and doesn't have to ask what I want. I want someone who gives me something better than the initial thrill of a first kiss; I want someone who gives me the peace of a best friend with a lot of hot sex thrown in to elevate it.

But I don't know how to look for that. Maybe it's foolish, but I'd like to believe that if it's out there—that kind of love—that it'll find me somehow.

But romantic ideals are easier to imagine than to achieve.

A perfect meal, on the other hand. Well, that can be done, start to finish, in a matter of hours or even minutes.

Chicken must be cooked perfectly so it's moist, not dry, and tender. No hard spots on the outside.

The difference between good shrimp and rubber is about ten seconds.

Cheap steak can be made better by dry aging in the fridge, but old steak is beyond hope.

Freezer burn is not dangerous to food, but it takes away flavor and reduces crisp vegetables to marbles.

In short, there are far more considerations than the average person thinks about to making a truly scrumptious meal. And that's where I come in. That is my passion, and I get great satisfaction from a job well done.

So in that sense—in that very real sense—I can succeed every single day.

And if I don't, I'm in trouble.

This is just one more thing I love about cooking. Recipes are certain. Use good ingredients, follow the directions, be sure your oven temperature is true and monitor your stove properly, and you are assured success. There are not many variables once you understand how cooking works.

Life, on the other hand, is full of variables. *Nothing* is predictable. Not the weather, not other people, not traffic, not even our own bodies. We are like seaweed, whipped around in the current of an erratic ocean.

I'd rather work with nori and know how it's going to come out.

Chapter 4

It was my first Lemurra-free Friday in months. Despite the financial panic that was growing in me, there was a certain thrill to not having to deal with Marie's antics anymore. I never would have been irresponsible enough to throw away good work because of a personality conflict, but I was able to see that maybe this was a blessing in disguise.

Especially since, by sheer coincidence, Lynn and I both happened to have the night off.

It had been too long since I'd done something just for fun. I'd gotten in a rut, so when she called, I took it as a sign.

"Everyone's talking about a new bar down in Woodley Park," she said when we talked by phone Friday afternoon. "I can't remember the name of it, but I can Yelp it."

"No Plans?" I'd driven past it and watched its construction every day since I started at Mr. Tuesday's. I loved the name.

"Yes! That's it! And my place is just a few blocks away, so you can come stay with me and we'll have a sleepover and it will be just like old times."

"I don't remember us having slumber parties."

She laughed. "I mean *really* old times. Like sixth grade. When we hadn't met yet. Come *on*, you *have* to do it! I love that neighborhood, and I haven't been since Jared and I broke up."

"Which one was Jared?"

"The one who lived in Woodley Park. I met him right after my divorce."

"Which one?"

"Second. Right before I met you. And you were dating that actor. . . . Shoot, what was his name?"

Oh God. "Skye." His name wasn't really Skye, of course. *No one's* name is really Skye. At least no one I knew. He had unashamedly told me that he'd decided on that stage name because of his—wait for it—"sky blue eyes." He thought it would help casting directors remember him.

As far as I knew, the only thing he was ever cast as was Scooby-Doo at Kings Dominion.

"Don't remind me. He's one of the many things that are wrong with dating."

"That's what you said about Alex with the hair plugs and the teddy bear."

My dating history is not dignified.

"Stop," I said. "Seriously, or I'll never leave my place again."

Lynn laughed. "This is *exactly* why you need to get out. So are you in for tonight?"

Given the week I'd had? No question. "I'm in!"

By nine that night, Lynn and I were cabbing it to No Plans. Maybe it was just the bubbles in the Prosecco we'd split while we were getting ready, or maybe it was sheer lack of responsibility for the night, but I felt good. I felt confident. And considering that every Friday for what felt like a *very* long time had been occupied by the peacock-purchasers, I felt kind of like I was playing hooky.

So that put us teetering on our bar stools, laughing crazily at the guy who had just hit on us. Us. At the same time. He was about an inch shorter than me, and the buttons on his shirt were straining a little, but he acted with the confidence of Javier Bardem. He had licked his lips at Lynn, bit the air at me, and invited us back to his "pad."

Unfailingly polite, I had smiled and told him, "No thanks, I have an . . . early morning. . . ."

But Lynn had just looked at him like he was insane until he wandered off.

"I think that the first hit-on of the night demands a celebration." She raised her hand and called, "Yoo-hoo!" at the bartender. Charmed by her as people usually were, he smiled and came over to us.

"What can I get for you ladies?"

"Two applesauce shots, please."

I gaped at her. "*Shots?* God, what are we, in college?"

She moved her wavy brown hair out of her eyes. "No, we don't have to be in *college* to have what I'm *sure*"—she looked at the bartender—"will be a fantastically prepared, perhaps overflowing shot."

He laughed with a shake of his head. "You got it."

"It's delicious," she said to me. "Goldschläger and something else. I don't remember. But it totally tastes like applesauce."

"Why would anyone want to *drink* applesauce?" But I was already wondering if it could be reduced to a glaze for pork chops, and made a mental note to find out what was in it.

When the bartender returned with the two slightly-bigger-than shots, we took them. I let it spin my head for a second, and then opened my mouth to tell Lynn she was right, they were delicious, but her attention had already been diverted by a tall, smart-looking guy in a T-shirt and glasses across the room.

"Is that—?" I started.

"Jared!" She nodded. "It's fate! Do you mind?"

I laughed. "Go for it."

And there it was. Suddenly I was no longer the carefree college kid but instead the rapidly-approaching-middle-aged woman sitting at a bar alone on a Friday night.

Of course, I remembered this from college, too. I'd never really been a partier; it didn't come all that naturally to me.

I was always the sort who'd be happier at home with a good book than out drinking and dancing.

But I'd come with Lynn tonight because that routine was getting old, so I had to give this night out a fair shot. I looked around at the mint-condition bar. The lights were blue, and all the surfaces were slick with black lacquer. The lights cast dramatic shadows on the happy-looking crowd. I looked around at them all, wondering who there would be going home together, and who would be breaking up. Who was meeting his or her soul mate, and who was just there to have fun and not meet anyone new.

Like me.

It was always easy to fit people into these types of categories at the bars, and when I was out with Lynn, it was something I often had time to do.

"Here, have this!" Lynn showed up at my side and handed me a plastic cup with an orange on the rim.

"What is it?"

"Sex on the Beach!"

"Oh my God, I haven't had one of these in years."

"Honey, we *all* need more sex on the beach!"

I laughed and sipped from the straw as she turned back to Jared.

I looked back around the room. In one corner was a red pool table. The men playing on it were all in suits, clearly just off work. I always kind of liked that look. The jacket off, the sleeves rolled up, the loosened tie . . . it worked for me. One of them—tall, thin, with dark blond hair—took a shot and sank two balls into two different pockets. I took another sip. That always worked for me, too. There's just something hot about a guy playing pool.

Then, as if he could read my thoughts, the guy suddenly looked at me. Startled, I swallowed the wrong way and coughed, sloshing some of the liquid onto my leg. I sopped it up with my napkin and looked back up to see him smiling. It did something wonderful to his already handsome face. When he smiled, it just made me . . . I don't know what exactly, but suddenly I felt hot, and couldn't tear my gaze away.

After another second, one of his friends evidently said something to him, and the moment was over. I looked back at Lynn, who was laughing heartily at something Jared had said.

With a moment of cheek-warming humiliation, I wondered if Pool Player had been looking at *her* and not me.

I rarely felt jealous of Lynn, but this time . . . I had really wanted him to be smiling at me. I slurped up the last of my Sex on the Beach and got the attention of the bartender again.

"Another applesauce shot?"

"Comin' right up, beautiful."

Well, at least I had that.

One shot and fifteen minutes later, Lynn was standing with her finger wound around Jared's belt loop, and I was wondering if I should just take a cab back to my place and get my things from her apartment tomorrow. I felt like a cockblock. But then I looked at Lynn, who seemed not to be feeling blocked, and decided that *no*, I was just kind of bored.

I glanced back to the rest of the room and saw Pool Player coming toward me. I looked around for something to stare fixedly at. But before I had a chance, he was in front of me.

"You wanna play?"

"What?"

He gestured back at the pool table.

"Oh," I said, feeling a little stupid. "Um . . . I'm just awful."

"I'm not."

I raised an eyebrow. "Well, that just doesn't sound like a fair game, does it?"

He grinned again. "Nope. And I'm not gonna go easy on you, either."

I couldn't say no. "Fine. Then I guess I'll just really have to try, then."

That was all I could come up with to say. It was lame, but I'd been out of this game, as well as pool, for a long time.

"You want another drink first?"

"Sure."

He nodded at the bartender and he came over. "What was it you spilled all over yourself?"

I smiled. "Applesauce. Oh no, that one was a Sex on the Beach."

"Which do you prefer?"

"Drinkwise?" I laughed. "Applesauce."

He looked amused, and then repeated the drink order. "I'm Mack," he said then. Or Max. I wasn't entirely sure.

"Sounds like an alias," I said stupidly. God, what was *with* me?

He laughed. "An *alias*? I can assure you, I haven't done anything interesting enough to need an alias."

"Disappointing."

"Tell me about it."

A few feet away, Lynn giggled a coquettish laugh and lay a hand on Jared's chest.

"She's having fun," Mack observed.

"Yes. She is."

"Are you?"

Until this moment, I had been fighting a growing desperation to be out of there. Now, I was content to stay just where I was. "Of course."

"Good." He took the drink from the bartender. "Then you won't be upset when I kick your ass on the pool table."

I laughed, decidedly less coquettishly than Lynn, and followed him. As we made our way through the crowd, he took my hand. Maybe it was weird, but it didn't feel that way. Once we had emerged on the other side, he let go and replaced it with a cue.

"You wanna break?" he asked as he began to rack the balls.

"I'm a terrible breaker."

"Then we'll rerack until you get it right." He pulled away the triangle and grabbed his own cue.

Luckily, the balls scattered across the felt on my first try. I even got in a solid.

"Beginner's luck." He took a swig from his Sam Adams.

I missed the next ball I tried to get in, more due to nerves than anything else. I glanced up to see Lynn looking thrilled at me. She gave me a thumbs-up, and I was glad that he had already started to shoot.

When he finally missed one, I gave an uncharacteristically victorious *"Ha!"* and took my next shot. Miraculously, I made the next four in a row.

"Phew," I said, making my way to my drink. "All this winning is making me *parched*."

I leaned my back against the wall to steady myself and take a sip. He was smiling again, and sauntered over to me. He put a hand on the wall behind me. My heart skipped, but I tried to look like it hadn't.

"So, you're a pool shark. And you just draw losers like me in from across the bar. Only to beat them after giving them the ol' oh-you-wouldn't-wanna-play-*me* routine. Huh? Is that your game?"

I smiled, my straw still in my mouth, and looked up at him. He had light brown eyes and dark lashes. "Yup. Sucker."

I didn't know if it was the shots that were doing it, but I had as much confidence as I *had* had in college. It felt like slipping into old stilettos.

He bit his bottom lip and moved just close enough to me that I got that chill you get when you're about to be kissed.

But then he just tilted his head slightly to the side and said, "This isn't over yet, Applesauce."

And he pushed away from the wall, and went back to the table.

We got down to the eight ball, my yellow seven, and his striped number eleven.

Right before I took my shot, he placed a hand on my arm. "Wait, there's nothing in the pot."

"Hm?" I stood up straight.

"We need to raise the stakes here. What do you get if you win?"

I gave a laugh. "I'm not sure."

"Well, what do you want?"

I swallowed my first answer and said, "A drink. Whoever wins has to buy the other a drink."

He considered it. "So cliché. But that's fine." He stepped backwards. "My drink's running low, anyway."

"So's mine." But I knew it was ill-advised for me to have another one.

I took my shot and missed. He took his, and sank his eleven effortlessly. He didn't look up at me, but he knew I was looking at him and he grinned.

"Left pocket." He gestured with his cue stick where he was going to aim the eight ball. Another smooth shot.

He stood up and splayed his arms in a gesture that clearly meant *What can I say?*

"Guess you're buying me a drink, then."

I shook my head and smiled. I couldn't stop smiling at this guy. "Guess so."

We put the cues away, and he led me back through the crowd. I squeezed my way into the bartender's line of vision and signaled for two more.

When the drinks arrived, I turned and saw him mouthing, *My tab*, to the bartender.

"Hey, that's not fair!"

"What?" He looked innocently at me.

I sipped from my straw and handed him his beer. "I was supposed to—"

He shook his head and came closer to me. "I couldn't hear you, what?"

"You were supposed to let *me* buy your—"

His eyes were close to mine again, and I noticed once more how nice they were. He shook his head again and looked at me. "Still can't hear you."

"Yes, you can!"

He laughed and came very close to me now, and spoke into my ear. "I still can't hear you."

I looked him in the eye and mouthed, *Liar*.

He looked at my lips, which had just formed the word. His clever grin faded a little, and he put a hand on my waist. I felt my breath catch and sipped from my drink for something to do other than throw myself at him.

He glanced around. "Do you . . . Do you want to go back to . . . to my place? For a drink?"

I never did that. Okay I never did *this* at all. Growing up near one of the most dangerous cities in the country had taught me to always be careful about invitations like this. Even when it was this guy.

But I wanted to. "Um . . ." This was foolish. I knew this was foolish. I didn't even know this guy. "I guess that would be okay for a few minutes. Maybe one drink."

He nodded. He shot a hand out to get the bartender. "I need to close my tab. Do you—?"

"Oh, no, my friend and I were on the same one. I'm gonna go tell her I'm leaving."

"I'll meet you at the door in a second."

I nodded. "Okay."

I slithered through the crowd and made my way to Lynn.

"I'm . . ." Suddenly I was embarrassed. "Going back to his place for a drink?" It sounded like a question.

Maybe a request for permission.

"Gemma! Are you crazy?"

I was a little startled by her accuracy. Because once again, this was not a normal thing for me. "It seems possible."

"Hm. I don't like him having a home advantage, just in case he's a weirdo."

"If I thought he was a weirdo, I wouldn't be going!"

"I know, but still . . ."

"You think *my* home advantage is better?"

"Of course not! You can't let him know where you live!"

I sighed. "Well, a hotel seems like overkill."

She looked back at Jared. "How would you like an overnight guest?"

For one startling moment, I thought she meant me, but then I realized what she was doing.

Jared nodded with a smile, and she reached in her purse and produced her keys. *"Mi casa es su casa."*

"But—"

"Tell him you're going to your friend's place. Tell him yours is too far away or whatever. If he knows it's not your place, he's not going to go looking for you there."

It made sense, though I really doubted he was anything other than what he seemed to be—a really nice, normal guy. "Thanks! Close out our tab, will you? I'll just get my card tomorrow."

"Of course! Have *fun*! Bet you're glad you ran over that peacock now, aren't you?"

Jared looked puzzled, and Lynn launched into an explanation as I left. I didn't need to relive that yet again.

I walked over to the door and then stepped outside. He was there. It might have been awkward, but somehow it just wasn't.

He gave me that smile one more time and we left side by side in silence.

Twenty minutes later, we were crossing Lynn's lobby, past the security guard, and into the tiny elevator. I never would have guessed *I* would be the one back here tonight with a guy. But he didn't give me much time to think.

We got to the apartment, fumbled with the key, and finally got the door open. I turned on the light switch, illuminating a small hall that opened to a modest sitting area. I paused. Was there any point in going in there? Were we just going to end up in the bedroom anyway? Just how far did I need to take this charade if we were both adults with the one intention and we knew it?

I never got the chance to really ponder the answer. No sooner were we in the hall than he had my back against the cool door, and his lips on mine. He pulled off my shirt, and I started to unbutton his. Underneath it was a toned, solid physique. I ran my hands along his stomach and up his shoulders as his shirt fell to the floor.

He unsnapped my bra with one quick, easy motion, just as he'd sunk the eight ball only minutes before. His hands felt strong and a little rough on my skin, and he let one trail up my spine and into my hair. I was glad I'd worn it down. When I wore it up and let it out of its band, it always came away looking like a crumpled umbrella.

When you have gone a long time without any kind of intimacy—as I had—this kind of touch was like a drug. Better than a drug. It was the kind of bliss that made foolish people weaken and make compromises they shouldn't. Compromises that maybe they wouldn't consider if they were of sound mind.

But it's hard to be of sound mind when your body is in such a state of ecstasy that it feels like your whole *soul* is being soothed. Under his touch, I had the strangest disconnect from the rest of the world. It was as if, for the first time in *quite* some time, I felt I didn't have a worry in the world.

That's the trick sex plays on us, I guess. It erases really important things from our consciousness. Things like, *Maybe I don't know this guy well enough to be doing this* and *I'm not prepared for this* and *Maybe this is a chance I shouldn't be taking.*

Instead, I listened to my body, which was all, *Wooooohooo! This is awesome! Let's go!*

So I did.

My fingers ran along his waistband and fumbled with his button. His skin was hot against my knuckles when they grazed his abdomen. As soon as I unfastened them, his pants fell to the ground and he kicked them off along with his shoes.

One hand still wrapped around me and holding me steadily, he slid the other one up my thigh and under my skirt. I sighed. He pulled down the black, lacy Victoria's Secret thong I was glad I'd chosen, and pulled it down my legs and I stepped out of them.

I was still wearing my heels.

Things were moving really far, really fast. And I couldn't wait for more. My body cried out for it. I think *I* cried out for it. I arched toward him, pressing against him, willing him closer, willing him in, never wanting this moment of exquisite anticipation to end, yet dying for the satisfaction of feeling him inside me.

Then it happened. He entered me and I gasped. It was familiar, even though it was new, and welcome even though it was crazy. Suddenly I didn't care that we were pounding against the door and that anyone could walk by. I didn't care that I could probably be heard through the walls and probably out the window and down to the parking lot. All I felt was him.

"We need," I gasped, "protection."

He drew back, looking a little shamed. "Of course . . . You're not—?"

"No. Maybe Lynn has some . . ." I went into the bedroom and scraped open the bedside table drawer. After a little digging, I found a three-pack of non-latex condoms, exactly where I would have kept them at my place. Relief filled me. I grabbed the box and went back to the hallway.

We didn't make it back to the bedroom. Even those few moments it would have taken between the hall and the bedroom felt too long. I needed to be with him *now*. My body moved toward his like steel filings to a magnet. He kissed my neck, and I let my head fall back against the door, unable to do anything but hold him tightly around his shoulders.

I took a condom out and opened it with hands that felt weak. It was a drag to stop and worry about it, but this was one thing I was absolutely vigilant about. Sex with a stranger was apparently okay, but not without protection.

I had my limits.

And, I've got to say, I didn't regret it.

He was amazing. His touch was perfect; it was as if he were inside my head as well as my body and he knew exactly what I wanted. Honestly, I can't even find words to describe it. It was . . . *perfect*. It was just what sex should be; it felt just how passion should feel. It was hungry and devoured and then, finally, satiated.

I caught my breath, or tried to, and looked at him.

He opened his mouth to say something, but instead just closed it and whispered, *"Wow."*

I was just about to respond when there was a hard knock on the door.

We both exchanged a look, and then he laughed and said, "Yes?"

"There was a noise complaint," a crisp female voice said from the other side. The security guard from downstairs, I was sure of it. "Just want to make sure everything's okay."

He stifled another laugh and said, "Yes, everything's fine."

There was a hesitation on the other side of the door, and the voice said, "Sir, could you open the door?"

"Um, yeah, one second."

I grabbed my clothes and dashed into the bathroom. He slid on his pants and opened the door.

A small dark woman in a light blue cop uniform—the kind that real cops never actually seem to wear—stood in the hall. She was the same one who had been behind the desk when we came through the lobby, but I made a point of coming into her line of vision anyway, just to make sure she wouldn't hold this against Lynn.

She took one look at Mack, his shirtless body, and then my face, which went hot the moment she glanced my way, and then she nodded.

"Quiet down, lovebirds."

She said it without humor, then left. He closed the door and came back over to me.

I could not help bursting out laughing. He did, too.

"That was really rude of us," I said, grimacing.

"Probably."

"Couldn't be ruder."

He raised an eyebrow. "I don't know that *that's* true. We could try."

I shrugged. "It's not like she can kick us out. It's my friend's apartment, not a hotel room."

"She'd need to get the police involved."

"That would be embarrassing."

He bent down and kissed my neck. "It's unlikely."

Before I knew it, he had his arms around me and his mouth on mine, and suddenly—unstoppably—we were doing it all over again.

Thank goodness the condoms came in a three-pack.

Chapter 5

Monday night.

The Van Houghten house in Chevy Chase, Maryland.

"I want to be raw."

I looked at Angela Burns-Van Houghten, who was sipping a large glass of chardonnay in her recently remodeled kitchen, and involuntarily took a step back. If she was going to get *raw* with me, that couldn't be pretty. She was the most abrasive person I'd ever met.

In the mid-'90s she'd been sort of a sub-supermodel. Not quite at the level of, say, Kate Moss, but she'd had a name and a lot of people knew her when they saw her still, partly because of that, and partly because she was a frenemy of Marie Lemurra and had made the final cut of several episodes of the reality show, though her screen time was never as much as I think she hoped it would be, based on the amount of loud laughing and broad movements I'd witnessed her making at one of the dinner parties I'd catered for Marie on the show.

So Angela was relegated to the netherworld of D.C. subcelebrities—not quite interesting enough to be famous but just famous enough to be interesting. Here in "Hollywood East," our celebs didn't tend to be attractive so much as powerful. Thus attractive-and-famous ruled supreme, and attractive-and-semi-famous came in at a very close second.

Close enough for someone like Angela Burns-Van Houghten to feel absolutely free to be an imperious bitch with a lowly servant like myself.

I braced myself for whatever "raw" truth she might be preparing to tell me. "Okay, go ahead."

She frowned slightly. "That's what I have *you* for."

"I'm sorry, I don't"—*have any idea what the fuck you're talking about*—"understand."

She sighed. "Do you know what raw means?"

It meant *several things.* "Yes. Of course. But I don't know what *you* mean by it."

"That's the way I want you to cook from now on."

"Raw?"

"Correct."

"In other words, *un*cooked?"

Uncertainty flashed across her features for just a split second. "Well, it's not really *uncooked*, is it?"

"Raw is, yes."

"I'm talking about a kind of cooking."

The raw food movement, yes, I got it. But still. "Yes, that is essentially uncooked food. Nothing is prepared at higher than something like a hundred and twenty degrees. Which means no more grilled turkey burgers."

She was undaunted. "That's just fine, we don't want the carcinogens."

The Van Houghtens had a gas grill—something I, personally, don't consider *real* grilling—which meant *there are no carcinogens in gas grilling.*

Her kohl-lined hazel eyes narrowed at me. "Do we need to argue about this, or can you just do it?"

I had the bad feeling it might end up being both. "We'll need to sit down and talk about your food preferences again."

"You already know my food preferences. No onion, no nuts, no garlic, no dairy, no cinnamon, and so on. Oh, and I'm starting to think about no herbs at all. The pesticides are just too prevalent."

Oh no. No, no, no. If she cut all herbs out of her diet, in addition to the no dairy and no dairy derivatives, no soy, et cetera, it was going to be *impossible* to cook for her.

Or at least seriously unfun.

"Let's back up a minute," I said quickly, hoping to derail that train before it picked up too much speed. "Let's get the basics down first. Are you looking for a very vegetable-heavy diet?"

"Yes."

"But you realize that things will be served at a cool

temperature, right?" She would take that as condescending—
I knew she would—so I added, "I only ask because I remember how much you enjoy things like turkey chili and
lentil soup in the cold weather."

She paused. "But it's a very healthy diet."

"It is."

The front door opened and closed. Peter was home. Angela's husband. He was a former Olympic decathlete and
current local sports radio host, playing the "good cop" to his
cohost's shock jock "bad cop" persona.

"And I do have Stephen to consider," she added, though
it sounded like it was an afterthought.

Stephen was her six-year-old son who could have used a
fucking cheeseburger, if you asked me, but no one was asking me for my opinion on the Van Houghten diet. At least,
the Van Houghtens weren't.

"Well, of course, a healthy diet is important for children, as well as variety—"

Her phone rang and she glanced at it. "Ugh, it's the
nanny. Excuse me."

I was 100 percent sure if she had been standing here
with the nanny and I had called, she would have looked at
her phone and said, *Ugh, it's the cook*. Which, in a way, spoke
better of her. She was nondiscriminatory in her discrimina-
tion toward anyone she felt was in any way *lesser* than she
was.

We were *all* lesser than she was, in her view.

I'd heard her complain about the maids putting the pillows on the bed wrong, the nanny arriving fifteen minutes

late in a blizzard, the babysitter going to a funeral and leaving Stephen to deal with a different caretaker . . . and so on. Angela was one of those people who felt entitled to everything, preferably at the expense of everyone else.

I didn't like working for her.

She put her finger in her free ear and walked away from me, as if concerned that I would eavesdrop on the super-private stuff she had to talk to the nanny about.

I returned to the task at hand, making *cooked* pasta sauce—no oil, no onions—for steamed vegetables. No noodles. No Parmesan (only a nutritional yeast substitute).

No fun.

Peter came into the kitchen and draped his jacket over the back of one of the chairs at the kitchen table. "Hi, there," he said, and came over to the pot I was stirring.

"Hi." I stepped aside as he bent down and sniffed the sauce.

Peter Van Houghten was a good-looking guy by almost anyone's definition. Tousled dark brown hair, dark blue eyes, and a tall, trim body, thanks to a painfully lean diet and the fact that he worked out regularly and ran a few marathons every year.

Under other circumstances, I might have found him attractive, but not under these circumstances.

I swear I have never had a romantic relationship of *any* sort with *any* of my clients. And I never would. Though with one bad almost-engagement behind me, it would figure if I did fall for a guy who was both attractive and unavailable. Whatever small appeal Peter Van Houghten's looks held for me, it was probably based mostly on the fact that nothing could ever happen.

With a chilling rush in my chest, I thought of Mack at the bar on Friday. This happened every time I thought of him. Right about now, I was feeling like I could just relive that night like *Groundhog Day*, over and over, and never get tired of it.

But then there'd been the Morning After, when I'd awoken, bleary-eyed and my head in a vise—and alone. For a horrible moment, I wondered if it had even happened. I fumbled for the bottle of water by the bed, but knocked it over. I muttered a curse word, and then flew to the bathroom for a washcloth. I came back and started sopping up the wet mess. I blinked the mascara out of my eyes a few times, and then saw that I'd been running the cloth over a soggy, ink-stained piece of paper. There had been words on it, I could tell. But now they were as illegible as could be.

So. I was probably never going to see that guy again. And in the meantime, I'd just have to think of him every five minutes and notice actively how different it felt to have someone else standing closely behind me.

I handed Peter the spoon and took a small step from him. "Go ahead and taste it. Tell me if you think it needs anything."

He lifted the wooden spoon to his lips, blew gently, then tasted. "Needs onion."

I sighed. Almost everything I cooked for them would benefit from onions. "I know." We both nodded a little sadly. "Other than that?"

"It's delicious." He met my eyes, his pupils dilated in that way my seventh grade science teacher said meant you like what you're looking at. "Just like everything you make."

My face grew warm and I went to the sink to wash my already-clean hands. "Thanks," I said casually, "but I think it needs something. Apart from the obvious." I gave a laugh. "I wished I could put something onion-ish in, but Angela is allergic to the entire onion family, so there's no getting away with that."

"Ahh." He gave a dismissive gesture. "She eats onion all the time and just doesn't know it. She's not allergic to anything, she just says that." He moved back and leaned on the counter. "You should cook the way you want to."

I shook my head with a smile. "No way. I cook the way the client wants me to. If I didn't, I wouldn't be in business long."

He gave a half shrug and was about to say something else when an exasperated Angela flounced back in.

"Honestly, we need two nannies just so they can cover each other's erratic schedule." She looked to Peter. "Kim needs to go to the doctor tomorrow while she's got Stephen, and wants to either bring in a friend of hers to cover for an hour or two, or take him with her. Like Stephen needs to go hang out in a doctor's office!" She gave a sharp laugh and shook her head.

"Why doesn't she go while he's in school?"

She raised her eyebrows. "Exactly. She said the only time she could get was one thirty, but, come on. She could go to an urgent care place any time in the morning and be back on time to get Stephen."

Unless, say, she wanted to see her *own* doctor. But what could I say? Like Kim, I was just the help. So I said nothing. Just stirred the sauce and sautéed the vegetables.

"So I was just telling Gemma how we want to go raw from now on," she said to Peter.

He looked completely confused. "Raw—?"

See? It wasn't that obvious what she was talking about.

"Food," she snapped.

"We do?"

"Absolutely. It's the healthiest diet there is. Cooking destroys the enzymes in food." She glanced disapprovingly at the stove, despite the fact that she had *loved* this very dish just last month. "It's almost better not to eat at all."

"That's certainly an option," Peter said. "Myself, I'd rather have spaghetti and meatballs once in a while."

"Gross!" Angela looked at him, scandalized and mouth agape, like he said he'd like live puppies dipped in ox blood. "We just don't need to consume rotting flesh. It's disgusting."

"Put that way, it is," he said at the exact same moment that I thought the exact same words.

"So from now on," she said to me, her posture suggesting she'd had enough of him, "it's all raw, all the time, okay?"

"Same constrictions as before, with regards to onions, garlic, and so on?" I asked.

"Yes. *Of course.*"

"What about Stephen?" I asked. "Do you want me to do

something"—*anything*—"to supplement his diet with a little more protein and calcium?"

She narrowed her eyes at me. "You're talking about cheese, right?"

"Not necessarily—"

"Cheese causes phlegm. Dairy is the most common allergy in the United States, but no one even knows it. Everyone just keeps on eating it, coughing, and eating it some more." She shook her head, a distinct look of they'll-all-see-one-day-when-it's-too-late. "People are so stupid."

Myself, I couldn't think of anything in the world better than stirring sharp white cheddar, smoked Gouda, creamy Havarti, Monterey Jack, and a touch of piquant Maytag blue cheese into a bubbling hot white sauce, stirring it to a thick honey consistency, and pouring it over al dente macaroni to toast to a crispy deep golden on top.

"Okay." I tried to sound patient, but it was hard. Because I wasn't. "But there are other options. Tofu. Textured vegetable protein. Nuts. Lean meats would be ideal."

She looked dubious. "I'll have to think about that. Except the tofu, of course. No tofu. Or meat." She turned away from me and started talking to Peter, clearly indicating her time with me was done.

I knew exactly what it meant because I'd experienced this same thing time and again with her. It was almost funny. It certainly didn't hurt my feelings, as it was nearly impossible to take someone like this personally.

"I don't like that we have to eat so late because you take so long to get home," she said to him, walking away but not so far that I couldn't hear every single word she said. "Why the hell don't you leave work earlier?"

"You're welcome to eat without me," he returned, completely calm in the face of her snappishness.

I silently cheered him on.

"That's how much you care for your son?" Her voice was demanding, immediately accusatory. "You don't even care if you eat with him? Wow, that is really . . . just *wow*."

He shook his head, but it looked like it was more to himself than at her. "Half the time, Kimberly has fed him dinner by the time I get home, anyway."

"That's because you take so long!" She said it through gritted teeth, each word carefully formed.

He looked weary. "I can't help the traffic, Angela."

"You can help what time you get into it! You're always staying well beyond the end of the show."

I cringed. The entire atmosphere had gotten thick and tense. The strongest mood in the house always wins, it's just a universal law, and Angela always seemed to have the strongest mood.

And she always seemed to win.

I stole a glance at Peter. His face was like something etched by a Renaissance artist, taking every cliché of masculinity and softening it just enough to keep him from looking like a caricature of Hercules. The gentle waves of brown hair also softened what was otherwise a fiercely masculine visage. But when he looked like he did now—angry but in control—he looked distinctly different. Maybe even more handsome.

His voice was quiet, but not weak. I'd never seen him back down, never heard him give in. Not that I knew everything that happened in this house. Far from it. I was here for two or three hours a week, but given the fact that Angela's bitching was consistently the same, it was hard to imagine she was sweet the rest of the time.

I used to ask myself how on earth Peter had gotten into this marriage in the first place, but that wasn't really the point. He had, and that was that. She'd probably been different once. Whether she'd changed or just been trying to land him, who knows?

All I know is that it was impossible to imagine him, or anyone, purposely signing up for the floggings I saw her issue almost constantly.

How did he live like that?

Why did he live like that?

I was pretty sure I knew the answer to that: Stephen. Peter was absolutely *devoted* to that little boy, and the child clearly loved his father, too. I'd seen them playing around, joking, laughing, a million times. If Peter was five minutes later getting home than Angela would have preferred, I don't know that it was having a huge impact on Stephen, but I knew she would make it *sound* as if it were.

And I was also pretty sure that Angela would be the type to use Stephen as a pawn, threatening to keep him away from Peter. I've known more than one guy who was so scared by the possibility that he wouldn't dare take a chance.

It was sad.

On the other hand, maybe I was just giving Peter excuses that didn't fit. Maybe he stayed because he liked his daily beatings. Maybe it was some sort of Stockholm syndrome and he was afraid to leave the known for the unknown.

Maybe he was just a total pussy.

All I knew for sure was that *I* could never live with the kind of acrimony I witnessed in this house virtually every minute I spent within its walls. I couldn't abide it as a bystander, and I absolutely couldn't imagine being a participant day after day.

The vegetables were cooked, and I turned the heat off and lifted the pan, almost hitting little Stephen—who had sneaked up on me—right in the face with it.

"Whoa, buddy!" I reared back, and a few pieces of zucchini flew out of the pan and hit the floor with a splat. I set down the pan, picked the zucchini slices up off the floor and tossed them into the sink. "You okay? I didn't get you, did I?"

Stephen shook his head.

"Are you hungry?"

He nodded.

"You want veggies with tomato sauce?"

He looked hesitant. "I don't know."

I bet he didn't. It was hard for anyone to know what was all right around here. "I'm going to make a topping for it right now. Want to help?"

"Yes!"

"We'll need to use the blender." I figured he'd be attracted to the noise and potential mess.

Apparently, I was right. "Okay!"

"Okay!" I got out the nutritional yeast and sesame seeds, and a scooper. "We need one of these scoops full of each of these things—can you measure it out?"

"Yeah." He looked uncertain.

"It's easy." I got the blender and set it on the counter in front of him. "Pull up one of those stools and you can reach better."

More noise. He dragged the stool across the wood floor and climbed onto it, smiling.

I could feel Angela's irritation at the noise—which I knew she was picturing creating deep rivets in the floor—radiating from the other room.

"So, here's the scoop." I handed it to him. "First get the flakes." I pushed the canister over to him and watched as he carefully lowered his hand into it and pulled up the measuring scoop.

"Is that too much?" he asked, fretful.

Jeez, this woman had everyone in the house totally cowed!

"Well, you're not finished yet. Now you make it even by taking a knife and scraping it evenly along the top." I demonstrated, running the blunt side of a butter knife along the cup. "See? Now you dump it into the blender."

He did, and looked delighted with himself.

Bless his heart.

"Now take another scoop and do what I just did."

Eagerly, he reached in, scooped out some yeast flakes, and pulled up the measuring cup. I handed him the butter knife, and he was just starting to scrape the measurement even when Angela shrilled loudly from the doorway.

"Exactly *what* is going on here?"

Stephen, startled, let the knife fly, and it clattered onto the countertop, making an edgy rough scraping sound.

"My *God*, that could have been his eye!" Angela hurried over to Stephen, but instead of taking him into her arms and coddling him like you might expect a normal mother to when freaked out about her child's safety, she pulled him roughly off the stool and said, "Go to your room. You *know* you're not allowed to play with knives."

Instantly, I felt horrible. "Please don't be mad at him— it's not his fault! I told him he could help me, so he probably thought it was okay to do what I said since I'm an adult."

She sniffed at me. *Sniffed!* As if it were debatable whether or not I was, in fact, an adult. "You're the *cook*. *You* are not authorized to tell him to do anything."

"No, of course not, I wasn't giving him orders. I just thought it might be nice for him to have a little bit of dis-traction while you and Peter . . . talked."

"Mr. Van Houghten and I—"

Mr. Van Houghten. She'd said it pointedly. Big Me, Little You. It was one of her favorite passive-aggressive tricks.

"—don't need you running interference for us. We're per-fectly capable of having a discussion *and* taking care of our child, thank you very much."

There was so much I wanted to say to her. But even if I

had the freedom to let fly with everything, without regard to losing my job, I wouldn't even know where to begin.

Besides which, I *couldn't* let fly without regard to my job. She was not only in charge of my Monday-night paycheck, but she held the purse strings for my country club job as well. I had already lost Fridays, so I *really* couldn't afford to lose another night.

"Of course, I was just trying to help. I thought he'd have fun helping out."

"It wouldn't have been very fun if he'd poked his eye out with that knife, would it?"

"It was a butter knife, and I was right here," I pointed out. I *had* to. "He really couldn't have gotten hurt."

She tilted her head at me like the old RCA Victor dog and narrowed her eyes. "Is that right?"

I tried to give a little laugh, but it was hard to do in the face of her steely resolve. "Well, I've had my share of knife injuries, believe me, but *none* of them ever came from a butter knife."

She assessed me, judging. Then just shook her head and left the kitchen, passing Peter on his way back in.

"*You* deal with her," she snapped. "I have a *splitting* headache."

If she had a headache, it was bound to be from malnutrition more than from me, her exhausting cook.

Peter ignored her and fastened his gaze on me, concerned. "What happened?"

"I let Stephen measure an ingredient out and gave him a butter knife to level the measure." I grimaced with the retelling, hoping it wouldn't seem so heinous a crime to him as it did to her. "I'm really sorry."

"A *butter* knife?" He laughed and reached for the knife on the counter. "This one?"

"Yes."

"Does it actually *say* Fisher-Price on it?" He turned the knife over, pretending to look for the toy branding, then set it down. "That couldn't have hurt him."

"Honestly, that's what I thought," I said. It was a relief that he wasn't mad. "But Angela came in, and I guess she was scared when she saw it in his hand, so she spoke"— *shrieked*—"and it made him jump and drop the knife. Which, admittedly, isn't something you ever want happening around a child."

Peter waved the notion away. "Don't worry about it. I think it's nice that you were letting him do something in here. She won't even let him come through here without hovering over him to make sure he doesn't eat something unhealthy. Not that you could *find* anything unhealthy in here. Or edible."

I smiled. "Well, she does have a lot of food allergies and whatnot." Onions, dairy, honey, cinnamon, peanuts, carrots, mushrooms, and any kind of root vegetable, to name a few. "That kind of limits what you can keep in the kitchen."

He gave a half shrug. "I don't know that she has *allergies* so much as there are things she doesn't like the idea of."

"They're really not allergies?" He'd said it earlier, but I thought he'd been kidding. I'd been driving myself crazy, scanning the tiny ingredient list on every box, can, bottle, or bag I bought for them for a year, absolutely vigilant about not even purchasing a bag of something that had been next to a bag of something else that was processed in a plant that may or may not have processed peanuts. What a waste of time!

"Not that I know of."

"Huh." Well, it wasn't like I could stop being vigilant about it, anyway. If she said she had allergies, I had to proceed as if that were true, even if it wasn't.

But *why* would she say it if it wasn't true?

There was no reason in the world she needed to lie and tell me she was allergic to stuff if she just didn't like it. She was the boss—if she hated cheese or onions, or if she preferred that I sauté everything in no more than a quarter teaspoon of oil and drew big yellow smiley faces on the napkins, she wouldn't get cheese or onions and I'd sauté everything in no more than a quarter teaspoon of oil and I'd draw big yellow smiley faces on the napkins.

There was no reason to make it seem like a bigger deal than it was for her to want her specifications met.

God, she was tiresome.

"Anyway, thanks for trying to take care of Stephen," Peter went on. "It was a lot better than letting him hear his parents argue. That's for damn sure."

I agreed, but of course couldn't do so out loud. "I was happy to have him here. He's adorable."

Silence stretched between us.

"I guess I'd better finish up here," I said.

"Here." He handed me the knife, and I held it in my left hand as I measured out sesame seeds with my right.

"Thanks."

"Is this the fake Parmesan?" Peter asked.

I nodded. "It's pretty rich, nutritionally."

"It ain't Parmesan."

I laughed. "No, but it also ain't dairy."

"Right." He looked at me, and I saw a distinct weariness in his eyes. This was a guy who'd made a bad deal, and he knew it and paid for it every day of his life. "But it's what she wants. And she gets what she wants."

"A lot of people would call that lucky."

"Yes, they might." A muscle tensed in his jaw. "You're not like her, though."

"Well." What could I say to that? If we were friends chatting in a bar, I could be honest. We weren't, and I couldn't. "We're all different, aren't we?"

His eyes flicked to mine, but he didn't answer.

So I followed my usual compulsion to fill a tense silence with empty chatter. "I have to say, I feel just awful about what happened earlier. It was my fault, not Stephen's. I hate to see him getting in trouble when I asked him for help." Not only asked, but in reflection, I had basically lured him right into a trap.

God, the poor kid was already skittish enough. He'd trusted me for a moment there, and it had led him to get into trouble.

I felt just terrible about that.

"The poor kid." A darkness I'd never seen before on him crossed his features. The bad deal wasn't just his. His son was paying the price, too. "Thanks again for trying to help. I'll go talk with her about it."

I could already anticipate how *that* would go, and I did *not* want to be anywhere near here when it blew. "Everything here will be ready in five minutes. I'll leave it on the counter and slip out."

"Thank you, Gemma." His eyes met mine again, and gratitude softened them. "You're the best."

He went upstairs, and before he reached the landing, I heard Angela's voice rising in anger.

I don't know what they said. I didn't want to know. I couldn't stand it.

It was quite telling that every time I left their house after cooking for them, I felt sick.

Quickly I finished the dish, pouring the hot tomato sauce over the vegetables on a platter, then grinding the nutritional yeast, sesame seeds, salt, and pepper in the blender to make Angela's poor substitute for Parmesan cheese.

I shook that into a bowl, set it next to the dinner platter, put a serving spoon next to it all, and did a quick cleanup so I could get the hell out of there.

This was not a good situation, and not just for Peter and Stephen. Angela had become increasingly . . . difficult (unhappy? hormonal? unbalanced? I had no idea) over the past few months. She'd always been sharp with her husband and son, but the worst she used to be with the nannies or me was condescending. Lately, she'd gotten downright snotty with me, and I wasn't at all confident about my place on their staff.

My days here felt numbered.

It was time to write an ad for the *Washingtonian* classifieds and start marketing myself again. Self-promotion was never my forte, but there was no choice. I needed to replace Fridays quick, before I needed to replace Mondays as well.

I was buzzing on my way home that night.

Irritation kept rising in my chest about Angela, and regret kept washing through me when I remembered the events of Friday night. I had to keep taking deep breaths to calm both emotions. I needed to do something to distract myself. I took a hard left, on an impulse, and decided to get my groceries for the next couple of days. It's not like I'd be able to sleep when I got home, anyway.

Privately rationalizing that I was going this way for convenience and not for any other reason, I drove down Connecticut Avenue and passed No Plans on my left. As soon as I passed it, I shook my head, feeling stupid. What had I expected, just to see him hanging out outside, waiting for me to drive by? And if so, that'd be weird.

I turned up the radio, trying to drown out my thoughts, and pulled up a few minutes later in front of Giant.

I grabbed a shopping cart and let my purse sling into the top compartment. I laughed as I thought of what Angela would do if she saw her cook touching a grocery cart handle without Purelling it first.

My cell phone rang, and I answered when I saw it was Lynn.

"Hey, Lynn—ugh, I've had the worst day."

"Oh, no, really?" She sounded genuinely disappointed. "What happened?"

I let loose, venting about all the frustrations of my evening. She listened carefully, agreeing in all the right spots. I finished with "She's just so . . . *eergh,* you know?"

"God, she sounds like it." She sighed. "You should just quit."

"Ha!" I said, resting the phone on my shoulder as I picked out a few cloves of garlic. "As if it were that easy."

"Once you get Fridays covered, you can just put out another ad for Mondays. Maybe someone will even need both nights!" She gasped at the convenience in her dream scenario.

I smiled at her support and interest in my personal dramas.

"So," she went on, "have you heard from him?"

"How would I have heard from him? He still doesn't have my number. And I still don't know what the note said. It could very well have said, 'Ehh, it was all right. Thanks, though.'"

She laughed appreciatively. "I don't know, I thought maybe he might have tried to track you down. It's like *Serendipity.*"

"Uh-huh, except with slimmer odds. By the way"—I lowered my voice—"I owe you condoms. I should pick them up now."

She laughed. "Um, did we make a bet I don't remember?"

"No, I dug them out of your bedside table on Friday night. It was kind of an emergency."

"Good Lord, I don't even remember having any there. Don't worry about it."

"Well, still, I rifled through your drawer like a truffle-sniffing pig and helped myself to your stuff, so I really should replace—" I turned down an aisle. I almost dropped my phone. I backed out of the aisle again. "Shit, shit, *shit*."

"*What?*"

"It's him!" I whispered. "The guy from the bar is here!"

"Go talk to him!"

"I—what do I say?"

"You might start by getting his last name."

"Very funny. I'm serious, *what* can I say? I've never had a one-night stand before. This is very awkward."

"Play your cards right, and maybe it won't end up being a one-night stand."

As soon as she said the words, a little zing went through my chest. The idea certainly had its appeal.

"Suddenly you're recommending long-term relationships?"

She laughed. "God no. But there's something in between a one-night stand and marriage. Just make sure you stop short of that crucial point."

"Marriage?"

"Engagement."

"I hear you."

"Good. Now, I'm hanging up!" Lynn said when I didn't answer right away. "Go talk to him, you dumb girl!"

And my phone went silent.

I mustered the courage and took a deep breath to steady the butterflies—no, they weren't butterflies; they were elephants trampling my stomach.

I turned down the aisle again, and I saw him reaching into his pocket. I was just about to call his name when I saw him pull out his phone.

"Is it bad?" he answered without preamble. He put his head in his hand and rubbed his eyebrows. "Shit . . . Yup. Yup, I can come back." He was nodding silently. He looked very tired, I was noticing. "I shouldn't be more than fifteen minutes or so."

I didn't know what to do, so I just stood there, frozen. This was not the time. This was clearly not the time. Not only was he obviously leaving, but he was leaving in a hurry and didn't need the inconvenient delay of a conversation he didn't have time for with a woman he didn't know.

I was ready to back out of the aisle once more (I must have looked like an idiot to anyone watching), when he saw me.

"What's the guy saying?" he asked into the phone. He held up a hand to wave at me. I held up my own.

I could say nothing. He mouthed, *One minute.*

I smiled and nodded, hoping he couldn't actually see or hear my heartbeat. *Okay,* I mouthed back.

He returned his attention to the phone, shook his head, and looked a little desperate. "Tell him not to say anything else." He patted his pockets and pulled out his wallet, cradling the phone awkwardly in the crook of his neck. He reached into the compartment and pulled out a card and handed it to me just before whoever was on the other end of the line said something that made him say, "Stop him *now!* Put him on the phone and let me talk to him."

He handed me the card and mouthed the words *Gotta go*, looking apologetic.

I nodded again, feeling like he was water running through my fingers.

He started to hurry out of the store, then stopped. "Hold on one second, Jason." He turned back to me. "Call me, okay? Please, I want to talk to you!"

And then he dropped his basket by the door, pulled keys from his pocket, and walked quickly out of the store. I just stood there, gaping. I'd had him, and then I'd lost him.

I looked at the card in my hand. SUSAN PILLINGTON, FLORAL ARRANGEMENTS.

What the fuck?

This had to be a mistake. Obviously *he* wasn't Susan Pillington. And I seriously doubted he was intentionally sending me on a scavenger hunt to find his name and identity via one obscure clue at a time. No, given the hurry he was in, he must have meant to hand me his card, not hers.

We'd missed again.

Was this fate? Was God, or whatever, going to great lengths to keep us so far apart that we didn't even know each other's whole names?

I called Lynn back as I grabbed the chips I'd walked into the aisle for to begin with. Mr. Tuesday's favorite, and ones he once told me in a note that he could never resist as a midnight snack. It was ironic that I was kind of pining for one man even while I was essentially acting as the perfect wife to another.

Not his real wife, but perhaps something better.

I threw them into my basket just as she answered. "Well, fuck," I said unceremoniously.

"Oh, no, what happened?"

I told her the whole thing.

"What were you gonna do, though?" she asked when I'd finished. "I mean, you could hardly go running after him to tell him you don't have his number."

I shrugged, and then remembering she couldn't see me, I said, "Yup."

"Maybe he'll be at No Plans this Friday. We could go back. Casually check the place out."

The idea was appealing, but I didn't know that I could just be That Girl.

"Maybe." I wound around a corner, suddenly feeling not at all like shopping. "I don't know. We'll talk about it later in the week, okay?"

"Okay. Feel better, babe."

"Okay."

And I hung up, leaving with a strange sense of emptiness, whereas I had gone into the store seeking only a few groceries.

. . .

The *Washingtonian* ad I placed advertising my services went pretty well. It appeared over the weekend and I interviewed with six possible clients, two of whom seemed . . . doable. Not great—honestly, the people who want to hire a private chef aren't always what you'd consider the most "normal" people in the world—but I was pretty comfortable with all the people I interviewed with that day. My instincts told me there weren't any serious wackos in the bunch, though my instincts had *also* told me that Cal was the right guy for the rest of my life, that Yugoslavia would be an "interesting" vacation destination in 1994, and that pillowcase blond would look good on me for my thirtieth birthday.

In short, my instincts were sometimes *way* off.

I would have preferred a personal referral. It also takes a lot of the guesswork out of the personalities involved. Look, you'd have to be a fool to think that in one half-hour interview you can really tell enough about someone's personality to know whether or not there's anything to be extra cautious about.

Obviously, the same is true of those people interviewing me, asking a stranger to come into their home and wield knives (and sometimes have a butterknife-on-the-counter-incident) one night a week. The relationship requires mutual trust, but basing it on someone else's personal knowledge of a person was a much more comfortable springboard into that relationship.

Unfortunately, I needed to earn a certain amount per

week, and I absolutely could not afford to lose one of those nights for long. Granted, I was able to pick up a Friday or Saturday catering job here and there, and luckily I'd done enough of those to sock away some money that would keep me afloat until I replaced the Lemurras, but like I said, Suze Orman would have torn me a new one if I'd called her TV show and told her the honest state of my financial affairs and savings at age thirty-seven.

This was my weakness. I was a right-brained person, a nurturer. Not a numbers girl. My left-brain capacity was not nearly so good as my right. So I was deficient in the savings department, but at least I knew enough to know I had to get more work, and quick. The old me might have taken those days off, combined them with my savings, and gone on vacation, but new me knew better than to sink in those waters.

Now all that new me had to do was find a good piece of driftwood.

And if driftwood couldn't be found in the form of the job I preferred—cooking—I would have to take it in whatever form I could find it.

Which was one of the most motivating things I could come up with: I did *not* want a desk job.

I had to get cooking.

Chapter 6

I have some special needs."

It wasn't the words—I'm used to talking to people about their dietary concerns, especially during a job interview. It was something about the *tone* the guy used when he said it.

And the fact that he was wearing half a clown suit.

The bottom half.

And the nose.

The minute I'd walked into his apartment, I knew it was a mistake and that this wasn't going to be a good fit. Part of me stayed out of morbid curiosity—what could he possibly perceive his special needs to be?—and part of me stayed out of sheer politeness. It just felt too awkward to turn tail and run the minute I'd gotten there.

It was Wednesday, and I had the afternoon and evening

off. Lex, my usual, had forgotten about a party he'd promised to attend, but paid me for the night anyway.

"What in particular?" I asked.

"Well, for one thing—" He shifted his weight and clapped
one huge-shoe-clad leg over the other. Something, somewhere, squeaked. "—do you have a problem with dogs?"

I looked around the apartment. There was no sign of a
dog. Or a maid, for that matter.

God, hopefully he didn't mean *cooking* them.

"I . . . like dogs," I answered cautiously.

"I like dogs, too." So it was the right answer. "And I
really *hate* people who don't like dogs."

Again, it wasn't 100 percent clear in what capacity he
liked dogs.

"Okay, you mean as pets?" I asked.

"Obviously." The red nose twitched. "What, do you think
I *eat* them?"

"Of course not!"

"I did once," he went on, as if he hadn't heard me. "Over-
seas. It was an accident."

"How do you accidentally—?" I stopped, thought better
of it.

He didn't seem to notice. "How much do you charge?"

I told him, explaining that the cost of food was depen-
dent upon, well, the cost of the food, but that my rate for
preparation was always the same.

He cocked his head. "Do you take payment in other
currencies?"

"No."

"What about in something other than money?" He uncrossed his legs and let them lag open, inviting the terrible question of what he was suggesting.

"No. What kind of—?" I stopped as I thought better of it. I didn't want to know his answer. The tamest of which that I could imagine would be Monopoly money and chocolate coins. "Actually, Mr. Lutz, I don't think this is going to work out."

"What isn't?"

"Me working here."

"Who asked you to work here?"

I opened my mouth and then breathed deeply instead of speaking right away. "Isn't that why you called and asked me to come talk to you about work?"

"It's Klutz."

"What?"

"You said *Mr. Lutz,* but it's *Mr. Klutz.*" He gestured, indicating a brown leather suitcase, presumably something he took to work when he went to scare children out of their wits at birthday parties. It had MR. KLUTZ written on it in what appeared to be black Sharpie. It also appeared that a left-handed person might have written it with their right hand. "I had it legally changed."

"You had your name legally changed from Lutz to Klutz?"

"From Lutz to Klutz? No."

I bit my tongue, regretting that we were both sounding like a Dr. Seuss rhyme.

He looked at me as if *I* were the one who was crazy. "From Rosenfeld."

"Wow. Okay." Honestly, if I could have been sure he wasn't about to whip out a bowie knife and call it a mitten before slicing my throat with it, I would have stayed just to see where else this conversation would go. "Anyway, Mr. Rosenfeld, it was very nice to meet you." I started for the door.

"You can call me Klutz."

I let out a noisy breath. "Right."

"You have the number, right?"

This was why I used a disposable phone when interviewing potential new clients. So *they* didn't have *my* number, or any way to find me, if they turned out to be nuts.

"Yes, I do," I said calmly. "My husband's waiting downstairs, so I wish you luck with . . . whatever it is you're looking for."

"Geraniums. I'm looking for geraniums."

I nodded, looking wide-eyed and wishing anyone else were around me to hear the conversation. "Perfect."

I took the stairs. I did *not* want to take a chance on getting stuck on the elevator in this whack job's building. But even as I ran down the stairwell, I had to laugh. I had run into some oddballs in my time—it wasn't all that rare—but that one was up there.

Most people were normal, or normal-ish. We all have our peculiarities. And just because a potential client falls under the umbrella of *normal,* that doesn't mean it's going to be a good fit. A lot of times, it's clear to both parties that it won't be.

But I have to say, those oddballs really are the spice of life sometimes.

The next appointment was more promising.

They were a middle-aged couple in southern Chevy Chase, right on the D.C. border. They'd lived there for all their thirty-odd-year marriage and had a solid reputation in the community.

"Can I get you some tea?" Reva, the wife, asked me. "It's fresh raspberry and basil."

We were sitting in their huge country kitchen. Every upgrade imaginable had been made, from the professional Wolf stove to the wide Sub-Zero fridge (an oldie but goodie) to the slightly angled cement counter with a movable stainless steel hose over it in order to make cleanup a breeze.

I was *dying* to cook in there.

And if great ingredients and combos, like raspberry and basil, were in the pipeline, it was going to be all that much better. "Wow. Sounds amazing. Thanks."

"She's into her witchy concoctions," her husband, Tom, told me. "Loves to make teas and those smelly sachet things, but I can't get her to make a salad." He smiled. "I assume you know your way around a salad?"

"Not a problem."

"We have an herb garden out back," Reva said from across the room.

"Of course," Tom added.

"As well as a very nice selection of lettuces, although I find they grow so slowly that it's not really an economical choice in a back garden like ours."

I nodded. "But at least it's organic."

"Oh, yes, we try to stick to all organic ingredients." Reva set a steaming mug in front of me. "Not that I want you to knock yourself out if you're finding it difficult to procure everything you need without going conventional. It must be difficult to act as a part-time wife in a household where personalities can be so divergent."

This was so refreshing, I could have cried.

Under the best circumstances, my clients were like family to me. Really, in many ways, they replaced the family I had never had myself. So it was unbelievably lucky to find a perfect fit like Tom and Reva seemed to be. They were kind, sensible, realistic, and having lived here—and with each other—for thirty years, they were arguably creatures of habit, which meant a good shot at job security for me.

Penny always joked that I was a wife-for-hire. She was going to love this story. "Yes," I agreed. "You just can't please everyone all the time." I thought of Peter and Angela and their wildly different diet tastes. "Very often, one person ends up feeling left out and that can create a lot of tension. For *all* of us."

"I think you'll find we're pretty easygoing," Tom said, and I believed him.

"Speaking of *not* easygoing, we were at one of Marie

Lemurra's parties one time when you cooked," Reva said, sitting down at the table next to me.

I froze. Marie Lemurra. This had the possibility of turning very bad, very fast. "Were you?"

"Oh, not the stupid *True Wife* one," Reva said with a laugh that immediately put me at ease. "Don't worry. She did kick up a storm about you for a couple of days after that, but everyone knew she was trying to save face."

"I hope that went okay for her," I said, trying to sound sincere.

"Went better for you," Tom said.

"She didn't deserve you," Reva went on. "Marie liked to take credit for the success of those parties, but everyone knew it was your delicious food that made everyone want to keep coming back."

My face flushed with pride. "Thank you," I said, meaning it. "That is so kind of you to say."

"Kindness has nothing to do with it—it's the truth. We wanted to steal you and bring you home the first time we saw you. But I bet you hear that all the time."

"Not really, but it's very flattering."

"Tom's tastes actually tend to run toward the more exotic usually, but . . ." She shrugged. "What can I say? You completely won him over."

"So what do you say?" Tom asked. "Are you interested?"

I looked around the kitchen and just knew I had to be as wide-eyed as a kid on Christmas morning. "Very. I think we could be a really good fit."

They beamed at each other. "I told you she would be perfect," Reva said.

He chuckled indulgently. "You're always right about these things." Then he turned to me. "I suppose you'll be wanting to see the rest of the package."

"Is there *more*?" What next? Their very own Whole Foods right in the basement? A full-time barista to serve me coffee and tea while I cooked?

"Honey, there's *always* more," he said.

Reva nodded. "He's not kidding."

Tom began to work at the buckle of his pants. "Sorry, these are new and they're a little stiff."

"Oh!" Reva clapped her hand to her mouth and laughed.

"No pun intended," he added, wrestling the button free and unzipping the zipper.

What the hell was *happening*?

I know you *think* in a situation like that, you'd just get up immediately and get out of there, but it was so surreal, so *completely* unexpected and inappropriate that my thought process couldn't keep up with what my eyes were actually seeing.

Until he actually stood up and dropped his trousers.

"We do prefer you don't stay overnight most of the time," Reva was saying. "The bed is a king, but three makes for a tight fit when you're trying to get some rest."

"I'm sorry." With surprising calm, I picked up my purse and stood, backing carefully away from the table. "I don't understand what you're thinking I'm going to do for you, and I'm really not sure I want to, but—I—" There was just no room for misinterpretation, even though the logical part of my brain told me to search for one. I mean, they could have taken it into a hundred even weirder directions from here, but this—*this*—was clear enough.

This was *never* going to happen.

"I thought you understood we wanted you to take over as a part-time wife," Reva said, looking genuinely confused. "You just said it yourself."

"Well. Yeah. I mean." What *had* I said? Hadn't I just agreed with their joke reference to my job as being a part-time wife? Yes, Tom had said it must be difficult sometimes. And *I'd* said . . . Oh, dear God. *I'd* said that it was hard to please everyone and that all too often one person ends up feeling left out.

Oh, gross.

"I think we've been at cross-purposes here tonight," Tom said, very sensibly.

"Yes." I nodded spastically. "Yes, we have."

"Oh, dear, I *am* sorry," Reva said. "So you *don't* go from the kitchen to the bedroom? Professionally, I mean."

"No!" Jesus, is *that* what Marie had been saying about me? Where else could they have gotten that impression? I scanned my memory, trying to recall if there had *ever* been an event or party where my role as cook had been open to *any* sort of interpretation.

"This is awkward," Tom observed.

"Yes." I clutched my bag closer to me. "I'm going to go now."

"So sorry for the misunderstanding," Reva said, walking me to the door, though I would have been *so* much happier if she'd just stayed in the kitchen and I could have run away and never looked back.

"It's . . ." What? Okay? No, it wasn't. On top of everything else, they thought I would cook for them *and* have sex with them for what I had believed had been our agreed-upon price for cooking? Incredibly I managed to feel both shocked that they thought I'd do it at all and insulted that they didn't think I was worth more. But they were nice people, and it had clearly been an honest mistake. "Don't . . . don't give it another thought." I smiled pitifully. "I'm going." I increased my stride and threw the door open.

"Give it some thought, won't you?" Reva called behind me as I raced down the wooden front steps and toward my car in the darkness. "We'd love to have you!"

I said nothing and pushed the key fob, and my car lights flared to life. Unfortunately, they weren't bright enough to light up the large divot in the gravel driveway, which I managed to turn my ankle in. No matter, I was like a racehorse, sprinting for the finish line, regardless of the pain of injury. I had to get out of there, and get out fast.

"That's not how *I* meant it," Penny said when she finally stopped laughing long enough to spit out a coherent sentence.

This is the kind of mockery you can take only from family, huh?

I shifted the bag of frozen peas I'd gotten from her freezer to put on my bruised ankle. "You probably *caused* this. You put *wife-for-hire* out into the universe and—boom!—suddenly that's what people expect me to do."

"The most degrading part of all this is the money."

"Tell me about it."

She reached for her water on the coffee table, but her nine months of pregnancy blocked her way. I nudged it closer so she could reach. "Thanks. So do you think Marie Lemurra told everyone that's what you do?"

"I thought of that, but it doesn't make her look so great, does it? Anyone who says they hire someone to come in and cook *and* sleep with her husband looks pretty sketchy."

"She didn't want to sleep with you, too, huh?"

"Ew, gah, I don't know. Just—ew." I shuddered. "Stop talking about it!"

"Oh, honey, I don't know how we can *ever* stop talking about this!"

"Stop talking about what?" Her husband, Dell, walked into the room with two bottles, one of beer and one of ginger ale. He handed me the beer and handed her the ginger ale. "This sounds like something I want to be in on."

"Gem just went to interview with some people about cooking for them, and it turns out they thought the price included sex."

"But not sleeping over," I added. "Don't forget that part of it. They wanted to make *really sure* I wasn't planning on staying over and cramping their style."

"Huh." Dell nodded thoughtfully. "How much extra do you usually charge for the sex?"

"Two hundred."

"That's the package price, right?"

"Of course."

He shrugged. "Seems reasonable to me."

"Oh, *stop*." Penny playfully batted at him with a decorative pillow. "What if Charlotte overhears?" Charlotte was their seven-year-old daughter.

"She is sound asleep," he said, sinking down onto the sofa next to Penny and draping an arm around her. "*Knocked out.* That swim party did her in today."

Penny relaxed under his touch. "Thank goodness."

I watched them, thinking that, if marriage had seemed to me the way it *looked like* it felt to them, I would have been the happiest girl in the world. In fact, Penny kind of *was* the happiest girl in the world. Her relationship with Dell seemed easy, the companionship undeniable. I could only imagine what it was like to go to sleep with someone I adored so much every night and wake up with him in the morning.

The babies were probably the icing on that cake for them. Butter cream, of course.

They were lucky.

"What's the matter?" Penny asked, looking at me, concerned.

"What do you mean? Nothing."

"You just looked upset. Dell didn't offend you by joking around about your price, did he?"

"No!" I said quickly, just as the idea seemed to take hold in him as well. "God no," I assured him quickly. "I totally know you were joking. We both were. I was actually thinking about something else."

"What?" Penny wanted to know.

How jealous I am of your happiness and how alone it sometimes makes me feel.

How incredibly different my life would be if I'd turned left instead of right all those years ago.

How I wonder if I'll ever be sure I made the right decision.

"I was thinking," I said, "that this would be a really good time for you to hurry up and go into labor because of all the unexpected days off I have."

Penny sighed. "I have tried *everything*. Every single thing I could find that might send me into labor without killing me. Nothing works!"

"Time, my love." Dell touched his knuckle to her cheek. "Time will work."

She made a miserable face but snuggled in closer to him.

Well, yes, it was always timing, wasn't it?

Everything in life comes down to timing. Stopping at a yellow light instead of accelerating sometimes makes the difference between life and death.

Problem is, you never know whether you're better off stopping or blasting through. Maybe I should have stopped a long time ago.

And, for just a minute, I really did feel like maybe I'd waited too long, focused too much on my career, and had inadvertently let something important slip away.

Chapter 7

Ah . . . Mr. Tuesday's apartment.

Its cool darkness was a welcome relief after walking in from an unseasonably hot October afternoon. It always felt like leather and soap and masculinity in there, probably less because of the furniture than because of whatever the cleaning lady used. Still, it was a distinctly dignified, manly feel that I loved.

I went to the kitchen area and turned on the overhead lights, bringing the room to life in filmworthy hues and textures. The black granite countertops gleamed, the brushed stainless steel appliances seemed to glow, the hardwood floors shone without a nick or scratch. Inside the fridge was sparkling clean, with a line of Sam Adams beers, the usual condiments on the door, milk, eggs, bacon, yogurt, fruit, and a jar of Wickles Pickles, coincidentally my favorite.

Either he was the tidiest man on earth or his cleaning lady also came on Tuesdays, because the place looked like a showroom every time I came in. I'm pretty sure it was the latter, though I can't say why I had that impression about someone I'd never met. Maybe it was the way the notes he left for me each week always seemed rushed and written in a messy scrawl.

Today's was no exception.

G—

Thanks for the roast chicken. It was awesome, as usual. But maybe next time you don't need to put in quite as much garlic.

I smelled like a buzzard all week.

—P

I smiled and shook my head. He didn't want me to put so much garlic in the chicken that calls for forty cloves of garlic? Would thirty-nine have been better?

I don't trust people who don't like garlic.

Of course, he always seemed to have a little something to say about everything I left for him. They weren't really *complaints*, exactly, just comments. I suspected he might have been goosing me sometimes, just to get a rise out of me. I mean, the buzzard thing *was* kind of funny, though arguably obnoxious.

Slightly disgruntled, I took out the four frozen meals I'd prepared for him over the weekend and put them in the freezer, clipping the instruction sheet I'd typed to a magnet on the side of the fridge.

Then I took out the ingredients I'd brought for tonight's hot meat loaf dinner and laid everything on the counter.

Look, I know everyone thinks their meat loaf is the best, but mine really is. For one thing, I use all beef—no veal, no pork. Why add complication or moral questionability if you don't have to? I make a ketchup and molasses glaze that is to die for, and I don't wrap it in bacon, because as great as bacon is for just about every reason, I don't love it withered and stringy around a filet mignon or draped like a limp dick over a meat loaf.

If your meat loaf depends on it, then forgive me. I'm sure it's excellent.

Mine's just better.

I heated some butter in a large Dutch oven on the stove and took out an onion and celery and my handy chef's knife and started to dice. Unlike the lively voices at the Olekseis' on Wednesdays, or the usually tense undertones of argument at the Van Houghtens', and even the constant din of traffic outside the thin walls of my own condo, the entire place was completely silent except for the quiet, rhythmic chopping and the subtle crisp yielding of the onion to the blade.

It was interrupted by my ringing phone. I set down the knife, wiped my hands on my apron, and took the phone out of my purse. It was him, Paul McMann, Mr. Tuesday himself.

"Hello?"

"Gemma." He always sounded so stern when he said my name. It used to give me pause every time. Now I knew it was just his way. Probably the lawyer in him.

I lowered my voice and imitated his tone. "Yes."

He laughed, obviously recognizing the fact that he was being mocked. "Are you at my place?"

"Yup."

"What are you doing?"

"Just rifling through the drawers and writing rude things on your underwear in Sharpie." I don't know what it was about him that made me so obnoxious, but we probably spoke at least every other week, and it always went like this. He was always walking through a noisy office, and half the time I couldn't hear him.

"Again?"

"What can I say? I'm a one-trick pony."

"Just make sure you write on the outside this time. I really had to jump through hoops to show it to people last time. I was nearly arrested."

"Ahh, good point."

"So what are you making this week?"

"Garlic meat loaf. With a side of garlic mashed potatoes. Garlic green beans. Maybe some garlic gelato for dessert."

"Good, you got my note."

"Yes, I got your note."

"Hey, look, I hate to ask—but maybe you could take a few minutes to make garlic muffins for breakfast?"

"Consider it done."

"All right. Well, here's the reason I'm calling. I'm expecting some really important papers to be couriered over, and they were supposed to bring them to the office, but there was a snafu and the courier is on his way to the apartment instead. I'm on my way out now and will be home before I get back here, so there's no point in having him rerouted. Would you mind waiting and signing for them? I'll pay you for any extra time you have to spend there, obviously."

Like I said, I never minded spending time there. "No problem," I said. "Don't worry about paying extra for my time. I'm waiting for the meat loaf to cook, anyway."

"You're a doll."

I had to smile. "Thanks. The ransom for the papers might be pretty steep, though."

"Will a hundred thousand in small, unmarked bills do?"

This time I laughed. "For now. Where do you want me to leave them?"

"The desk in the study?"

"You got it."

"Great, thanks. I really do appreciate it. Maybe you could text me when they get there."

"Sure thing."

"You are the best." He sounded seriously relieved. "It's been a crazy week here, I'm glad there's at least one damn thing I don't have to worry about."

I smiled to myself. This was, after all, what I found most gratifying about this business. As clichéd as it was—and as big a setback for feminist values—I really liked taking care of people and making things easier and nicer for them. I'm not even sure you could call it generosity on my part, since I got such a charge out of being needed and indispensable in some small way now and then.

To me, this was like having one of the more gratifying parts of a romantic relationship without all the hassle.

"Don't worry about it," I said. "It's really not a problem."

"Now, get back to your garlic extravaganza."

"The vampires are cowering in anticipation."

"Ah, yes, an added benefit." He laughed. "I will repel vampires *and* women."

"You're welcome!"

We hung up and I went back to work but found myself smiling. He was a pain in the neck in a lot of ways—I mean, seriously, not so much garlic in the garlic chicken next time? He might as well have asked me to make it less "chickeny," too. But then again, he was the most *normal* out of all the people I worked for, and there were many weeks where that fact alone saved my sanity. And even when he was being finicky, he was amusing.

The butter was getting too brown, so I turned the burner down and went back to chopping the vegetables and putting the rest of the ingredients together. It was easy to get lost in the simplicity of this task. It was like the old Buddhist "chop wood and carry water" thing—and it had saved me from heartbreak, depression, and stress time and again.

I assembled the meat loaf and put it in the oven, then started working on the glaze. Ketchup doesn't usually excite me. I *use* it, I do put it on my burgers, and I like to dip my fries in ketchup and mayonnaise sometimes, but as an ingredient, it doesn't normally make my heart sing. As an ingredient in the meat loaf glaze, however, it is operatic. I mixed together the ketchup, molasses, cider vinegar, and a few spices in a small saucepan, turned up the heat, and waited for it to start bubbling and reducing down to a thick confection.

Slowly it morphed from orangey red to deep mahogany, and the smell—tangy and savory but with that hint of sweet—filled the kitchen. This was the real key to meat loaf—the almost candied glazing on the top. My ideal meal would be the semi-chewy top of a broiled glazed meat loaf; the crispy, buttery, cheesy top of macaroni and cheese; and the fragile, sweet, crumbly top of brownies.

I also save the top of Hostess cupcakes for last because that's the best part.

I'm a topper, I guess.

I tasted the glaze. It was perfect. Bliss. So I turned the burner off and looked around for something to do.

It would still be an hour before the meat loaf was ready, and I would normally go out and get shopping and whatnot done in the neighborhood while I waited, but since he needed me to be here for the courier, I went into the living room to look for something to read.

There were two large dark wooden bookcases full of books. Hemingway, Joseph Conrad, a few Kinky Friedman mystery novels, and a bunch of tomes on economics and investments.

There was also a photo of an unbelievably hot guy standing in a tropical setting with his arm around a ridiculously thin, pretty blonde. Mr. Tuesday, I assumed, though I didn't know who the woman was. I hadn't seen any obvious signs of a feminine presence here, but that wasn't to say she didn't have a drawer in his bedroom and maybe a few inches of closet space.

Even though much of my work involved having a key to my clients' homes and going in when they weren't there, I had firm rules about not snooping. For one thing, it's wrong. Obviously. And for another, you never know when someone has the equivalent of a nanny cam hidden away, waiting for you to slip up. For all I knew, Mr. Tuesday's edition of *Heart of Darkness* could have a pinhole camera in the spine, recording everything I did every Tuesday.

Actually, it was a creepy thought, and I was pretty sure he wasn't that interested in what I did.

But standing here, looking at the picture, speculating . . . there was nothing wrong with *that*.

It was impossible to tell how tall he was, but easy to tell that under the tropical print shirt and linen pants he wore in the photo, his body was pretty effing solid. His shoulders were broad and the fabric clung just enough to show that he had a muscular chest. His arms were also powerful looking, wide at the biceps but not flexed. I hate it when guys do that thing for pictures where they're flexing but they think you don't know it. For me, the masculinity lies in the guy's self-confidence in knowing he's got it, rather than the needy urge to prove it.

Mr. Tuesday had it. His hair was dark and glossy, his jaw strong and square without being cartoonish. His smile was more beautiful than a movie star's, and his eyes—I couldn't tell the color—crinkled with laugh lines, which I've always found pretty hot.

In short, he was one good-looking man.

Obnoxious, though. Don't get me wrong; I liked him a lot, but I could tell from our interaction that he'd be a pain in the neck to date.

Not that the option was on the table. Like I said, I don't date clients. Besides which, even if he didn't still have the picture of this gorgeous girlfriend displayed—evidence that they were still together, surely—I'd never even met the guy. He was just interesting to try to figure out. A mystery man with a nice voice and plush material surroundings, but no physical body. That is, no physical body I'd ever seen.

As I looked into the eyes of the smiling man, I remembered Mack. Not so technically good-looking as this guy, but man . . . there was just something about him.

I moved away from the bookshelf and studied the pictures on the walls. Most of them were sort of obscure paintings done by people I'd never heard of. There was an unusual theme of tropical shapes done in dark, almost sinister, muted colors.

The furniture was also dark, and almost everything was that thick, solid mission style. Most of my girlfriends would have found it too masculine for their own tastes, but I liked the clean lines.

I was standing by a table, looking down at the items on

it—knowing it was *kind of* snooping, yet following my personal rule not to *touch* anything and not to move anything—when the door buzzed, scaring the crap out of me.

Funny how a guilty conscience will do that to you.

Hand to my pounding heart, I went to the intercom and pressed TALK. "Yes?"

"This is Barney with Crowly Couriers. I have a delivery for Mr. McMann?"

"Okay, I'll buzz you in." I pushed the button for about ten seconds, assuming that was long enough.

About a minute later, there was a knock at the door. I opened it up to find a pimply young guy with dark red hair and faint blue eyes standing there, holding a large envelope. "Is Mr. McMann here?" he asked, glancing behind me.

"No, I'll sign for it."

He looked hesitant and bit his lower lip. "But it's addressed to Mr. McMann."

"Right. I'll make sure he gets it."

He tucked the envelope under his arm and drew it back, as if I'd reached for it. "I don't know—"

"Look," I said, "I've been waiting here for an hour and a half to get this parcel, so let me sign for it. He told me to wait. All you need is a signature. Not *his* signature. After all, you're at *his* apartment, as you know. You made it up here yourself. Obviously, I'm not some sort of thief who broke into the apartment with the hopes that a delivery man would show up with something more interesting than all the stuff that's in here."

He glanced behind me again, as if he had to see what was in there before he could agree with me.

I sighed.

"And what's your name?" he asked, hesitating.

"Gemma Craig."

"Like the diet lady?"

It was incredible that I'd never realized this before and now, for the second time in a week, someone else was pointing it out to me.

"Yes," I said, figuring it was easier than trying to explain the difference between *Jenny* and *Gemma*. "Almost exactly."

He clenched his jaw. "Listen, ma'am, I really don't think I should leave this with anyone but Mr. McMann. No offense, but I don't want to lose my job."

"Look, Barney?"

He nodded.

"I totally understand your concern. So how about this—do you have a number for Mr. McMann there?"

He looked at his log. "Yes."

I handed him my phone. "Okay, then. Why don't you dial it yourself, so you know there's no funny business, and ask him if you can leave the papers with the woman at his address."

He looked doubtful, but took the phone and said, "All right." It seemed to take twenty minutes for him to check the number and the phone and get it dialed.

When he did, he handed it to me.

"No, I meant, you should—," I started, but then Paul answered the phone.

His voice was hard and rushed, and it sounded like he was outside in the wind. "Lisa, we've got them down to manslaughter, but they're still going for time, and I don't think Schlesinger's going to agree to it, because he's convinced their evidence is inadmissible."

Suddenly I was in an episode of *Law & Order* or something. "I'm sorry . . . what?"

"Wait, what?"

"This is Gemma? Not Lisa?" I was, of course, certain of both those facts, but I'm not good when I'm confused. It makes me come off as stupid.

"Gemma?" He sounded equally perplexed.

"Yes . . . at your house?" Again, I knew I was at his place, but the very mention of anything even vaguely criminal apparently made me act guilty of something.

"Oh. Gemma." Understanding pinged in his tone. "What the hell are you doing on the phone?"

"I called you."

He let out a breath. "Sorry, I didn't mean— Never mind, my call forwarding is obviously fucked up. I thought you were my secretary. What do you need?"

"The courier's here, but he won't hand over the package unless you tell him he can."

"What?"

"I said, the courier's here? With the papers you were expecting? But he won't—"

"Put him on the phone!"

Wow, *someone* was sure impatient when he was busy.

I handed the phone to Barney.

He took a short breath. "Hello, this is Barney with Crowly Couriers, and I have a delivery for—"

Even from my place across from Barney, I could hear Paul say, "Give her the fucking papers!"

Barney cleared his throat. "The package is addressed to a Mr. Paul McMann. Is that you?"

"Yes. Now, give her the damn papers."

"Okay." He handed the phone back to me.

"Sorry," I said.

"No, not your fault," Paul said. He didn't sound so irked anymore. "I'm sorry I snapped at you. I'm just distracted by work—innocent guy about to serve time."

"Don't worry about me."

"I pay you to cook, not act as an ad hoc secretary and absorb my impatience."

I laughed. "Look, with that temper, I'm just glad I'm not your wife." Immediately I worried if I'd gone too far.

Fortunately, he gave a chuckle. "You're not the first woman to express that exact sentiment."

I doubted that, but I said, "I'm sure. Now, where did you say you wanted me to leave the papers?"

"Leave 'em on the study desk, please."

"Done." I hung up the phone.

Barney, a shade paler than when he'd first arrived, handed over the package and took out a small electronic box with a stylus. "Sign here, please, Mrs. McMann."

Really no point in correcting him on that one. Then we would have started a whole new cycle of doubts, and I didn't think either Barney *or* I was up for that. I reached for the signature thing, but he held on tight, apparently thinking I was out to steal useless business-specific electronics as well as possibly helping myself to other people's boring work papers.

So I signed. It wasn't neat and no one in a court of law would ever think it was my signature if comparing it to my usual signature, but at this point, I just wanted this kid to hand the thing over and leave so I could finish my job.

And he did.

I took the thick envelope and headed for the den, a room I'd been aware of but never actually entered. It was much the same as the rest of the apartment. Actually, Mr. Tuesday might have been a little bit on dark wood overload, because you could have knocked the wall out and the den would have fit seamlessly into the corner of the living room. It all looked the same to me.

Well, I assumed it was, anyway. The bedroom door was closed. For some reason, the bedroom door was *always* closed. I don't believe there was anything sinister back there—maybe he was just a slob who never made his bed or something.

I was.

Possibly he didn't want anyone else to see that. So I walked past the closed door—yes, totally tempted to open it up and look—and dropped the envelope on the desk in the den.

I went back into the kitchen and took the meat loaf out of the oven, then reheated the glaze and added a little Frank's hot sauce. As soon as it was melty, I poured the mixture over the meat loaf, broiled the dish for two minutes, and—voilà!—it was done.

I took it out of the oven and just beheld my masterpiece for a moment. This happens to me with making meat loaf: I always wish I'd set a tiny bit aside on another baking sheet so I could eat it myself. It was torture looking at this beautiful thing and knowing there was no way in the world I could cut into it without being obvious.

So I put an aluminum foil tent over it, par-steamed some French-cut green beans and almonds, and poked a couple of potatoes with a fork before dropping them into a ziplock with instructions on heating in the microwave. (Basically, "Put in microwave and push 'potato' button twice," since pushing that button once was *never* enough, not in any microwave I'd ever tried.)

Once everything was done and ready to be reheated whenever he (and she?) got home, I put it all in Tupperware and into the fridge with clear directions for everything. I'd learned the importance of extra-clear instructions way back when one of my first clients heated a whole dish of chicken and biscuits with the plastic wrap still on. You could just never assume people had common sense.

I started to leave, then hesitated and turned back. It was hard to resist messing with him. Honestly, if we'd met in a college civics class or something, we probably would have been best friends, I could just tell. Even when he exasperated me—which was much of the time—he made me laugh a lot, too.

He was just that kind of guy.

Of course, if he ever said something seriously obnoxious about my cooking, I probably wouldn't feel so kindly toward him. But he never did. For the most part, he was really appreciative, often noticing even subtle additions and changes of spice or flavoring. He complimented me on my work frequently, and honestly, there's almost nothing I like better than praise for my cooking.

I'm not too proud to admit it.

So I took a pen off the desk and went back into the kitchen. I'd tossed his note, but there was a plain lined pad with a magnetic back on the refrigerator. I took a sheet off that and wrote:

P—

    This is the last of the garlic—don't worry, I'll pick up some more before next week. They sell pounds of it in a jar at Costco, already peeled. I already have plans for Chicken with Seventy-five Cloves of Garlic, and of course, garlic bread and a nice sharp pesto spread to go with it.

    I know this pleases you.

—G

I laid it on the counter and took a head of garlic from the vegetable bin and put it down as a paperweight. I wondered what his response would be.

And with that, I was done with Mr. Tuesday for the week. But I wasn't done thinking about him.

Chapter 8

Wednesday.

"Hello, hello, hello!" Lex hurried into the kitchen, set his leather valise down on the granite-top desk, and came over to kiss my cheek. "I have been *dying* to see you and hear about the party in Georgetown—when—two weekends ago? Were the true wives there?"

"*They* were there. I wasn't." I mixed an Algonquin, his favorite martini with rye, vermouth, and pineapple juice, into a sterling shaker and shook it with ice. I poured it into a martini glass and handed it to him, feeling—as I did every time—like a poor man's Myrna Loy.

He took a sip and closed his eyes in a moment of apparent ecstasy. "I don't know how you do it, but this is better than Mother's. Don't tell her I said so!" He laughed.

No danger of that. "Thanks." I put three eggs in a pan of cold water and put it on the stove to simmer.

He took another sip and set the glass down. "So why weren't you there?"

I told him about the peacock incident. At the end, he laughed and asked, "So do you think any of it made it onto the show?"

"God, I hope not." I explained the whole thing as I chopped lettuce, chicory, and watercress for his Cobb salad. "I never signed a release, so they can't put me on, right?"

"Well"—he gave a skeptical look—"I don't know what the rules are about blurring faces and license plate numbers."

"Oh, no, I didn't even think of that!"

He tapped his finger on his temple. "Always have to use the noodle. And be paranoid." He sipped his drink again. "And *always* look your best." This was something he clearly took to heart. Not one of his silver hairs was ever out of place, he was always dressed immaculately, even when in his "workout clothes." (These consisted of a velour tracksuit that would have looked perfect on any wealthy sitcom character you can think of—Mr. Drummond, from *Diff'rent Strokes* comes to mind.) Somehow everything Lex wore worked for him.

I, on the other hand, had my mousy hair pulled back in a messy ponytail and was wearing green sweats I got from Target a million years ago along with a USMC T-shirt I've had since dating a marine a couple of years ago.

In short, I was *not* camera ready.

"Unless you plan on having a reality show, I don't think I'm in a lot of danger of ending up on TV in the near future," I said to him.

He raised an eyebrow mischievously. "Not a bad idea. The goings-on behind the scenes of a department store."

I laughed and started dicing tomatoes. "Lex, you would hate having cameras follow you around every waking moment. Even *you* couldn't control your close-ups all the time."

He frowned. "Good point."

I nodded. "So are you having another book club tonight?" I loved the idea of him having that group of equally elegant, old-fashioned guests over to shoot the shit.

"Not tonight." He gave a small smile. "I canceled. Tonight there will be just one guest."

"Ooooh! Are you divulging details? Who is it?"

He pressed his lips together for a moment, then said, "Terry. We have some very exciting things to discuss. But that's all I'm going to say. I don't want to jinx things."

"I understand." I didn't, though, and I *totally* wanted to. Was Terry a man or a woman? There didn't seem to be a way to ask that without seeming really nosy and inappropriate.

Which, of course, I was.

He took the shaker to the sink and rinsed it out. It had probably been driving him crazy, sitting there, empty and uncleaned. "Back to your dinner-party-that-wasn't, what will you do on Friday nights now that you're not working for the Lemurras?"

"Good question." I took out ziplock bags I'd brought of

diced turkey breast and crisp bacon and made columns of them on a platter. "I have a few prospects, but nothing I feel really good about." I went to the stove, turned it off, and let the eggs sit to continue cooking until they were hard-boiled.

"There have got to be some nice, normal prospects for you."

"You'd think. But there are all kinds of difficults out there." Understatement. "It's kind of chancy every time you go into someone's private domain."

"Indeed. However, if you don't mind my saying so, *I'd* feel better if you worked for a woman."

"*But* all too often, it's the women who are the *most* difficult." I raised an eyebrow. "Marie Lemurra."

He nodded, but raised one silver eyebrow knowingly. "Yet less likely to try to impose themselves on you."

I rolled my eyes. "You'd be surprised how little the men I work for seem to notice me."

He looked me up and down, but I think he thought I didn't notice. I just *knew* he was assessing my current appearance and deciding that I was not only not *camera ready*, but I was not *man ready*, either, and he was, in fact, not the least bit surprised that the men I worked for didn't notice me.

And, really, he was right.

"Stop judging," I said lightly. "I'm not saying they *should* be noticing me sexually, only that half the time they bump into me like they're not even aware there's another human being in the room."

Lex waved a hand. "I'm sure that's an exaggeration."

"Only a little."

"You know"—he sighed—"you'd look so pretty with the right clothes. . . . Let me take you to the store and have a shopper work with you. On the house!"

"I *have* clothes." I laughed. The clothes I had probably wouldn't qualify as clothes to him. "But if you want me to get dressed up to come cook for you, it's gonna cost you extra."

He laughed, too. "Now, Gemma, this is starting to sound like an illegal operation."

"It probably should be. I'd make a lot more money!"

"Naughty, naughty." He wagged a finger, joking. "Yet so true. I'm going to change my clothes for dinner. Do you need me to do anything here?"

He was the only one of my clients who ever bothered to ask, though I would never have any of them do work in the kitchen when that was what they'd hired me to do. "No, thanks, Lex. You just get ready for your"—I hesitated over the word but said it—"date." My hope was that he would elaborate, but he didn't.

"Will do!" was all he said.

I worked alone in the kitchen while he was gone. This was my meditation. I didn't have the patience to sit for twenty minutes, chanting *om* in the lotus position twice a day, but I could chop, peel, slice, simmer, and bake for hours in complete silence.

I could also do it with anything from Maroon 5 to the Partridge Family blasting, too. It was the Zen of the action that did it for me, not the distraction or lack thereof.

About twenty-five minutes later, Lex came back, wearing the kind of cigarette slacks Rob Petrie would have worn to dance in his living room on *The Dick Van Dyke Show* and a crisp pin-striped shirt. He smelled of expensive cologne.

"Do you know," he said thoughtfully, walking into the kitchen. He went for his drink and took a sip, all the while considering me over the rim. "I have an idea."

"What's that?" I peeled and sliced avocados and popped a piece into my mouth. Avocados are one of my weaknesses. Creamy but firm, even plain, they call margaritas, chips, and good times to mind. Fortunately, they are so nutritious that the fat content is pretty much canceled out. I ate one more small piece, wishing I had some Frank's to drizzle on it, then arranged the rest on the platter.

"If you're serious about needing another client for Friday nights," Lex said. "I might have the solution."

My heart leaped. If Lex had a referral, that would be great. *So* much better than taking a chance on a complete stranger.

Plus, Lex's people were always so fun!

"I'm very serious about it," I said excitedly. "Who do you have in mind?"

He perched on one of the Pottery Barn barstools next to the counter. "Today I was speaking with my niece, Willa, and told her you were coming tonight to do the Cobb salad—which is looking fabulous, by the way—as I was trying to get her out of her house. . . ."

"And—?"

"And it was a no-go." He sighed. "Not surprising, really.

She hasn't left in ages. Honestly, I was trying to tempt her here with your food. Anyway, she declined, but *actually* . . . she needs a private chef."

"Really?" How incredibly fortuitous.

"Yes. But . . ."

There always seemed to be a *but*.

But she just got out of prison for accidentally hacking her last chef into pieces?

But she likes to eat the meat of domestic animals?

But she'll have to pay in buttons instead of cash because she's a little strapped right now?

"But what?" I asked, bracing myself for the answer.

"But she might not agree. I'm thinking about making that particular executive decision for her."

"I don't understand."

"Hiring you to work for her."

"Wow." Sounded good to me. "That's generous of you. All around."

He looked dubious. "You might not say that when you know all the facts."

I paused and looked at him. "What are you getting at?"

"She is somewhat . . . challenging."

"Challenging in what way, exactly?"

"Well . . ."

"Come on, Lex. Hit me with it." I piled the chopped greens into the middle of the platter, then went to the sink to rinse the hard-boiled eggs in cold water.

"It's the reason she never leaves home, actually. She's very . . . heavy."

"Heavy?"

He nodded gravely. "Yes."

"You mean she's into deep, philosophical conversations about being and creation? Or that she's fat?"

"I don't like to use such derogatory terms as 'fat,' especially about my friends or family, but"—he sucked air in through his teeth—"yes, that might be the way many people would describe her."

I cracked the eggshells and peeled them off. "Why would that be a problem? Sounds like the perfect client, actually. Someone who loves food."

"Well, she needs a private chef because frankly, she can't be trusted in the kitchen. She needs all the food out of there except the things that are 'safe,' meals you could leave for her to heat and eat."

"There are a lot of diet services that do that," I said. "I think it's pretty successful for people. Does she cook, or what? You said she doesn't leave the house much."

"Delivery," he said with a shake of his head. "Delivery delivery delivery. Chinese, Peapod from Giant"—Giant was the local grocery store, and Peapod was its delivery service—"pizza . . . you name it."

Who on earth could afford that? "Does she work?"

He took a deep breath that indicated this was another bone of contention for him, though not one I could solve, in any event. "She *gambles.*"

"What?"

He nodded. "Online. Poker." He closed his eyes in disdain. "Of course, her inheritance was not inconsiderable, either. Now, listen, I can tell you right now she's not going to like this. She can be rather a pill. You need to just bulldoze her. Otherwise, she'll bulldoze you."

I laughed. "Gotcha."

He looked concerned. "This might not be a lot of fun for you."

Might not be a lot of fun? He'd never met the Van Houghtens. I could definitely rise to the challenge of reinventing comfort food. Neufchâtel and low-fat sour cream were my friends! Low-carb pasta with omega-3s and protein were the greatest inventions ever! I'd had luck using all of them.

Granted, even though I couldn't resist a good fatty slice of prime rib every now and then, and Fromager d'Affinois bursting into cream in my mouth was like heaven for me— and certainly I had the curves to show for it—but even if I didn't follow a strict diet, I could *certainly* cook one!

I would convert this Willa from a nonbeliever to a believer!

"Compared to some of the people I've worked for, she sounds like a dream," I told him.

"Are you sure?" His face took on an expression of great uncertainty. "I'd hate to have you so overwhelmed by the reality when you meet her that you decide you're not interested. She's had a lot of hard knocks in this life."

"Don't be ridiculous. Give her my number!"

"All right, I will. As long as you understand what I'm saying." His tone was careful. "She's *very* heavy." He drained his glass.

"I hear you." I gave him a querulous look as I passed him on my way back to the sink. "I'm sure it won't be a problem."

"She's morbidly obese."

"I'm still not seeing the problem."

"Perhaps *hundreds* of pounds overweight."

I paused, the water running over my hands. "Wow." The challenge was still alluring, though.

"So you see what I mean? It might not be that much fun to cook celery."

"Oh, it won't be celery." I turned off the water and took the eggs back over to the counter, slicing them slowly and placing them on the platter. "There's the mistake skinny people always make, thinking you have to eat horrid, flavorless food in order to lose weight."

Lex shrugged. "I must say, I'm very glad that is not something I have to be concerned with."

"I'm glad you're not concerned with it, too." I looked at the Cobb salad and wondered how many gazillions of calories were in it.

And I hadn't even made the creamy dressing yet.

It would be fun to try to transform it into a low-calorie meal.

I knew I could do it.

"Tell her to call me," I said, getting out a bowl to make the dressing.

He looked pleased. "I sincerely hope this works out. My sister passed away more than ten years ago now, and my brother-in-law . . ." He rolled his eyes and shook his head.

"Anyway, I'm all Willa really has, and I want to see her get well."

"That's really nice of you, Lex." It was funny. He'd always felt kind of like an uncle to me, and here he was, being all wonderfully uncle-y, just as I could have expected. "And I'm thrilled. She's related to you, so that's a plus right there, and it's a different kind of cooking than I'm doing the rest of the week, which mixes things up." This was sounding better to me all the time.

"All right. All right, then! Let's call her now!" Lex took out his cell phone and began scrolling through the contacts. "I just love getting people together!"

I had to smile. What Lex loved was taking care of people. It was nice that he had this niece, as it seemed unlikely that he'd ever have kids. He was in his late fifties now, a good twenty years older than me, but he would have made a great dad.

My father had died when I was three; I really never knew him. I didn't have even foggy memories. My mother never remarried, but the stress of his death and being a single mother took a toll on her. She smoked nonstop and resorted to fast food and junk for as long as I can remember. She died when I was twenty-two, three days after having a massive heart attack. So there was something very nice about having Lex around. He was sort of *adult* without being *parental,* or even distinctly masculine *or* feminine. He just felt like a grown-up to me. It felt like I could call on him in an emergency, though I'm not sure what kind of emergency he'd be best equipped to deal with.

Fashion emergency, certainly.

But I was pretty sure he'd be a calm head in just about any kind of crisis, and my world was better for having him in it.

I added the spices and oils to the bowl and whisked while he called Willa and introduced my services to her. By the time he was finished describing me, I was pretty sure he had the Barefoot Contessa or perhaps Julia Child herself working for him.

". . . hold on, let me ask her." He put his hand over the mouthpiece and asked me, "Can you meet with her tomorrow morning at her place in Woodley Park?"

"Sure." I tasted the dressing and shook a little more Worcestershire into the bowl. "How's ten?"

He asked her and gave me the thumbs-up.

I tasted the dressing again—now it was perfect.

Maybe things were going to work out after all.

Willa lived in a glorious apartment building near the National Zoo. As I walked through the brisk fall air, and leaves skittered across the sidewalk in front of me, I could really picture myself coming here every Friday night. Every season was beautiful in this part of town, *and* there were two Whole Foods and the Chevy Chase supermarket right on the way there.

I had a good feeling about this.

Right up until I got to the door and rang the buzzer.

A voice inside called, "Go away!"

Lex had warned me about this. Still, I was very uneasy about being heavy-handed with someone I didn't know.

I texted him.

I'm at the door. She said go away.

His response dinged immediately.

Go in anyway.
I can't do that!!!
Okay, wait a minute.

I stood there, and a moment later I heard a phone ringing inside and her voice murmuring like Charlie Brown's teacher.

Next thing I knew, my text tone dinged again.

Go in, she's expecting you.

"Hello?" I opened the door to a beautiful slate foyer. It smelled like crème brûlée. "Wow, it smells great in here!"

"It's no substitute for the real thing," she answered. "So don't start in on any bullshit about replacing one sense for another and fooling my brain into thinking I'm satisfied."

I followed the voice into a white-on-white living room, where sat, on the sofa, the largest human being I'd ever seen. This was not Tyra in a fat suit. It wasn't even Divine in *Polyester.*

This was just a couple of Twinkies short of *What's Eating*

Gilbert Grape. It was largeness on a scale I'd rarely seen in real life. It was arms that looked like puffy sleeves, cutting at the wrist before a hand that looked the way a rubber dishwashing glove looks when you blow it up.

I was shocked, and immediately felt guilty. I wasn't being an asshole—she was just . . . very big.

But my shock clearly registered on my face.

Her expression fell almost imperceptibly, along with her brow. "Is something wrong?" she asked, unmistakably defensive, which was ironic, given the cheerful bright pink, purple, and green hibiscus pattern on the muumuu she wore.

I faked a bright smile. "Wrong?" As if I didn't have any idea what she could possibly be referring to. Ridiculous. God, who did I think I was fooling? "Of course not."

She cocked her head and looked at me in a way that said she totally had my number. "So it's not my weight problem that's giving you trouble."

Now, I have a terrible confession to make. My first thought upon seeing Willa was that she had to be stupid. I mean, most of us have struggled with weight issues to *some* degree. I've cooked for people who had fifty, a hundred pounds to lose. I know there are medical reasons, I know there are emotional reasons, and I know that sometimes the two intersect in seriously damaging ways.

However, I have never understood how someone gets *hundreds* of pounds overweight. It seems like it has to be a self-control issue. What else could it be? Maybe something metabolic, but the body can't convert *nothing* into fat, and it also can't convert a sensible diet into *that much* fat.

Clearly, it seemed to me, this was someone who had zero self-control. Who had somehow passed all the "point of no return" warning signs and thundered on, eating her way out of even semi-reasonable health, social acceptability, even *clothing.*

"Don't pretend Lex didn't tell you that's why you're here," she went on. Her face knotted in something like anger. "And do *not* try and tell me you didn't notice. I see that look you have on your face all the time."

You know the old cliché about "such a pretty face" and so forth? The idea that the diamond can clearly be seen in the rough? Well, in this case, the truth was that I couldn't see what Willa would look like without the weight. Her face was like risen bread dough with a few finger dents poked into it for eyes and a mouth. Her nose was there, of course, but indistinct. If she lost weight, maybe it would remain a bulbous bump or maybe it would become a refined slice; it was impossible to guess.

"I'm sorry," was all I could say. I went into the room and reached out to shake her hand. "It's very nice to meet you. I'm Gemma Craig."

She ignored my outstretched hand and met my eye. "You're joking, right?"

A million thoughts whizzed through my mind. Joking? Why? Was she a germophobe, too? Did I look like I couldn't cook? "What do you mean?"

"Gemma Craig?" She looked at me expectantly, then, when I didn't take the bait, added, "Like Jenny Craig? The whole diet guru thing?"

"Oh!" I felt warmth flush into my face. "You know, I never even thought about that until someone pointed it out last week."

For the first time, her face softened into something approaching a smile, though it didn't quite get there. "Are you serious?"

"Totally."

She shook her head. "You're a professional chef, and it's never occurred to you that your name rhymes with Jenny Craig?"

I tried to laugh. Here I'd been thinking maybe *she* was stupid, and for years I'd missed the most obvious pun possible.

"Well," she went on, "I hope you cook better than you rhyme."

"I think I do."

She looked me up and down, then gestured at the chair adjacent to the sofa. "Have a seat. Please."

I sat.

"As I'm sure you've gathered, and as I'm even more sure you've been told, I'm not really into this idea of having someone come in and cook."

I hedged, trying to figure out what to say that wouldn't be obviously patronizing. "I don't really know—"

"Yes, you do."

I nodded.

"I like flavor," she said. "Not rabbit food. I know that doesn't go with the whole weight-loss thing, so I'd like to know what you think you can make that I'll actually want to *eat*."

"I can make *anything* you want to eat."

"Fried chicken?"

It was such a cliché, I doubted she even really liked it, but still I said, "Baked that's better than fried."

She rolled her eyes.

"I bet you wouldn't know the difference, in a taste test."

She raised a brow. "I'll take that bet."

No small statement for a gambler. "What else?"

"Pizza."

"Easy. Child's play. What else?"

"Dessert."

"You like chocolate?"

"Eh." She held out her hand and tipped it side to side. "Ice cream. The *real* thing, not ice milk, not low-fat ice cream, not frozen yogurt, but full-fat, Ben and Jerry's *ice cream*."

I thought of a recipe I'd been making recently for strawberries with chocolate balsamic vinegar and cracked pepper, spilled over a small amount of dense premium vanilla ice cream. The whole thing had comparatively few calories but was satisfying because it had such a huge punch of flavor. "No problem," I told her confidently.

"Seriously?" She narrowed her eyes.

"Absolutely."

"No tricks? You're not going to try and slip no-fat frozen yogurt by me as the real thing?"

"Never."

"Huh." She considered for a moment.

"It's worth a try, isn't it?" And at this point, that was the best I could say for my end of it. Lex was right: This woman was a pill. But not a real bitch. She was no Angela, for example. Still, it wasn't hard to see that this could go badly.

"I don't think I'm going to like it, and usually if I think I'm not going to like something, I'm right—"

Well, sure, if you *decide* you feel a certain way about something, you're apt to go ahead and feel that way.

"—but I'll give it a shot," she finished, surprising me.

"I didn't see that coming," I said honestly. It was obvious that honesty was going to be the best policy with her.

"It's my job to keep a poker face," she said, doing just that. I had no idea if she was being ironic or serious.

"Okay, well, if you're willing to try this, so am I. After all, it's a pretty simple formula. Fewer calories in, a little more movement . . . It's tried and true. I'm sure we can succeed together."

"Don't get cocky," she warned, and all trace of humor was gone. Her face was a wide, blank landscape, like the surface of the moon with no discernible life or energy to it. "I said I'll give it a *shot*. But I *really* don't think this is going to work."

Unfortunately, I didn't think so, either. It was hard to sell someone something they were sure they didn't want to buy.

Chapter 9

The Oleksei family lived in a house on Wyndham Place in Northwest D.C., in a neighborhood that could once have been populated by Cleavers, Petries, Stones, and Haskells. It was a Cape Cod that looked small from the outside, but somehow managed to have five fairly large levels, and five larger-than-life occupants, on the inside.

But there was a weird tension in the house. Nothing I could put my finger on. Just something . . . indefinable . . . that made me vaguely uncomfortable every time I went in there. Not uncomfortable like I was in danger, just uncomfortable like there was some creepy essence in there.

Like the ghost of a mean old woman, standing next to me, glaring.

Therefore, I usually tried to do most of my prep work for the hot meal in advance, so I didn't have to stand there with the various members of the family, tediously chopping, mixing, and so on while wishing they weren't there. But with tonight's eggplant with walnut sauce, there wasn't a lot that could be done in advance.

So when I showed up and Viktor—the eldest son—was having a screaming match with his wife, Cindy, all I could do was try to blend into the woodwork and be as invisible as possible.

Fortunately, most of the people I worked for *did* find me invisible, so disappearing wasn't usually too difficult, though it's never really easy to be around two people who are all-out screaming at each other.

"You did not have to speak to him!" Viktor threw his arms up. "There was *no reason* for you to speak to him!"

I took the groceries out and set them on the counter.

"He asked for *directions*!" Cindy returned, just as heatedly.

Eggplant, garlic, coriander, pomegranate juice, walnuts . . .

"He could have found his way!"

I opened my knife case and took out a chef's knife and reached for the cutting board behind the sink.

"To the Leicesters'? Two doors down? I would have looked like a fool if I'd just shrugged and walked away."

Viktor slammed his hand down on the tabletop, making me jump, but not Cindy. Fortunately, I had a good grip on the knife, because it would have been just like me to drop it and chop off a toe.

"It's all about *appearances* with you!" Viktor shouted. "*You* don't want to look like a fool, so you make your husband look like one instead! Very nice. Very, very nice."

Cindy had been bitchy to me on more than one occasion, but I have to say I was completely on her side with this one, even though I didn't know all the details. Nevertheless, even if it was a carful of men she'd had one-night stands with, if they were simply asking which house belonged to the people they were visiting, it would have been nuts for her to ignore them or to pretend not to know.

"Ask Jenna!" Cindy said.

That was the other thing. In a year and counting, she still thought my name was Jenna. Maybe all of them did, but she was the only one who spoke completely unaccented English, so she was the only one I could really hear the mispronunciation with.

They wrote the checks to the right name. That was the only thing that really mattered to me.

"Okay, we'll ask her."

All I could think was, *Please don't ask me, please don't ask me, please don't ask me. . . .*

Both of them approached the counter, and I—in an acting job worthy of either Gabor sister but no Streep—pretended I didn't hear them and turned to rinse the eggplant in the sink.

"Jenna!"

I rolled my eyes to myself, then turned around. "Did you need something?"

"Do you think a married woman should be fraternizing with other men?" Viktor asked.

Oh, God. That was *not* the question. What a jerk. "Depends what you mean by fraternizing, I guess. I don't know." Play dumb. Play possum if necessary.

"Giving directions to neighbors," Cindy supplied.

I sliced cleanly into the eggplant and set the slice aside on a plate. "There's probably nothing wrong with giving directions," I said carefully. "We all need help getting where we're going sometimes."

She crossed her arms in front of her and gave her husband a smug smile. "See?"

Viktor's face darkened. "And if a woman does it with her, how do you say it, with her *tits* hanging out. Is it okay then?"

Slice.

"Oh my *God*, Viktor. You don't talk to the damn *maid* that way!"

Chef.

Slice.

"You are going to be really sorry about this," he said to her in a low, fierce voice.

"You don't scare me."

Everything Dell and Penny made look *good* about marriage, Cindy and Viktor made look *horrible.*

The doorbell rang, and I looked at the two of them glaring at each other, challenging each other in a strangely fierce game of chicken, to move.

I needed no such challenge. "Why don't I just get that?" I suggested, and neither of them made a move. I could have said, *I think that's Santa Claus over there giving John Lennon a back rub*, and they wouldn't have moved their eyes from each other.

I went to the front door, wiping my hands on a dish towel and wondering if I should find a new Thursday night in addition to a new Friday night. Except I really liked making the Russian food. It made for an interesting change from the norm, and it seemed unlikely that there was someone else in the D.C. area looking for a weekly infusion of noodles, potatoes, and other starches all mixed together.

I opened the door. A small, balding man in an ill-fitting suit was on the front step, and he jumped, apparently startled, when I opened the door. What did he think, that someone was just going to vaporize out there to usher him in?

"Can I help you?" I asked, knowing immediately that I couldn't. I didn't normally get the door, and I suddenly realized that no matter who this guy was here to see, I wasn't going to be sure how to direct him.

Particularly given the scene that had just taken place in the kitchen over Cindy giving driving directions to a house twenty yards away.

"I'm here to see"—he looked left and right, then lowered his voice—"*Vlad*."

"Oh. Okay." Most people came to see Vlad. I, on the other hand, rarely laid eyes on him. What was I going to do now? Go to the secret room where he was always holed up and bang on the door, telling him he had a gentleman caller?

Fortunately, Viktor showed up and pushed me out of the way. Well, *pushed* might be a little strong, but it was a bit more than a nudge. I bristled at his touch, but then remembered the ugly scene that had just taken place with Cindy and decided it was better not to cross him under any circumstances.

"What do you want?" he asked the man, and I could swear his accent got stronger.

"I—I'm here to see Vlad? Vlad Oleksei? I'm not sure if this is the right place. I was expecting an office, but I was told—"

"You're in the right place." Viktor flashed me an impatient look that left no doubt that I was not supposed to be there.

So I went back to the kitchen and salted the sliced eggplant while the man was shuffled into Vlad's office. Or torture chamber. Or whatever it was.

Borya and Serge came in then. Like rambunctious adolescents being called in for dinner when they would rather keep roughhousing. They were small and sturdy— Tweedledum and Tweedledee to Viktor's taller, darker, arguably handsome looks. I mean, if Viktor weren't such a dick to Cindy, I might have thought he was kind of hot.

Clearly *he* thought he was hot.

"Who was at the door?" Borya asked, then wiped his nose with the back of his hand.

Lovely.

"I'm not sure." I put a pan on the stove and heated the burner to medium, focusing hard on the task. "Someone to see your father."

I could swear they exchanged a look.

What did *that* mean?

I put a big slab of butter into the pan. The Olekseis didn't give one tiny damn about health, which made them refreshing to cook for, and my motto was pretty much, *When in doubt, add butter.*

Right now, I was definitely in doubt.

I added more butter.

"So what is it your father does?" I asked, as if it had been explained to me previously but I'd simply forgotten.

This time they definitely exchanged a look.

"We are in the cleaning business," Serge said, and Borya nodded.

He paused over *cleaning business;* I'm sure of it. I was tempted to point out that Vlad wasn't dry-cleaning wedding dresses and ironing shirts for people in the back room when they came in, but I held my tongue. Instead, I started frying the eggplant and dissolving into the background, which was understood by everyone to be my role.

"Is it the last one today?" Serge asked Borya.

"Of course." Borya gestured at me. I pretended not to notice but a chill went down my spine.

I placed three eggplant slices in the hot pan and they sizzled.

Serge said, "Oh, yes, yes." As if I were somehow the key

to *him* (whoever *he* was, presumably the guy who was seeing Vlad) being *the last one* (last what?). "What are you making?" he asked me.

"Eggplant with a pomegranate walnut sauce." It was nice to be able to answer at least something with certainty. I turned the eggplant over in the pan. The sauce was just a mixture of pomegranate juice, good red wine vinegar, garlic, red pepper flakes, and salt. Nothing else. It was hard for me to resist embellishing recipes that called for so little, but the complexity of the juice itself transformed what would otherwise be the world's most basic support ingredients into a symphony of flavor.

"It's from my grandmother's recipe collection?"

"Yes." My friend who was translating had run low on time this week, so I'd just told him to pick the shortest recipe in the book and give me that one. Some of the grandmother's recipes were quite long and involved, and I was dying to try them, too. "So . . . this should be ready in about twenty minutes, give or take." I took the eggplant slices out and put them on a paper towel, then put more in, saying, "When do you think your father will be available?"

He glanced at the clock and said, with complete certainty, "Twenty-five minutes."

"That works perfectly, then." I waited, hoping he'd elaborate, but he didn't.

Borya disappeared down the hall, toward the back room where Vlad took his meetings. After a moment, Serge joined him.

I was glad to be alone.

It was short-lived, though. Cindy came into the kitchen about five minutes later. "Sorry about before," she said. "Viktor can be a real jerk sometimes. He's all worried about this *thing* his father's involved in, so he's even worse than usual."

"Oh, that's . . ." What? Okay? Uncomfortable? Your problem, not mine? I couldn't think of a way to end the sentence, so I didn't.

She nodded. Apparently my silence was the most profound thing I could have come up with for her. "Have you ever been married?" she asked me.

This personal question, particularly from someone who'd been calling me Jenna for almost a year, took me by surprise. "No, I haven't."

"Why not?" She looked me over—her manicured, made-up, designer-clad self shining like a beacon next to the shrub that was me—and frowned, as if such a thing seemed impossible.

"I guess I never found the right man." I hated giving her the answer that would make sense to her for all the wrong reasons.

She nodded. "It's a jungle out there. Have you tried a lot of dating services and things?"

The assumption that I not only had been to dating services but that I had also obviously burned through *a lot* of them was insulting. "None, actually." I turned the eggplant slices over in the pan. "I don't really have a lot of time for dating."

"Really? What do you spend your time doing?"

I looked at the stove and then at her. "Working."

"At . . . this?" She smiled, but it wasn't charming. "I mean, is this your only job?"

"Yes." My voice was getting as crisp as the eggplant. "This is what I do. I have other clients to fill up the week and special events on the weekends at the country club."

"Oh."

I took the eggplant out of the pan. Suddenly it looked dark, gray, and depressing to me.

The smell made me feel a little ill.

"I love my job," I added, though it was probably a bit too defensively.

She sighed. "I need a lawyer."

"What?" My question had been automatic, but I immediately wished I could take it back.

"A divorce lawyer. I need a good divorce lawyer."

"Well." Why was she saying this to me?

"Do you know one?"

This was starting to make me nervous. I had no way of knowing for sure, of course, but my impression was that Viktor wasn't privy to these thoughts she was having. Or, if he was, he wasn't worried about them. But it didn't make sense that a man worried about his wife divorcing him would be hammering her about something as petty as giving driving directions to another man. So if Cindy was thinking of divorcing Viktor but Viktor didn't know it, I sure as shit didn't want to get caught talking to her about it.

"I'm sorry?" I hedged. I was bad at improvisation. Focus on work. Pour pomegranate juice into the pan to reduce it to a syrup. Chop the garlic. Add the salt and red pepper flakes.

Toasted walnuts were the garnish.

Perfect.

"Could you recommend a divorce lawyer for me?" she pressed.

Ugh. "Wow, I really—"

"*Divorce lawyer?*" The question came with such ferocity that there could be no doubt who was asking, even before Viktor rounded the corner, red-faced and wide-eyed. "Do my ears deceive me, or did you just ask the maid for a divorce lawyer?"

Chef.

But *really* not the time to argue that.

Cindy's face paled. "It wasn't for *me*," she lied badly. "I was asking Jenna about her divorce because my friend Ramona is looking for someone."

Somehow his expression darkened. "I've never heard of this Ramona."

"She's in my Yogilates class."

He didn't look like he believed her one bit. "Ramona."

"Yes."

I turned and stirred the chopped nuts, garlic, and spices into the sauce and turned off the burner.

Behind me, I heard Cindy say, "She's a new friend. You haven't met her yet."

I assembled the eggplant slices onto a platter, then poured the sauce into a gravy boat. Incredibly, and luckily, I was invisible to the two of them again. Viktor and Cindy, whatever their supposedly "humble" upbringings, had an amazing capacity for completely ignoring the "help"—this was not a conversation I would have had within fifty feet and three locked doors of anyone, if I could help it.

"*You listen to me*," Viktor said, capturing both Cindy's attention and mine.

Now, believe me, *I* didn't want to listen. I absolutely love a good story, and the gossipier it is, the better usually, but this was not a scene I wanted to witness. I'd learned a long time ago it was really hard to rebound from witnessing a personal scene in a client's home because *most* people are well aware that the hired help tends not to be blind, deaf, and dumb. (And all too often, the hired help then goes out and tries to make a buck off what they see, hear, and can say for the right price . . . particularly if the client in question is either famous or rich enough to be blackmailed.)

That said, they were across from me on the counter that was my workspace. However much I tried to ignore them, it was impossible.

Especially when he swooped in closer to his wife's face and said, "Make no mistake. I will see you *dead* before I will see you in divorce court."

Ah. True love.

I was trying to bolt out the door and get away from yet more marital acrimony when the great Vlad Oleksei himself showed up in the kitchen.

This was a rare thing, believe me. Most of the time,

people showed up at the door, as they had tonight, looking nervous and agitated, ready for an appointment with Vlad. Once I came up with the whole Russian Mob Theory, I imagined that they left as emotional basket cases—which at least half, maybe more, of them did—because their family's lives or kneecaps had been threatened.

So when Vlad showed up in the kitchen, pointed a gnarled finger at me, and said, "*You*. I need to talk to you in private," believe me, I was scared to death.

"Me?" I touched a hand to my chest and looked around, as if there were any possibility that he was actually talking to someone else.

I was, of course, the only one there.

"Yes, you." He snorted, like I was an idiot. "Who you think I's talking to?"

"Well . . ." There was no answer. Best not to try. "I don't know."

"Come." He gave the universal *come with me now* arm gesture. "We talk."

I didn't want to talk.

I didn't want to hear.

I didn't want to die.

But this was more crazy stuff from my imagination. I knew that. I'd been working for them for ages; they knew I was a good employee, discreet and trustworthy.

Maybe he wanted to talk to me about a raise!

Okay, stop laughing. I know that sounds a little overly optimistic, but I didn't do super well with middle ground. My imagination tended toward either the very grim or the very great. And there was no reason *not* to hope this could be great. I mean, for real, I'd made their Russian meals seriously kick-ass.

In any event, he beckoned and I followed, well aware that I was about to see, at last—for better or for worse—the locked room in which Vlad conducted the business that made people nervous coming in and, a good percentage of the time, weeping copiously on their way out of the house.

It smelled funny.

He paused outside the door. "I don't normally do this," he said to me with a significant nod of the head.

Trepidation gripped my chest. "Maybe you shouldn't then? . . . I don't want to make you uncomfortable."

He shook his head with great impatience. "I *have* to. Sometimes God does not give choice."

Okay, shit. *God* was telling him he had to do something here? That sounded like crazy "talking to the devil" stuff to me. I didn't normally believe in that, truly, but my friend Jamie totally believed, and though I dismissed it out of hand over drinks at a nice restaurant, it was harder simply to dismiss it at this moment.

"What is . . . God telling you to do?" I asked as gently as I could manage.

Vlad was older, and definitely weird, but he knew when he was being condescended to. "God gives me vision. Vision for you."

Okay, I don't know if the rest of the world would have had this figured out by now, but all I can tell you is that I did not. I didn't know what he was talking about, and if I was worth my salt at all, I would have told him I was uncomfortable with the meeting he was trying to coordinate and either we could do it in the open—and easy-to-escape-from—living room, or we could not do it at all.

Naturally, I opted for the wimp path.

So, thinking that Vlad *might* be a Russian Mafia kingpin, but fearing being rude above all else, I followed him back to the mysterious room where I'd seen countless people walk in smiling and walk out crying.

It was a small room, with deep mauve walls and no pictures or decorations. The only furniture was a utilitarian wooden desk—with no drawers or shelves—an orthopedic office chair, and three folding chairs opposite it. The only light came from one of those green glass banker's lamps on the desk.

He indicated that I should sit in one of the folding chairs, while he creaked painfully over to the executive chair on the other side of the desk.

Any second now, he might start talking about that raise.

But no, he took out a deck of cards and handed them to me. "Shuffle."

Yes, I was still confused. "I'm sorry, do what?"

He looked at me like I was an idiot. In retrospect, I can't say I blame him. "Shuffle the cards."

"Why?"

"So they absorb your energy."

"But—" Finally it dawned on me. "Wait, are you a *psychic* or something?"

Now, here's a fact you might want to keep in your back

pocket: If you work for one of the most famous clairvoyants in the Metro area for almost a year and don't realize it, you might want to keep that little bit of ignorance to yourself.

Unless you really want to insult them, that is.

"Is this joke?" he asked, his expression darkening.

"No, I"—I just didn't know what to say—"I work in your home, so I try to mind my own business as much as possible when I'm here. More so than if I were, say, your neighbor, or—"

He snatched the unshuffled cards from my hands. "I try to *help* you!"

"Oh! Well, thanks, but I think I'm okay. . . ."

He scoffed. Actually *scoffed*. "You do not know what Vlad knows!"

I have never believed in psychics. At least not since I realized the gypsy at the carnival was Mrs. Rooks. I believe some of them might believe they're psychic, so they may come at it from a well-intentioned place, but I think at best they are people who are very good at reading other people.

The rest are just thieves.

I'm not sure it's that hard to be either one of those things. If you think about it, almost everyone you know is wrestling with either a money, job, or romance issue to some degree. Even most happy people would probably agree they'd like to better their lot in at least one of those areas.

Mrs. Rooks was one of the best examples of that, actually. Apart from the bitter tirade against men and marriage that she'd unleashed on me, she'd evidently done a pretty good job of convincing my classmates she was the real deal.

Obviously, she'd had a few pat, universal "predictions" and she'd divvied them out to the amazement of my friends.

She knew I don't like school!

She said a new boy was going to come into my life and ask me out!

How could she know my best friend wouldn't keep my secret?

It was all just basic body-language reading. Almost anyone could do it.

However, Vlad Oleksei did it for a living, and whatever his gift actually was, he was apparently good enough at it to have people coming to him all day long and taking him very seriously.

Besides which, I couldn't afford to insult him and lose my job.

"I'm sorry," I said to him. "You're right, I don't know what you know."

He eyed me. "You *need* to know."

"Okay—?"

He thrust the cards in my direction again. "Shuffle."

So I shuffled. "Is that enough?"

He splayed his hands. "If you say it's enough, it's enough. Cut three times to the left."

I wondered if he meant cut three times, to make *four* piles, or make three piles, but I didn't dare ask. I made three piles.

Apparently that was right, because he gathered them up and spread them in a line in front of him. "I see a man here, a man in your life—"

And here we go.

"—it's not romantic," he added, looking sharply at me.

Okay, I'm a private chef. I work in people's homes. Obviously, I interact with men on a nonromantic basis. Hell, he could have claimed to have been talking about any one of his sons, or even himself!

I waited for more.

After a loud rattle of breath, he said, "You're making some sort of movie with him."

"Movie?"

He nodded. "Film. You know, a—what do you call it?—a video, a movie."

I frowned. "I don't know what that could be." I think it was the sheer unexpectedness of such a specific and odd detail, but I did find myself trying to imagine what he could be talking about. "You mean, like, at a family gathering?" We were sure to have a party once Penny's baby was born.

Vlad frowned. "I don't think so." He pushed some of the cards around, looking at them like he was trying to read a menu without his glasses on. "It's just two of you."

I know what you're thinking. But, no, I'm not a sex tape kind of girl.

"I seriously don't know what that could be," I said.

He shrugged. "It will reveal later. Also, there is a woman. Lighter hair than you. Light eyes. She looks close, you see her often. Do you know who this could be?"

"Maybe my cousin." This is just how it works. He asks a vague question, I feed him the answer, and he turns it around and gives it back to me in a way designed to make me think he came up with it himself. It was dazzling, really.

"She's very thin?"

"Well . . ." Normally, but she was pregnant. "She's been up and down."

"She's angry." He continued to scrutinize the cards.

"Angry?"

He nodded. "Do you know this?"

"I don't know."

He didn't answer, just gave a shrug like *that* no longer mattered, and he was on to something else. "There's another man here." He sounded surprised. "You were married before?"

"No." This was bullshit.

Vlad nodded, his forehead creasing like origami. "You will. Soon."

I gave a laugh. "Nooo, I don't think that's going to happen." In fact, my last gypsy experience had warned me specifically against it. Granted, it was Mrs. Rooks, but it had made an impression.

And *soon*? How could I marry anyone *soon* when I didn't know anyone I'd even sleep with?

Except, of course, for Mack—whose last name I didn't even know.

"You will," Vlad insisted. He was not going to let me disagree. "It's the man you're with now."

"I'm not dating anyone right now." There you go, I was going to marry no one and spend the rest of my life with him. Mr. Nobody. *That* I could believe.

He looked at the cards again, then at me. "Yes, you are, I see him right here." He pointed at the King of Clubs, like that would prove it to me. "You've been with him for quite some time."

"Seriously, I'm not seeing anyone." Though I didn't want to, I thought of Mack again. I almost shook my head at the thought. He was a one-night stand. Our *Affair to Remember* moment had come and gone at the grocery store.

"But you are right here." He thumped his index finger on the Queen of Diamonds. "And he is here. Next to you." He looked at me like he'd caught me in a lie.

"Honestly, I don't know who that is. I don't recognize him." Obviously. I almost laughed at the idea of the little cartoon man being someone recognizable. "I mean, I can't even imagine who it could be. Unless you're getting my cousin and me mixed up, and that's *her* husband."

It's easy to get wrapped up in this stuff and try to make it make sense.

"No, this is you." He shook his head. "I see it clearly."

"Well . . . all right." This was getting boring. I just wanted it to end. "I guess . . . I don't know."

"If you don't now, you will."

He went on to say a few more things. Something about minor car trouble, look out for getting speeding tickets, the kind of warnings you could reasonably issue to anyone as they were leaving the house in anything other than a plastic bubble surrounded by armed guards.

When he finished, maybe twenty minutes after we'd sat

down, he drew the cards back up into a single pile and plopped it down on the desk.

"That's all I see right now."

I stood up. "Well, thanks. I appreciate your taking the time to do this for me."

"The woman is very angry. Be careful."

I racked my brain again, even though I didn't believe a word of this, and came up with Marie Lemurra. But she didn't care about me. I'd seen her get angry time and again; it blew over as soon as she removed the source of her anger. In this case, firing me.

There was no way he was seeing any sort of real future. At best—at absolute *best*—he could get me so psyched out about certain things that I'd start to expect things like speeding tickets, and I'd drive faster subconsciously, get a ticket, and then think he was right.

But there was no point in trying to debunk the man to his face.

"I will watch out," I said, and gave him what I hoped was a reassuring smile. "Thank you."

I left, but cooking their meal had left a bad taste in my mouth this time.

Chapter 10

No one was there when I got to the Van Houghten house, but Angela had left a note with very specific instructions. Apparently, she suspected something I'd cooked the week before had hidden soy in it and she wanted me to be triple sure there was no soy or soy derivative in any of her food, since it would "wreak havoc" on her skin.

We couldn't have that.

So I looked at the ingredients I'd just bought for a sushi-grade raw tuna Caesar salad—no croutons (gluten), cheese (dairy), or anchovy (garlic oil)—and scanned the labels for soy.

I was making the dressing—a difficult task, given my additional restrictions—when Peter came in.

"Hey, there." He was dressed in his running gear: long-sleeved Under Armour shirt and running pants that, mercifully, were not too tight. "What're you making? Smells good."

"That's probably the tuna you're smelling." I gestured with the whisk to where the tuna was sitting on the counter. At this point, Angela's food sensitivities had reached such epic proportions that all I could use to season her meals was salt and pepper. Tonight I'd put multicolored peppercorns into my grinder with the hopes that what the food would now lack in taste complexity it might make up for a little bit visually. And that was going to have to carry the whole meal, I was afraid.

"Mmmmm." He walked up behind me to take a look. He smelled like cold air. "You are the best, Gemma. I don't know what we'd do without you."

"You're reaching the point where I'm not sure I make much of a difference," I said. "Soon you'll just be having raw celery for dinner, I'm afraid."

He laughed. "But you'd be able to make that taste good."

"I don't know."

I reached for the pepper grinder at the same moment he did, and our hands knocked. I drew back liked I'd touched a snake.

He handed it to me. "So she's still allowing pepper."

I laughed. "So far." Pepper was pepper. She didn't have an allergy or anything like that, but it was all too easy to imagine her getting a gander at the colorful flecks on the chicken tonight and imagining there was some hidden allergen in them.

"Well, it looks good to me." He smiled and leaned back on the counter. "So, tell me, what is your favorite food to cook?"

"Oh, wow, I don't know. I like cooking just about anything. Every time it's a challenge, you know? But if I had to pick, I'd probably say comfort food. Full fat, full butter, sour cream, the whole nine yards. Almost no one eats like that anymore." Mr. Tuesday was the only exception I knew of. And me, on Tuesdays, when I couldn't help taste-testing an unnecessary amount.

He nodded. "I would just love a good old-fashioned pot roast one night."

I laughed. "That will never happen in this house, right?"

"Oh, hell no." He laughed, too. "But I bet you make a killer pot roast."

"Maybe if Angela goes away sometime." I used the heel of my palm to move a piece of hair from my eyes. "My pot roast is excellent. Well, all my food is."

"Lucky for me." He smiled faintly and looked off in the distance. "I think I'll have a Bloody Mary," he said suddenly, moving toward the fridge. "Do you want one?"

"Me?" This was weird. "No thanks. Not while I'm working. But I appreciate the offer."

"I haven't had one in ages, but I think it would really hit the spot tonight." He poured the tomato juice into a glass, then asked, "Can I use some of that pepper?"

"Sure!" I handed him the grinder. "Have at it." I transferred the tuna to a cutting board.

"Angela can be tough to work for, huh?"

"Oh, she's not too bad," I said, slicing the tuna. I was mindful of the fact that (1) I was talking to her husband, and (2) she could walk in at any moment and overhear whatever we were saying. "It would be boring if everyone wanted the same thing every single night."

"Predictability certainly has its drawbacks."

He went to the freezer and took out a bottle of Belvedere Vodka. I was amazed Angela allowed it in the house. He poured a splash into his glass, hesitated, then poured another splash.

I wondered if he did this a lot.

Maybe it was the only way to live with her.

I watched from the corner of my eye as he tasted it, added a little salt, then tasted again. I would have put Worcestershire in, of course, but Angela objected to anchovy, so there was none in the house.

"You're sure you don't want one?" he asked. "It's not like you're a cop on duty."

I smiled. "I know, but I'm working with sharp objects." I held up the knife.

"True. I concede."

I don't know exactly how it happened, but somehow he went left and I went right, and I guess I knocked into his hand, sending his almost-entirely-full glass of Bloody Mary spilling down my shirt.

"Oh, shit, Gemma. I'm so sorry." He put the glass down and grabbed a dish towel to hand to me. "What a mess!"

"It's okay." I started to dab at my shirt, but there was too much there—this was never going to do.

"Come with me, I'll give you a T-shirt to change into. You should rinse that right away before it stains."

Normally, I would have demurred at the offer of a new shirt, but I was completely soaked. There was no way I could hit the streets looking like this. Honestly, I was just lucky it hadn't gotten all over my pants as well. "Thanks," I said. "Yeah, if I could just give this a quick rinse in the laundry sink, I'm sure it will be fine."

"Come with me. I'll show you where everything is."

I followed him upstairs to the landing and waited while he dodged into what I assume was his and Angela's bedroom. He came back out with a plain navy blue T-shirt and handed it to me.

"Less likely to show stains," he joked. "You can change in Stephen's room."

I took the shirt and went into the small bedroom opposite theirs. It was adorably decorated in a zoo theme, with giraffe, lion, and tiger decals on the walls and a neatly organized row of stuffed animals lining one wall.

I removed my shirt carefully, turning it inside out so it wouldn't drip tomato juice on the floor or drag it across my face and hair. I was about to put the T-shirt on when the door opened.

"What was that?" Peter asked.

Startled, I dropped the shirt.

"Oh, I'm sorry." He hurried over to pick it up and hand it back to me.

Why didn't he just back out of the room and close the door?

I clutched the shirt to me and waited a moment for him to go, but he didn't make a move.

"Excuse me," I said, annoyance rising rapidly in me. I looked pointedly toward the door.

"I thought you called out for something."

I shook my head. "I didn't. Everything's fine here, so if you could just go—"

"Gemma." He came toward me.

My nerves sprang to alert. "Peter, I'm not dressed!"

"I know."

I took a step back. "This isn't happening."

"What isn't?" He closed the distance between us and put a hand on my shoulder.

I took another step back. "Whatever you have in mind. *Nothing* is happening."

"Right." He put his other hand on my other shoulder and moved closer, so he was just a couple of inches from me, looking down into my face. Even though this was quickly feeling like an emergency, I could not help remembering the stark difference between this situation and the one with Mack. This was *definitely* not wanted.

I put a hand to his chest to push him away, but he was stronger. He didn't budge. *"Please."*

"I've wanted this for such a long time," he said, as if I hadn't said a word. "Haven't you seen how I look at you?"

"You're *married.*" I pushed again, but he was immovable. My hand just slid down his stomach.

"I won't be married forever."

"You're also my *employer.*"

"People have met in stranger ways." He dipped closer and grazed my cheek with his lips.

"*Stop* it." I turned, but he captured my mouth with his. I shoved him away.

Then he looked at me, shocked, as if he had no idea where he was or what he was doing here. "I'm so sorry," he said.

"Go. Please."

"Of course. I'm so—I'm sorry." He nodded, gave a brief embarrassed smile, then moved out of the room.

As soon as he was gone, I scrambled to put the shirt on in case he came back in. But then I froze. What was I supposed to do now? Obviously, I had to handle this in some grown-up way, but I didn't know what, exactly, that meant. Go back out there and pretend nothing had happened? Address it and scold him like a child? Turn in my resignation immediately, even though there was no way in the world I could afford to lose not only another night but also my substantial country club gig—which Angela was in charge of, by virtue of recommending me as the caterer for people who rented the club for weddings, bar or bat mitzvahs, anniversary parties, whatever. The profit on events was tremendous, and a wedding could easily equal or outprofit an entire week of cooking for my regulars.

I needed the club events, so I needed Angela.

Peter had never imposed himself on me before in any way. Maybe this was just a glitch. A moment of bad judgment. On the other hand, what if it wasn't? It wasn't like I could just start carrying Mace around with me. At least not the spray kind. Although, truth be told, I couldn't carry the spice mace around here either, because it was exactly the kind of thing Angela would have a reaction to.

What was I going to do?

The longer I stood in Stephen's bedroom, the more lost I felt. There was no obvious answer here. No clear solution to the problem. I didn't want to lose any more work—I really couldn't afford to—but I also didn't want to feel apprehensive every time I came here.

Clearly I had to talk to him about this.

I went downstairs and paused in the hallway, taking a bracing breath before going into the kitchen, where he was making another Bloody Mary.

Great. What if he was now buzzed?

"Peter?" I stood straight and went in.

He looked up at me.

"Can we talk about what just happened?" I asked.

"What just happened?" a razor-sharp voice asked behind me.

Angela! When did she get here? What had he already told her?

"I . . ." What? *What?*

"Again, I'm sorry for spilling tomato all over you," Peter said pointedly. "I hope your shirt isn't ruined. Obviously, I'll pay for cleaning or replacement."

"Oh." It was true, he had spilled on me. I don't know why I had to sound so damn surprised. "Well, that's fine, then."

I could feel Angela's eyes on me from behind, and I turned to her. "It's a tuna Caesar salad for tonight."

Her gaze shifted from me to her husband, and back. Then her brow lowered fractionally. "I see."

What kind of response was that?

What did she see?

This was a new kind of uncomfortable.

"Okay, then, I guess I'll be on my way." I needed to get out of here. Whatever had happened, the evening had taken a weird turn, and I needed to get out. "I'm just going to put the finishing touches on the salad and put it in the fridge."

Peter raised his glass to his lips but first added, "It looks terrific, as always." His return to a normal conversation that fit in with the one from fifteen minutes ago was unnerving.

I hurried to arrange the sliced tuna on top of the salad, covered the whole thing in plastic wrap, and put it in the refrigerator, all under what felt like two watchful gazes.

It felt like hours crept by before I was finally finished and left, but the weird feeling that had bubbled up the moment Peter touched me stayed with me for the rest of the night.

Chapter 11

You have to quit," Penny said the minute I told her what had happened with Peter Van Houghten. "Ask Lynn. She'll agree with me. You have to quit."

We were sitting on the sofa, having mocktails. Penny always insisted that she didn't mind if I went ahead and had wine when she couldn't drink, but it felt rude. So instead, we were drinking seltzer with cranberry and a twist of lime, which she declared unsatisfying just about every time she sipped it.

"I can't afford to."

"You can't afford *not* to!"

I sighed. "Be real, Pen. I don't have the kind of reserves that can keep me afloat indefinitely while I look for another job. Willa, tough as she might be, was a godsend. I can't expect to get that lucky every time. Besides"—I set down my glass and she poured more into it—"that's just how some men are. You know it and I know it. There's no guarantee that that won't happen again with someone else. In fact, there's pretty much a guarantee it will."

"Yeah." She sipped thoughtfully. "Remember that Bernard Liski guy I worked for down on Connecticut? Older than dirt and made a stinking, gross attempt to kiss me."

"Then told you that you were mentally unstable when you quit, right?"

"That's the one."

"See? There are a million of them out there." I leaned back against the embroidered pillows my grandmother had made for both Penny and myself to put in our hope chests when I was twelve. Now it was a "hope not" chest. "Anyway, Vlad didn't mention anything about me finding a new job, so I don't think it's in the stars right now." I gave a laugh.

"Excuse me? Who is Vlad?"

"You know. Vlad Oleksei. The psychic? Well, the guy I work for who turns out to be a psychic? Come on, I told you about that!"

"You did not! Vlad Oleksei is a *psychic*?" She leaned forward, as much as she could with that baby in her, wide-eyed. "How do you know that?"

"The other night when I was there, he pulled me into his office because he had something important to tell me. Or warn me about. Actually, I'm not totally sure because it ended up being pretty nebulous, whatever it was."

"Wait a minute. Wait just a minute. Tell me everything. Every single detail."

I told her as much as I could remember. It was the oddness of the whole thing that had stuck with me more than the details of his predictions. Like I said, I didn't believe in that stuff.

Penny, on the other hand, did. "You're going to have a TV show. I *know* it. Now you have proof positive."

I laughed. "Okay, despite the fact that you know me, and you know I have never so much as liked having my picture taken, you're going to twist the words of a psychic into meaning I'll have a TV show rather than consider the possibility that the guy's not right?"

"Um, hello? He's *psychic*."

"Well . . ."

"How much does he charge?"

"I don't know. He didn't charge *me* anything. Why?" She'd always been into this kind of thing. "Don't tell me you want a consultation."

"Actually, that could be interesting." She looked thoughtful for a moment. "Good chance to test him on a basic boy-or-girl thing"—she indicated her belly—"but, no, I was asking because the really good ones either charge a fortune or nothing. None of this five-dollar psychic reading shit like they have in storefronts. They're criminals. Somehow, it always ends up that you're 'cursed,' and for a mere five hundred dollars, they can fix you—"

I looked at her. "Are you serious?"

"What?"

"Have you paid some lying gypsy five hundred bucks to lift a curse from you?"

"Of course not!" But I could tell from the way she said it that she had.

"Good Lord, Penny, who raised you? Why don't you have more sense than that?"

"Can we get back to the point?" She shifted uneasily in her seat. "What else did Vlad say to you?"

"Something about a woman around me being really angry."

"Marie Lemurra."

"I guess. If *anyone*, I mean. See, they say all this vague stuff, like the speeding ticket stuff, and then you make it fit."

"What speeding ticket stuff?"

"He saw me talking to someone in uniform and warned me to drive safely so I don't get a speeding ticket." Funny enough, that I'd taken a little bit seriously. Not that I thought he was predicting anything real, but if it impacted my already-depleted bank account, I tended to be extra careful.

"Maybe you're going to *date* someone in uniform."

I drained my "wine" and set down the glass. "You are such a sucker."

She put down her glass, too, though it was still half full. "Say what you will, but you can't prove he's a fake any more than I can prove he's real. All you can do is wait and see what happens."

"Right."

A quiet moment passed. Then she asked, "Gemma?"

"Yeah?"

She touched her hand to her belly, a gesture I later thought had to have been subconscious. "Do you ever think about . . . you know . . ." Her eyes met mine. "The baby?"

I knew exactly what she meant. No need to play coy. "Yes. Not as much now as I used to, but, of course, there are times when I think about it more than others." I gestured at her stomach and smiled. "Little reminders."

She looked concerned. "Is that hard for you?"

"What?"

"Me being pregnant, sitting here with me, waiting for the big moment. Is that all really melancholy for you?"

What did she want? The truth or some vague reassurance that her happiness didn't equal pain for me? "No," I said. Then, when she looked at me skeptically, I added sincerely, "That was a long time ago. I will never forget and of *course*, seeing you pregnant reminds me of my own experience, but it doesn't make me feel bad. In a way, it's interesting to remember."

"Good."

"And I'm also glad I'm not pregnant now," I added, then laughed.

She laughed as well. "Right? This ninth-month business sucks."

"*That* I remember. The not being able to bend without this huge and seemingly permanent obstacle in your way."

"Not being able to see your toes."

"Sometimes not being able to *feel* your toes."

"And what about peeing every three minutes?"

"I don't miss that!"

We laughed; then she sobered and asked, "Do you ever hope he or she will come looking for you?"

I shook my head. "That is one thing I think I did right. For every other decision I have made and questioned, I made *sure* that this was a closed adoption."

"But surely there's a way around that!"

"No. And I don't want there to be."

"You don't want to meet her or him?" she asked incredulously.

I sighed and looked at a woman who was completely immersed in motherhood right now, a woman who loved her children so much that she couldn't imagine another woman loving her own children in a different way. Of course, she couldn't imagine not wanting to meet her own child . . . because imagining that required her to put Charlotte's face on the baby or to come nine months in her current pregnancy, set up the nursery and study sonogram pictures for hours, and then reject him.

"I knew," I said evenly, "that I would spend the rest of my life wondering if every child who looked even vaguely like Cal or me, and who appeared to be about the right age, was the One. And I have." My throat tightened. I didn't usually feel this emotional about this anymore. Something about looking at Penny, in her full bloom of pregnancy, reminded me of my last moments of thinking I was going to keep my baby before suddenly, and irrevocably, deciding on adoption. "If I had to wonder now if every knock at the door might be him or her, or any ring of the phone, or even every stupid spam e-mail that gets caught in the junk file might be an attempt at contact, I'd go mad."

Her eyes filled with tears. "I can imagine. I think I'm just being overly romantic or something, dreaming of the great reunion."

"It's not romantic," I said sternly. "It's just wrong. I wanted the baby to have a life free of any possible eventual feeling of obligation to the woman who conceived her or him. Free of any stray idea that his or her mother—the adoptive mother—is anything less than a *real* mother. Whatever they say about his or her origins"—now tears burned in my eyes—"I never wanted there to be one iota of conflict because of the circumstances of the birth."

She was crying openly now. "I'm sorry I brought it up. I didn't mean to sound judgmental."

"You didn't. I understand where you're coming from. Totally." I gave what I hoped was a reassuring smile. I certainly didn't want her to feel bad. How could she understand? She was a grown woman with a good husband and a solid family. She couldn't imagine what it was like to be seventeen, pregnant, and terrified. "This isn't a hot button for me anymore. Honest."

"I'm glad you're okay."

"I'm *absolutely* okay."

"Do you ever hear from Cal? Like on Facebook or anything?"

It had been so long since I'd heard his name out loud

that he'd started to feel like a dream, or something I'd made up. "Never. Once in a while he'll show up as 'someone you might know' because we have mutual friends, but he never contacts me and I never contact him."

"Did you see his picture?"

"Of course." I laughed. "Don't we all do that after a few drinks, Internet-stalk people we used to know? When they leave all their information open, it's like Christmas morning."

"Right? So what does he look like now?"

"He's big. Kind of doughy. I wouldn't have known it was him, to be honest." Funny how time shakes things out. Once, I had thought I'd never get over him. That he was this gorgeous, hot Prince Charming, and no guy could ever compete with him.

Now, he just looked like some guy who worked a job he hated in the accounting department of some large, anonymous company.

And when I saw his pictures—I'd seen maybe fifteen or twenty of them—I felt nothing. Truly, nothing.

I only wished I could go back and tell my seventeen-year-old self that someday none of the stuff she was so worried about would matter much anymore.

"Good," Penny said. "I'm glad. I hope he never gets laid."

"He's married," I said, remembering the woman in the pictures with him. A woman who actually looked so middle-aged, it was hard to imagine her with the Cal I used to know. "So, yeah, he probably doesn't."

"Um." She gestured at her stomach. "Don't count on it." After a pause, she asked, "Does he have any kids as far as you can tell?"

I shook my head. "I wondered, but I don't think so."

"That's probably best. The SOB."

"Come on, Penny. He was just a scared eighteen-year-old himself."

She shrugged. "Well, he didn't demonstrate a lot of character, and at that age, he should have."

"Good that I'm not stuck with him, then, right?"

"Right."

I stood up. "I'm *exhausted,* and I'm sure you are, too. Get some sleep."

"I *am* pretty tired."

"Let me know if you need anything, okay? I'm waiting eagerly for the Call. I don't want to put any undue pressure on you or anything, but I'm completely psyched about this baby."

"Well, I'm completely psyched about not being pregnant anymore, so we have something in common." She laughed, but there was a weariness under it. "Call me if you think of anything else Vlad said. I'm serious. You know I absolutely love this stuff."

Chapter 12

I was on my way to Mr. Tuesday's when my phone rang. It was Makena Gallagher, one of my contacts at the country club.

"Bad news," she said. "The Foutys have canceled."

For a moment, this didn't compute. Foutys was a major local construction company that was having a huge party at the club next month. I was catering and had already hired a considerable support staff to assist. The job paid three times what normal weekend jobs paid—and they were already half my income—and promised to become an annual event if they were pleased with my work.

"How can they just *cancel* that party this late in the game?" I asked. "They're going to lose thousands on the deposit!"

"Well, they didn't cancel the party," Makena said carefully. It was obvious she'd gotten stuck with the job of delivering news she didn't want responsibility for. "They just canceled you."

"They're canceling me."

"I'm afraid so. They're going with someone else instead."

"Why?"

She took a breath and, I could tell, held it for a moment before saying, "I'm not sure."

"Come on, Makena. I can tell that's not true. What happened?"

"I really don't want to get in the middle of this."

There is little I hate more than finding myself in the midst of some sort of conflict that is not of my own making and having someone say, *I don't want to get in the middle of this.*

"Makena, there is no *middle of this.* I just want to know what's going on. This is my livelihood we're talking about, not a seventh grade squabble."

"All I know is that they said they heard some negative things about your menu and your cooking, and since this is their first big blowout like this, they wanted to be really sure it was the best it could be."

"But they sampled everything I made," I argued. "I offered five different variations of—" I stopped. This wasn't Makena's fault, and it certainly wasn't her decision; she was just the messenger. "Never mind that. Do you know who they heard this from?"

"No." This time she sounded like she meant it. "But it

had to be someone pretty powerful because there's been a huge scramble to replace you. In fact, I need to get back on that now. Do you remember the name of that pit barbecue company that works out of Chevy Chase?"

I sighed. "Trilling Farms."

"That's right! Thanks a million, it's been driving me crazy. And sorry about the party."

There were so many more things I wanted to ask, but it was clear Makena didn't have the answers.

"Thanks, Makena," I said, forcing cheer I didn't feel. "Let me know if you hear anything else. And especially if another job comes up."

"You got it!" she said, and clicked off.

What on earth had happened? I felt shell-shocked. I couldn't afford to lose *any* work, much less staple jobs like this! Who on earth could have been "powerful" enough to influence the Fouty company's choice of caterer? The only person I'd had any conflict with lately was Marie Lemurra, and she didn't have any significant social influence. In fact, she wasn't even a member of the country club.

Angela Van Houghten came to mind, but surely she didn't know anything to hold against me. It felt more likely that the problem was coming from one of the competitive caterers who wanted to take over the jobs. That sort of subversive trickery happened all the time in this business.

Feeling completely defeated, I went in to Mr. Tuesday's apartment hoping to feel calmed by the normally soothing atmosphere.

Instead, I was surprised by his note:

G—

Please make tonight's very simple. Bland even. Thanks.
—P

I stood there for a long time, unmoving. Make it simple. Bland. What did this mean? I thought back on the last week's meals I'd made and tried to remember if there had been anything insanely spicy, but it was all the usual stuff.

Was he suddenly put off by my cooking as well?

Was this the first move in another job loss?

I took out the ingredients for dinner. Chicken Francese over rice pilaf. Not exactly Spicy Bang Bang Chicken to begin with, but I supposed I could make it even more bland by making plain white rice and going light on the lemon.

He was the boss, after all. I don't know what it was about him that made me feel so belligerent sometimes. Probably the fact that he was usually pretty jocular with me, and fun. We had a rapport, even though we'd never met.

But something about this instruction seemed cold. It was a lot to infuse into seven little words, of course, but I really didn't think I was wrong.

My mind grew chatty, my emotions taking on a crazy life of their own. All at once, I could imagine losing everything. How long could I subsist on my ever-dwindling cash flow, and what would I do when it completely ran out? Should I be contacting temp agencies about doing freelance administrative work? Did I need to find a regular job and somehow work what was left of my cooking around it?

I put on my Bluetooth and called Penny.

"I think Mr. Tuesday is going to sack me and I'm going to lose everything and end up living in a cardboard box under the Fourteenth Street Bridge," I said the minute she picked up.

There was a pause, then an alarmed little, "Hello?"

Charlotte. Shit. "I said I think Mr. Tuesday is on the Fourteenth Street Bridge," I improvised, badly. "Wait a minute, is this Penny?"

Giggle. "No, it's *Charlotte.*"

"Oh, my gosh, Charlotte, you sound older every day! This is Gemma. Is your mom around?"

"Yes, just a minute, please."

I waited, taking chicken breasts out of the Costco packaging, and laid them out on the cutting board. It smelled . . . funny. I lifted a piece and sniffed it. It smelled like chicken. That was all, just a very chickeny chicken scent.

I was getting too sensitive. If I was going to start thinking my chicken smelled too chickeny, I was sliding onto a path of paranoia I'd never get off of.

"What's going on?" Penny asked when she got on the line a couple of minutes later.

"Oh, nothing." I sliced the breasts into cutlets, still wondering why it smelled so strong to me. "I just told Charlotte that I'm going to be moving into a cardboard box under a bridge."

"What?"

Slice. "The Fouty construction company just canceled a big job I had coming up for them." Slice. "And I just got to Mr. Tuesday's, and he left me a really chilly note."

"How can you tell how warm he's being or not being in a note?"

"I just . . . can." I sliced the last bit of chicken and piled it on the rest, then moved to the sink, knocking the faucet on with the back of my hand. Because I am scrupulous about cross contamination.

"You're nuts. You're PMSing or something."

"I'm not." I scrubbed with soap. "That's the problem. I think I'm right about this."

"Hang on a minute, Gem." She covered the receiver with her hand, and I heard her say, "Get a piece of fruit, Char. That's all you can have for dessert. You barely touched your broccoli."

"I hate fruit!" Charlotte wailed in response.

Penny really needed to be careful not to give Charlotte major food aversions that would last a lifetime. Charlotte needed to know that fruit was her friend. Instead, she was going to be one of those weird adults with fussy food habits.

Like Angela Van Houghten.

"God, she can be a pain in the ass," Penny whispered when she came back on the line. "It's just *broccoli*, for Pete's sake. You'd think she'd *want* to be healthy. She's so stubborn, it's unbelievable."

I started to give her my philosophy on creating food-phobic adults but thought better of it. Now probably wasn't the time for me to be lecturing anyone on anything. Granted, I hadn't done anything wrong, certainly nothing criminal, but as long as this uncertainty hung in the air like a big, sticky cobweb, I was probably better off keeping my mouth shut.

"We all are sometimes" was all I said, shaking some flour onto a plate and seasoning it with salt and pepper. "You, for example. Are you in labor yet?"

"Not as far as I know."

I laughed. "Hurry *up!*"

"Yeah, I'll do that for you."

My call waiting beeped, so I stepped toward my phone to glance at the screen.

"It's him! It's Mr. Tuesday. Let me call you back."

"Go!"

I clicked over. "Hello?"

"Gemma." He sounded grim. I thought. I mean, it could have been my imagination, but he definitely didn't sound friendly.

"Yes?"

"Did you get my note?"

"Y-yes—?" I wanted to ask what was going on. If he was planning to fire me. "Is something wrong? Do you have some . . . concerns I should know about?"

"My brother's coming into town tonight," he said, then expelled a tense breath. "He's allergic to *everything*. Going to a restaurant with him is fucking murder. It takes forever for him to go through the list of possible ingredients with the server."

Relief flooded through me. "I understand. "What, in particular, are his allergies to?"

"Flavor, I think. He hates just about everything I like. So just do the opposite of what you usually do."

"So pick something up from McDonald's?" Ugh.

"Not with those reckless sesame seed buns they serve." He gave a dry laugh. "Actually, he's allergic to a few spices, but I can't remember which ones, so if you stick with salt and pepper, we should be all right."

"That's it?" I asked, extra cautious. "Wheat, eggs, and milk are okay?"

"If he can't have bread, eggs, and milk, he's going to have a hard time surviving at my place."

"Are you *sure* that will be okay?" I took out a bowl and cracked two eggs into it. "Food allergies can be very serious."

"It will be fine."

I poured a little milk in with the eggs and whisked with a fork, worrying more by the moment. "You know, just to be sure, I'm going to write down all of the ingredients, just in case he has sensitivities you're not aware of."

"Excellent idea," he said, but I could hear the smile in his voice. "If he gets there before me, just tell him to help himself to whatever. He can find his way around."

"All right."

"Thanks." He hesitated, then asked, "Hey, has anyone called the house phone?"

"I haven't heard it ring since I've been here. But that's only been a few minutes."

"Okay. Well if someone calls . . . can you just answer

and take a message? I want to make sure I don't miss the call, and sometimes people don't want to leave voice mail. . . ."

"True."

"And can you be sure you say you're the chef?"

I gave a laugh and asked, "Expecting a call from a girl?"

"Good-bye, Gemma." But I thought I heard a little bit of embarrassment in his voice.

I felt better, having had a normal conversation with him. If I'd left after just seeing that note, I probably would have chewed on it all night, making it bigger and bigger in my mind until eventually I decided he was about to fire me and that I should preempt him by quitting.

I worked quietly for the next forty-five minutes, dredging the chicken through the flour, dipping it in egg, then sautéing in a pan with butter and lemon. They were simple ingredients. Hopefully, Mr. Tuesday was right and there was nothing potentially harmful there.

Nevertheless, once the dinner was made and in stoneware in a warm oven, I took down the pad of paper and wrote down everything I could think of about the ingredients I'd used, including—again—where I'd bought them: Kirkland brand chicken breasts (Costco), Gold Medal flour and large brown eggs (Giant), salt and pepper (Costco), 365 brand long-grain rice (Whole Foods), bagged lemons and generic salted butter (Trader Joe's), and Shenandoah's Pride 2 percent milk (7-Eleven) (it had been an emergency run). It took three pages of the small paper to write it all down, and

I went over it three times before I was satisfied that I'd covered everything. Then I went to the reusable Trader Joe's bag I'd brought it all in and removed the bag of Mr. Tuesday's favorite chips. I put them in the pantry with a note.

P—

I am very sure you will need these tonight.
—G

That was just luck. I'd picked them up before I knew I'd be cooking a bland meal.

With that done, I gathered my tools, piled them on the counter, and gave the sink area a second go with hot soapy water, just to make sure there was no raw chicken juice anywhere.

All in all, the meal took about three times as long to make as it normally would. But once it was done, I felt confident that it was 100 percent safe.

Since he'd only mentioned tonight as the problem, I assumed the rest of the week's meals, which I'd put in the freezer, were okay, but just to be sure, I hastily went back and added that to the note.

I was walking through the living room when I heard a key at the front door and it opened.

Mr. Tuesday.

He looked just like he did in the picture: tall, dark, and unbelievably hot. Really hot. Even hotter than he looked in the pictures. He was probably six feet tall, with gorgeously unkempt black hair, unlined tan skin, and just the shadow of a beard, which served to make him look even darker and his blue eyes look even bluer.

He smelled delicious.

But you could tell just from looking at his pictures that he would.

"Hey!" I shifted everything into my left arm and reached out my right. "We meet in person at last. I'm Gemma." A flush rose in my cheeks. "Obviously."

He smiled and it made his face even more handsome. Great smile. Perfect teeth. "The cook."

I nodded, because what else could I do? Yes, I was the cook. "There's food ready in the oven if you're hungry."

"Good." He came in and set his bag down by the sofa. "Thanks. I'll wait for my brother, though. It'll be okay in there for a while?"

He sounded different. Less playful or something.

"Yes, sure, it's just warming." I headed for the front door. "Also, I wrote down everything that's in it, so you can be sure there are no hidden allergens. I wasn't sure what to worry about, so I detailed it all, including the sources."

He gave that movie star smile and headed for the kitchen, doing a double take at the many pages of notes I'd left. "You really went beyond the call of duty."

I shook my head. "It's just my job. So is there anything I can do for you before I leave?" That sounded dirty. "I mean, do you have any questions?"

"Nope. Smells good." He opened the oven and looked in. "Looks great."

"Good. Well, it was nice meeting you. I hope you have a good visit with your brother."

"Thanks."

Okay, he was somewhat lacking in the personality department in person. Maybe he was just shy. I mean, he was such a smart-ass in all his notes, but here and now, he was just so . . . meh.

Maybe he was disappointed in me.

Maybe he'd pictured me as some hot Victoria's Secret model in a French maid's outfit, cooking away for him in some sexy manner while he toiled at work.

It wasn't a big deal. Seriously, I knew that it wasn't a big deal. I didn't know the guy, it was impossible for me to actually say what I was reading in his expression anyway, so why I decided it was disappointment in my appearance, I don't know.

I'm even less clear on why that hurt my feelings so much if it *were* true.

The whole thing was stupid, but I couldn't control my emotions and felt like I might cry.

"So if there's nothing else . . ." I just needed to get out of there. "I've got to go. Have a nice time. I hope you like dinner!"

I got on the elevator and pushed the CLOSE DOORS button madly until finally the doors closed.

It was only then that I realized I'd been holding my breath.

I sank back against the wall and put my hand to my chest. I could feel my heart pounding so hard, I wouldn't have been surprised to see it pulsing under my shirt, like Popeye's when Olive Oyl kissed his cheek.

"The whole gang is here!" Lex sang, coming over to kiss my cheek.

It was his twice-a-month mystery book club meeting, and I'd brought the makings for finger foods, like his favorite cheese puffs, shrimp cocktail with horseradish, and asparagus knots.

"Hello, Chef-girl!" Rose called out. She was a staple of the book group, the one who had the most opinions. She was probably only in her early forties, but there was something distinctly old-fashioned about her, like she was a character from an old Fred Astaire movie or something, with her barrel chest, tiny legs, big face, and huge smile. I really liked her. "Aren't you looking beautiful?"

If it were anyone but Rose, I would have thought she was being sarcastic about my plain attire, hair pulled back, lack of makeup, but Rose was so kind that, even though I thought she was crazy, I knew she meant it. "Thanks, Rose."

"It's true," Lex said. "You're just glowing." He raised an eyebrow. "What have you been up to?"

I laughed. "Nothing nearly as interesting as you think." My mind flew to Mack. It seemed to do that a lot, actually. I had replayed our night together in my mind so many times, it was ridiculous.

"That doesn't look like nothing to me," Rose said, cluck-

ing her tongue against her teeth. "I think you've got someone special on your mind."

I felt my face go warm. "I don't," I objected. "I mean, I
know it *looks* that way, but—"

"But what?" Lex patted the satin chaise for me to sit.
"Come on, tell us everything."

This wasn't *quite* so awkward as it seems, because I'd
seen these people a hundred times before and we'd had
some lively conversations, but at the same time, I felt pretty
adolescent. "I met a guy," I confirmed. "He was cute and we
flirted," I hedged, "but there's truly nothing more to it. I
don't even know his last name."

"Maybe this is a mystery we can solve," a little mouse of
a man named Melvin said from the sofa across the room.
"Tell us everything you do know."

"I know I can't go chasing some guy I met one time
without seeming psychotic."

"Or romantic." Rose clapped a hand to her chest. "Maybe
this is meant to be! Maybe that's why you're here tonight
talking to us. Because we're meant to help you find him!"

I reached for a chunk of cheese from a platter on the coffee table and hesitated before dipping it in what I recognized as Provençal grainy mustard. Did Lex have any Frank's
hot sauce? Because that would be a perfect complement to
cheddar. How had I never thought of this before, given
how amazing it was on macaroni and cheese?

"I'm *not* having you lot search this guy down," I said,
laughing. I could totally picture it, and that was *not* what I

wanted my next impression—if there was a next impression, that is—to be.

"Absolutely not," Lex said, and handed me a bottle of Tŷ Nant water. "We need to be much more subtle than that. Don't want to scare him off. After all, when was the last time you had a boyfriend?"

My face felt hot. "Date or boyfriend?"

"Boyfriend, dear. You haven't been interested in *any* of the dates you've been on this year. Except, of course, this one. . . ."

"Is it a friend of that hottie, Peter Van Houghten?" Rose asked. "You cook for him, right?"

"He just got a new show at the network," Melvin said. I always forgot he worked for a cable sports station because not one thing about him was consistent with that.

"Did he?"

Melvin nodded. "And they're throwing a *lot* of dough at him."

"Does he have any friends for *me*?" Rose asked with a giggle. "I'd like a lot of dough."

And on the conversation went, the group's speculation moving from whom I'd met to how much Peter Van Houghten would be making at his new gig, to how much other local D.C. celebs made, and eventually, to whether or not the famous mystery writer Angus Barton had been murdered or committed suicide.

Finally, around 11 P.M., everyone had left and I was doing the last of the cleanup.

"You don't have to do that, you know," Lex said. "It's not part of your job."

"It's not part of my job to sit and laugh all night with your guests either, but you let me do that, so let me help out."

"We love it when you stay, you know that."

"Thanks, Lex."

"Come sit down and talk to me for a minute," he said, returning to the chaise where we'd started the night.

"What's up?" I asked, drying my hands on the dish towel before going to him.

"That's what I'm wondering. Are you okay? You seem a little"—he shrugged—"off."

"I know." I sighed and leaned back. Suddenly I was exhausted. "I'm very stressed out about my work situation," I explained.

"That's tough," he said when I'd finished. "I had no idea you were doing all that catering on the side as well. When do you breathe?"

"Oh, I slip it in here and there."

"It would be pretty hard to have a social life on top of all that, though."

"Probably. But sometimes that feels important, maybe *more* important than the rest. I don't often admit this, but even though I'm busy, it can be pretty lonely to go home to an empty apartment every night."

He gave a sweep of his arm, indicating the large space he inhabited himself. "But isn't there something lovely about the peace and quiet at the end of the day?"

I looked at him. This was one of the lessons I had to keep learning in my life: that everyone was different, sometimes to the point where I couldn't relate, but that didn't mean they were more right or more wrong than I was. "You never wanted a companion? Someone to just drape across at the end of a long day and cry to when things are hard? Or laugh with when things are good?"

"I have all that when I want it," he said, and watching him, I could see that he meant it. That he truly was fulfilled and didn't want anything else. "But it's on my terms."

And there it was. Myself, I was weary from drawing up terms for everything. Sometimes I just wanted to share it, to let someone else take half the burden and share half the glory.

Then, inexplicably, I started to cry.

"Honey, honey." He put an arm around me and shushed me gently. "It's okay. You'll have what you want. You'll have everything you want."

"I'm okay, really," I said, all evidence to the contrary notwithstanding. "I've just been a mess lately."

"And who wouldn't be? Look, we sometimes have events at the store. I'm going to get that department to make sure you cater all of them."

"Oh, Lex." I sniffled unattractively. "That's not necessary."

"Hey." He pointed a finger at me. "I want the best, and *you* are the best."

I mustered a smile. "Thanks."

"We're also going to get your love life straightened out."

"Good luck with that."

"Gemma."

I looked at him, knowing I was kind of a sad sack right now, and had to smile. "Yes, Lex?"

"If you expect the worst, you're going to get it. You know what that means?"

"Yes, Lex."

"It means," he went on anyway, "that if you expect the best, you're apt to get that, too. So expect the best."

I nodded. "Yes, Lex."

"I *mean* it!"

"Thank you, Lex."

I left his apartment that night realizing that what I'd seen of his life tonight—including our time alone at the end of it—was exactly enough for him.

And that, despite my years of protestations against love and anything like it, it wasn't enough for me.

Chapter 13

It was with a strange mix of nervousness and confidence that I went to the Van Houghtens' the next Monday night. Nervous because of Peter's pass, but confident because bland food was so easy to make (if not fun) that I wasn't too concerned about disappointing Angela. The trick was to be able to do my work without having to tangle with him in any personal way. *Especially* not if she was anywhere nearby.

So it was a surprise when she said, "You might want to spice up Peter's portion tonight."

I stopped dicing tomatoes and looked at her. "I'm sorry?"

She paused, lips pursed, then said, "He seems to be wanting a bit more spice." Another pause. "So I'm just suggesting you might give it to him."

"Well, I'm just making gazpacho, so he can add salt and

pepper to it if he wants. That's all it needs, as far as I'm concerned."

She looked at me critically—a look I'd seen before and that usually preceded some elementary lesson in bland cooking—but then she just shrugged. "I think it's time for some change around here."

"Angela, are you trying to say you're unhappy with my cooking?" I was not going to make any assumptions. If she wanted something done differently, I wanted to know it now, not until it was too late and I'd lost another client.

"What makes you ask that?"

I set down the knife and turned to her. "You just said I should put more flavor in Peter's—"

"*Spice,*" she corrected crisply. "He seems to want more spice."

Same thing, right? "If you want me to make your food separately, I'd be glad to do that, just let me know. I'm glad to accommodate you however I can."

"Do that."

I couldn't figure out what was going on here. "O . . . kay—?"

"Give him whatever he wants, I don't care. In fact, I *want* you to give him what he wants, since I clearly can't."

All right, clearly they were having personal problems. And obviously, I could have guessed that from the fact that he made a pass at me.

But what was my best response?

She probably didn't know he'd made a pass at me, or for

one thing, she would have sacked me on the spot. She was exactly the sort of person to go all "Queen in *Snow White*" if she was afraid someone thought she was not the fairest in the land.

"He seems to be good with your choices," I said. Then, worried that it sounded as if I knew more about her husband than she did, I added, "But if you want me to switch things up, I certainly can. You're the boss."

He came into the kitchen then, and wordlessly went to the fridge and took out the almond milk.

"I was just telling Gemma you seem to want more spice these days," she told him, her voice both sharp and cold.

He looked at her, puzzled. "Do I?"

"Evidently." She looked at me. "If you make our food separately, it should be fine." She took a short breath, idly ran her hand along the counter edge, then, tossing a hostile look over her shoulder at her husband, left the room.

Leaving him and me alone.

I wished he would leave as well, but he didn't. Instead he leaned on the counter and said, "Look, about the last time you were here—"

No. I did *not* want to go there. "You already apologized," I said. "I'm really uncomfortable revisiting it. Again."

"I understand," he said, and I felt his gaze on me like a wet washcloth. "I just wanted to explain."

I shook my head. "No explanation is necessary. It shouldn't have happened, it won't happen again, let's just leave it at that. Please. You're my employer, it's just not my place to be having personal conversations with you. Let's leave it."

So much for spicing up his meals, right? I only wished that was the biggest of my problems here. Flavor, spice, organic or not organic, oil or water . . . these were all issues I was ready and able to address at any moment. But stuff with Peter wasn't about cooking. It was the age-old business of a lonely or desperate or ignored or fill-in-the-blank husband looking to someone else for comfort. Or just plain old sex. I honestly didn't think he was taking advantage of his position as my employer, but the fact that he *was* my employer just made it that much more awkward for me.

And then some.

He nodded. "You're right. Again, I apologize." He left the kitchen without waiting for me to respond.

But even after he'd gone, I had the strange feeling he was still watching me.

"I haven't heard a thing," Lynn said the next Saturday night, when we were at the country club for a forty-fifth wedding anniversary. "Believe me, if someone was bad-mouthing you, I would let them have it."

"Thanks," I said, arranging chocolate-dipped strawberries onto small china plates. "Do you know if there have been *any* complaints at all? It won't hurt my feelings—I just really need to know if my work hasn't been up to par."

"The response to your cooking is always outrageous," she said, moving the plates onto serving trays. "You know that!"

"I don't know anything anymore," I said, and pushed a stray hair back out of my eyes. "Losing the Fouty party is throwing off my finances for the whole month. I don't know what I'll do if I lose any more."

"Well, for all her *peculiarities*, at least you have Angela on your side," Lynn pointed out.

I thought about it for a moment. It was true, Angela had a tendency to be pissy with me, heaven knew, but where else was she going to find someone to cook to her exact— and ever-changing—specifications? "True, but if someone doesn't like what I do, she can't change their mind."

A waiter came in and took the platter just as Lynn put the last plate on it, and then she started on another.

I plated, she plattered.

"Not unless she's sleeping with them or something," she said flippantly.

"Not likely." I gave a laugh. "I don't even think she's sleeping with her own husband."

"No?"

"Nope."

"Okay, spill it." She paused and looked at me with interest. "What do you mean?"

I told her about Peter's pass at me and how awkward it was in the house now.

"Girl, you need to get some new work," she said, giving a low whistle. "If Angela finds out about that, you will lose every job here."

"Do you really think she's that powerful?"

"Oh, yeah." She lifted the platter. "Listen, if I were you, I'd go back to that psychic guy and see if *he* can tell you where to find some new jobs." She gave a quick smile. "And take me with you. I have a bad feeling that if you get screwed by this, I'm going to get screwed by association."

"No pressure there."

"Aw, don't worry about it. Jimmy, my first husband, is an attorney. If I get fired unfairly, he'll have their asses in a sling."

"I didn't know he was a lawyer!"

She nodded. "In some ways, I marry well."

"And in others . . ."

"Yeah, well. I won't make *that* mistake again. And if I try, I'm counting on you to stop me."

I sucked air in through my teeth. "I don't know about that. I'm with you in theory, but I'm afraid I'm a real sucker for romance. If you tell me you're in love and want to go for it, I'm going to be hard-pressed to be a big buzzkill on that."

"I know." She shrugged, then leaned against the counter and said earnestly, "For all my kidding around about it, the truth is, I'd *love* to be happily married. I didn't go into either of my marriages with the idea that divorce was an option."

I nodded. "I'm sure you didn't. What happened?"

"Oh, the typical stupid story you don't think happens in real life. I married for the wrong reasons. I had daddy issues and married two men who were older and who could 'take care of' me, then the age difference took hold and"— she shrugged again—"it didn't work."

"So at least you know, now, what you were doing wrong."

"Oh, yes. The problem is, knowing what you're doing

wrong and getting it right don't necessarily go hand in hand. Romance is tough. Everyone wants a soul mate. But maybe we don't all have them out there."

It was a depressing thought to contemplate. When I was young, I'd assumed it was there if I ever wanted it, which made it easy to shun the idea and declare I'd never get married. Now and then over the years, though, I'd revisited the idea, only to feel that maybe I'd been wrong all along. Maybe it wasn't a choice I'd made, but a decision that had been made for me by forces more powerful than myself.

Or maybe love was really only the domain of the young and lucky. In high school or college, it was easy to get a boyfriend. As time passed and people paired off, life became lonelier.

And despite the fact that a huge number of people seemed to be facing that and feeling that, the fact remained.

Life could be cold.

"Anyway," Lynn said, breaking my melancholy mood. "Jared and I are going to give it another try, so . . . who knows?"

I looked at her. Her smile was tentative but unmistakably hopeful. And I felt an odd twinge that maybe she was right, maybe this time it was going to happen for her. "No one knows," I said, and smiled. "That's the point. We never, ever know what's coming."

Chapter 14

"Now you want to see me?" Vlad asked, his mouth drawn into a tight little line.

This was stupid. It had been a stupid idea to begin with, and an even stupider thing to pursue. Worse, I had cash in my pocket—cash I couldn't afford to spend—in case he wanted payment for his psychic services this time.

"I was hoping you could help solve a mystery," I said, like I was trying to entice a six-year-old into telling me where he'd hidden the TV remote.

"Shuffle the cards." He nudged a large deck toward me across his desk.

"Don't you want to know what I'm asking about?"

He looked at me. "If you must. But I think it's about money, no?"

"You can *see* that?" I had the sudden thought that my

situation must be even more dire than I'd thought if he could tell the minute I walked in.

He scoffed at me like I was an idiot. "Everyone worries about money. Money and love." He nodded toward the cards. "Shuffle."

Okay, wow. That's how far gone I was. Was I so desperate for some easy solution to this situation that I was willing to leap to magical explanations and methods of detecting them?

Yes. Yes, I was.

I picked up the deck. Tarot cards this time. It was much taller than the playing cards he'd used before, and so wide, I had trouble keeping them from flying out of my hands while I shuffled. "How long should I do this?"

"Until you're done."

Helpful. I shuffled a few more times, felt as *done* as I was going to, and handed the cards back to him.

He set them down in an elaborate layout, then looked at them like a forensic scientist trying to study a minuscule drop of blood.

"What's wrong?" I asked when it started to feel like a lot of time had passed with him saying nothing. "Don't I have a future?"

He looked at me, sharp-eyed. "You have a future. Everyone has a future."

Somehow that wasn't reassuring. What if he was seeing that my future was just another hour or so?

I was being ridiculous. Psyching myself out over nonsense that had no credence. Really, I couldn't even believe I was here doing this at all.

"I see a blond man here. Something about the arts. And film. Again with the film."

"Ah." I gave a dry laugh. "Is it Brad Pitt?"

"Who?"

"Never mind."

He knew I'd made a stupid joke, but he didn't care to understand it. "I do not know who it is, but you make some movie with him."

"Okay, well, I don't know what that means, but maybe it will become clear later." It didn't take psychic powers to detect that I was being short, so I softened it by adding, "What I really need your help with is figuring out if there's someone out there trying to sabotage my work."

"What, like poison your food?"

"No, just"—I gestured vaguely—"I don't know, someone who didn't like my food."

"Your food is wonderful."

He said it with such uncharacteristic enthusiasm, I had to laugh.

"Thank you!"

"If someone doesn't like your food, they are crazy."

Any crazier than the girl going to the psychic to find out who doesn't like her? "That's very kind of you. But I think someone out there might have lost a big job for me, and I'm wondering if this is something I need to worry about."

"Nah. No worry." He made a dismissive gesture with his hand. "You will always have work."

I could have quibbled with that, but he wasn't in a

position to do anything about it one way or the other—unless he fired me, too, of course—so I let it go.

"There is a child on the way." He frowned at the cards. "Do you know this?"

"Yes," I said, thinking Penny would *freak* if she knew the psychic saw her baby. "Is everything all right with that? Is the baby healthy?"

He nodded. "Everything is very good. No problems."

Okay, but Penny would be glad to hear that. Good that I could give her the positive report, since she took this stuff seriously. "When will the baby be born?" I know it's silly, but I thought it would be pretty fun if, somehow, he could peg the date and I could impress everyone with my own "psychic powers."

He shook his head and said, "It's undetermined so far. I don't know."

"Rats."

He gave a light chuckle before saying, "You have other things to worry about first."

"Great. Bad things?"

"Not too bad. But you must be very careful," Vlad went on.

"I'm always careful," I said quickly. "About *everything*. Honestly, I am very mindful of keeping my equipment clean, the food fresh, and so on—"

"I don't mean with food." He gave a small smile then. "But it's true, you are. I can see here, and in my home, you are scrupulous about such things."

"Thank you." *I think.*

He frowned. "The thing that comes up over and over is that movie you make."

Crazy. The one thing that was never going to happen. But then it occurred to me: Marie Lemurra's party. The film crew, the peacock . . . the screams. Could Vlad possibly be seeing my footage ending up on TV even though I hadn't signed a release? Would it be legal for them to blur out my face or bloody license plate or both, and would anyone who knew me *not* recognize me and my car anyway? If they blurred out a license plate for legal reasons, would they still be free to leave the distinct EAT BERTHA'S MUSSELS bumper sticker I had on there? I'd gotten it in Fells Point a few years ago because it cracked me up, but would it now be the thing that identified me as an exotic pet murderer?

"Your future is very uncertain," Vlad said, breaking into my thoughts. "You're moving, do you know that?"

"What?" I met his eyes. "Do I go broke? Do I have to move because I'm broke? Will I be living in a cardboard box somewhere on Wisconsin Avenue?"

He looked at the cards and shook his head again. "No. I don't think so. This is your choice."

Good. That was good. I breathed my relief. "So my work is secure."

"I didn't say that."

"What?"

He tipped his hand side to side. "Your work is flexible, no? You have a free night since your lady is gone."

Gone seemed like unfortunate wording, but I knew what

he meant. "Yes, that's true." I glanced at the cards, as if a peek could tell me what I needed to know.

"And someone else will no longer be hiring you, too."

"I'm losing another client?"

He frowned once more at the cards. "Something changes there."

Great, so someone might fire me. Probably Willa. I'd been there one time since meeting her, and she'd been so intent on her online stuff that she hadn't even made eye contact with me the entire time, though it was evident that she didn't like having someone else in her house. She was probably going to sack me. "Will someone new hire me?"

"Not right away." He paused and looked thoughtful for a moment; then his face returned to his stony set.

"Is anyone else going to let me go?" I asked carefully, knowing there was always the possibility that he, himself, might do exactly that. Might, in fact, be planning it right now.

But again, he shook his head and gave a raspy chuckle. "Not Olekseis," he reassured me. "No one makes a kugel like you do."

I smiled. "Thank you."

He gathered the cards. "You have any other questions?"

"No, I don't think so. Just the same ones over and over again."

"Nothing about romance and love?" He raised an eyebrow. "Almost everyone who come here has questions about romance and love."

"That's the *one* thing I'm *not* worried about right now." I laughed. "Thank God."

He turned down the corners of his mouth as he nodded. "And you are right. Your love life is good. This is when it usually hits. When you are not expecting."

I stood up. "Yeah, well, I'm *definitely* not expecting." I opened my purse and took out the cash I'd brought, hoping it was enough. "I wasn't sure how much—"

"Pffft!" He waved it away. "No charge."

"But I can't take advantage of you that way. You pay *me* for what *I* do."

"You can't afford Vlad Oleksei on that." For the first time in my presence, he really laughed. "Besides, I am eager to see how your story comes out. You keep coming, yes?"

I nodded. "Thank you." I started to leave, but his voice stopped me.

"One more thing."

I stopped. Oh, no. What could it be? An IRS audit? I turned to him. "Yes?"

"The borscht you will make tonight—I like extra garlics and onions."

I'm sure he heard my sigh of relief. "You've got it," I said. "And light on the cabbage?" They always wanted me to go light on the cabbage. Never eliminate it, just go light. I suspected that was Vlad's preference.

He smiled and nodded. "Just right."

So at least I had something right.

I guess everyone likes praise for what they do, but that

night I enjoyed cooking for the Olekseis more than I ever had before. Everything about the ingredients, the smells, the textures, *everything* delighted me.

Maybe I should specialize in Russian food.

I sliced the garlic and dropped it into the pan. It started to sizzle, and I turned the heat down and began slicing the onion. It was very fresh, very pungent. My eyes watered, and I got sniffly. Then I smelled a hint of burn on the garlic and hurried back to the stove and shook the pan. Just in time. The slices were brown but not too brown.

I was getting good at this. I could detect the smell of burning just before it happened. That had to be some sort of superpower.

As I put the rest of the dish together—dicing deep, ruby beets; slicing carrots and Yukon gold potatoes; sizzling spicy sausage in the pan; spicing and tasting, and mixing, and finally pureeing the whole thing into a savory maroon liquid—I continued to marvel at the perfect ripeness and freshness of every ingredient I'd picked out. This was going to be the best batch of borscht I'd ever made, and normally I didn't even *like* it! I took a spoon out of the drawer and tried it.

Perfect.

I could have eaten the entire bowl.

For all my worry about losing jobs, this was a good reminder: As long as I continued to do a great job at what I was hired to do—that is, cook nourishing, satisfying food—my livelihood would be safe.

Wouldn't it?

Chapter 15

It wasn't any of Vlad's words that ended up haunting me that night, but my own.

I'm not expecting.

Forget the context, whatever he meant, whatever *I* meant at the time, the upshot is that I heard my own words and realized with all the chaos and craziness that had been going on around me lately, there might have been something wrong that I hadn't been paying attention to.

Sensitivity to smells, like chicken or onion.

Unexpected queasiness, like when I was making the eggplant for the Olekseis.

Hair-trigger moods, like freaking out because Mr. Tuesday might not have found me attractive when I was at his apartment, looking like total shit, *being his employee.*

The constant appetite for hot sauce, especially with sharp cheddar cheese.

None of this stuff was normal. At least not for me. How on earth had I not stopped and wondered, if not what these strange changes in my mind and body meant, at *least* where the hell my period was.

I was wondering now. As I scrolled through iCal on my computer, dread grew in my heart with every week that had passed without me notating five days with red *X*'s. Back, back, back . . . There it was.

Seven and a half weeks ago, I'd had my last period.

Five and a half weeks ago, I'd had my one-night stand.

Look, you're probably already thinking I'm no genius for taking even that long to put two and two together, and I see why, but I was not the kind of girl who got pregnant. (Well, not anymore.) It never even occurred to me as being a possibility. I had always been so *incredibly* vigilant about being protected (or doing nothing at all), that the idea that there might ever be a mishap or problem was absolutely out of the question.

Unacceptable.

Silly, I know. It was obviously a possibility. Until you no longer have the equipment, it's a possibility. And even then, you still hear the stories of "miracle births" sometimes.

It's just that it didn't feel that way to me. To me it had never, ever in my adult life seemed like a possibility because I straight-up, flat-out did not want it.

I'm going to be honest about this now: I was never the little girl who played with baby dolls. One of my earliest memories is of Penny trying to steal a Baby Tender Love from the Toys R Us on Rockville Pike. She was caught immediately, of course—an eight-year-old with a box shoved up under her Snoopy T-shirt is hardly subtle, but still, anyone who wants a baby so badly that she's willing to have DOLL THIEF stamped on her record forever is clearly meant to have babies.

I, on the other hand, played dolls with her only halfheartedly. If asked by a grown-up what I wanted to be when I grew up, I would say I wanted to be *like my mother.* Talk about a self-fulfilling prophecy! I got my chance to be like my mother, a struggling single mom with no good man in sight.

As time went on and boyfriends disappointed me, I began to call the hope chest my mom had given me for my twelfth birthday a "hope not" chest. The wife-beater-wearing, beer-swilling jerk Mrs. Rooks had put into my head never fully left my mind.

But the whole kid thing . . . The images of myself watching *The Bishop's Wife* with a glass of wine and half-eating the (delicious) cookies my son or daughter had left out for Santa were all new for me. The desire to have a little person sleeping soundly upstairs, and someone to uncork the wine while I picked out the movie—I'd never thought of them as being nice before. But lately . . .

First I called Lynn.

"Those condoms."

She didn't ask what I meant. "Huh?"

"From your drawer. How old were they?"

"Honest to God, I don't know. Like I said, I'd forgotten

they were even there. I think I must have gotten them when I lived on Calvert Street like seven years ago. Maybe more. Why? What's the problem?"

"Nothing. I hope." My throat tightened. "I really, really hope."

There was a long silence.

Then: "You're thinking they failed."

"At least one of them. Maybe."

"Oh God, Gem, you have to get a test."

"I don't want to get a test!"

"Because you don't want the answer?"

"That's exactly why." My stomach hurt. There was a lump in my throat. I'd been here before. I didn't want to go back.

"Gemma." Her voice was firm. "Get the test. I'm sure there's nothing to worry about and you'll feel better. Then call me back and tell me what happened so *I* can feel better, okay?"

I told her I would, but the words rang hollow to me. I didn't want to. I didn't want to. I didn't want to.

But I knew I had to.

But first I called Penny.

"How did you know you were pregnant?"

She didn't miss a beat. "My stomach got really huge, and started moving around by itself, and then a baby came out."

"Funny."

"What do you mean, how did I know I was pregnant? You were there when I took the test!"

"I know, I know, but what made you think you should take the test? What were the symptoms?"

"Whoa, wait a minute. I don't think I like where this is going. Why are you asking?"

"No reason."

All right, yes, I know exactly how stupid this conversation is. Though many have tried, no one in the history of the world has ever been able to talk themselves out of being pregnant. The human body is a miracle and so on, but not so much of a miracle that you can simply *will* yourself into or out of a pregnancy.

But denial is a powerful thing, and that's exactly the pool I was swimming in.

Penny was having none of it. "Holy cow, Gemma, you are *not* pregnant from that one-night stand, are you?"

"Well, I *hope* not!"

"How long ago was it?"

"Five weeks, give or take."

I heard her sigh. "No period, I guess."

Irritation niggled at me. "Yes, Penny, I have my period right now—isn't that a major sign of pregnancy?"

"I had to ask!"

"No, you didn't! It's not helpful!" Wasn't impatience another sign of pregnancy? My heart began to pound. This was starting to feel real. What was I going to do? What if I was pregnant? What would I do?

No, no, no, no, this wasn't possible.

Not again!

"Okay, so five weeks isn't *that* long," Penny said. "That makes your period, what, three weeks late?"

"About."

She sighed again. I wanted to tell her to stop, but that would, literally, be telling someone how to breathe. "This could be perimenopause."

"That's what I thought!" Though I hated to admit it out loud.

"Or even menopause, really."

"Slow down, Cloris Leachman, you're older than I am, this is *not* menopause."

"Okay, then, it's pregnancy!"

"I'll take menopause!"

We were silent for a moment.

"Seriously, do you have symptoms or did you just look at the calendar and realize things were off?"

I closed my eyes, knowing just how this was going to sound. "I'm suddenly really sensitive to smells—"

"Oh my God."

"I know. I *remember*."

"Remember that time Dell was cooking bacon, and I had to leave the house because it smelled like he was frying up the old man next door?"

My gag reflex tightened. "Stop."

"Okay, sorry. Go on."

"I'm a little oversensitive."

"All right, all right, I'm sorry," she said. "I'll be more respectful. Just go on."

"I am. I mean that lately I've been a little oversensitive emotionally. I feel like crying easily."

She sucked air in through her teeth. "Okay—?"

"And I nearly puked the other day when I was making

eggplant for the Olekseis. I mean, seriously, it just suddenly seemed completely revolting to me."

"Get over here."

"What?"

"Get over here *now*. You're taking a pregnancy test."

An hour later, we stood side by side in her bathroom, the mirror reflecting our shocked expressions as we looked down at the extravaganza on the counter.

"Do you think there's any chance that they made a bad batch and the indicators are in wrong so two lines means *negative* instead of positive?" I said in a voice that sounded questioning but really wasn't. Obviously, I knew.

"And all five of these tests are from the same bad batch from different brands?" Penny shook her head. "Seems unlikely."

The sticks were lined up on the counter like some ironic little picket fence. If just one of them—just *one*—had had a different answer, I would have felt at least a little hope.

But no, they were all the same.

"You're gonna have to find the guy, you know," Penny said.

"First I'm going to have to decide what I'm going to do."

"Okay . . . yes, you're right." She put her hand on my arm. "You have time for that. You know that. There's no point in pretending you haven't been to this crossroads before."

"Right." I took a shaking breath.

"It's okay, Gem. It will be okay. No matter what."

"I'm not sure that's true."

She hesitated. A hesitation that spoke volumes before she said unconvincingly, "It's true."

"I know what I'm going to do."

"What?"

"I can't have an abortion." I'd thought about it. God help me, I had thought about it. Faced with an unexpected crisis, it's hard not to think of *all* the options, but that was one I just couldn't face. I was all too aware—whether right or wrong—that this was my last chance, and having an abortion would be a firm cap on any ideas I might ever have about having children, even if I had only a few years left to entertain the idea. "And I can't give this baby up," I went on. "I know I'm going to have the baby. No matter what I say, or whether I go through the motions of making a decision here, the bottom line is I already know I'm keeping the baby."

"Okay, then."

I turned to her. Her swollen belly hovered between us like a big sign from God. I knew how hard she and Dell had tried for Charlotte and how much harder they'd tried for this baby. The options I felt I had were not options she ever would have felt herself.

And they were choices I never would have dreamed I'd have to make again.

Most of the time, I pride myself on being a strong and decisive person—at least about big things. I know what I want and I know how to get there. If a roadblock pops up

in the way, I'm usually pretty easy and flexible about finding a way around it.

Usually.

But this time, I was out of my depth.

This time I didn't know what to do.

So I did the only thing I could at that moment: I cried.

Chapter 16

I t's all about odds," Willa said. "Even when something bad happens to you against the odds, in a way, that's a form of luck."

She wasn't talking about my pregnancy, though she could have been. No, she was explaining her livelihood to me—and it was clear she was really passionately interested in it, Lex's disdain aside. The odds, the numbers, the chance, the adrenaline—all of that made her come alive.

It was hard to find fault with that.

"Luck, huh?" I laughed. "There are a lot of people walking away from casinos in Atlantic City, Vegas, et cetera right now—minus their mortgage payment—who would disagree."

I was making a carrot ginger soup, which, to my surprise, she declared smelled delicious, even though the ginger smelled so perfumy to me, I almost gagged.

"Well, that's just bad sense." She shrugged. "People come up with all kinds of *systems* for gambling, like the triple martingale at the roulette table, where you dominate two-thirds of the table and double your bets until you, theoretically, win, but the fact is, each roll of the dice is a Bernoulli trial."

I waited for her to elaborate, but she didn't, so I said, "It's like you're speaking a foreign language to me."

"I mean each roll of the dice is random. You have an equal chance of any outcome each time. If you're betting red or black, you have a fifty–fifty chance of either. You can't predict anything that way. That's why it's better to stick to games that have more obvious chances of success."

"Like—?"

"Poker. That's where I make most of my money. The number of cards is finite and the values are clear."

I got that.

Until she added, "It's like dealing with people."

"People," I said, stirring the pot but turning my nose away from the gingery smell, "are never clear."

"Not true. Everyone has their tells. You just have to figure them out."

"Hm."

I guess that was mine, because she narrowed her eyes and asked, "Who are you trying to figure out?"

I paused and turned to her. "I'm not sure. Someone seems

to be sabotaging my work at the country club, and I don't know who or why." I wondered at the wisdom of admitting that anyone might be saying bad stuff about my cooking, but it was too late, I'd already said it. "Actually, yes, I do. I think it's Angela Van Houghten, a woman I work for."

It was quickly clear that she was undaunted by it. "Why? What's her story?"

"Her husband made a pass at me." I sighed.

As soon as I'd spilled it, I regretted it. Willa had warmed up a tiny bit to me, but it wasn't like we were *pals*. This was just the kind of information that would prove to her I was more trouble to have around than I was worth. I was un-trustworthy, whether with your husband, your cutlery, or your computer.

So it surprised me when Willa simply shrugged and said, "So you need to stop her."

I met her eyes. Emotion wasn't getting me anywhere. "*How?* She probably wouldn't even admit it, much less stop it. This is *exactly* the kind of humiliation she would hate. *Hate*."

"Well, no one likes public humiliation."

"True. But no one likes it less than someone like Angela. I'm screwed."

"Maybe. But you're looking at the negatives instead of the positives, and believe me, if you look at the negatives, you're going to see plenty. It's like statistics that can prove whatever theory you want. So turn it around a little."

"How?"

"You're still working for her, right?"

"Incredibly, yes." I couldn't quit. I would have loved to, but I couldn't.

"So watch her. Be aware that she might be behind this and watch for a vulnerability and then"—she flipped her palm in front of her—"turn it on her."

She wasn't entirely wrong. If Angela tipped her hand, I could address this directly. "Good advice."

She smiled and sat back. "Hey, it's how I make my living."

"How long have you been doing that?" I asked her.

"What, being a shut-in, making money anonymously in front of the computer screen?"

I smiled. "Yes, that."

"Since I was twenty. Ten years."

It had never occurred to me to wonder how old she was, but the news that she was thirty somehow surprised me. She seemed older.

She must have read my thoughts in my eyes—and if anyone could, it would be her—because she said, "I know, you thought I was older. Most people do. I think it's because I don't have that youthful spring in my step." She smiled, but I could tell she didn't feel it.

"Is that why you started doing this? Because it was hard to get around?"

"Ah. No. Believe it or not, when I was twenty, I weighed a hundred thirty-three pounds."

"Really?" I couldn't mask the surprise in my voice. I wanted to ask what happened, but there wasn't a way to do that without sounding incredibly rude.

"My mother was a rail, but my father was very heavy," she said. "Still is. Nothing like me, though." She gave an awkward shrug. "I was so determined to be like my mother that I dieted insanely in high school and college. Barely ate a thing. Almost no nutrition, I realize now. Celery isn't exactly a powerhouse of vitamins."

"That's for sure."

"So I got no exercise. But I was thin enough to model for the store. Until I 'ballooned' to a hundred and thirty-five pounds, that is. Then I looked like a blimp next to the other models and *plus size* wasn't cool in those days. On the runway or on the street. My boyfriend dumped me, and I guess that's when I just stopped caring."

She sounded so defeated, it broke my heart.

"A hundred and thirty-five on your frame is nothing," I said. "How tall are you?"

"Five eight and a half." She nodded. "I see now just how ridiculous it was that I bought in to that, but at the time, it was very painful. Obviously, it's more painful now. . . ." She looked down at her form, sitting on the sofa like an unsteady pile of tires.

I won't pretend for a moment that I knew how she felt or how hard it really was for her, but I have struggled with weight in my own way as well. After the baby was born when I was eighteen, my body changed in a lot of ways. In many ways, it never came back. To this day, I have the faint white road map on my hips and lower abdomen that shows the astute observer exactly where I've been in my life.

After the baby, like Willa, I was vigilant about diet and

exercise in college, and like Willa, I had experienced the draining effects of lack of fuel in the body.

Unlike Willa, I kept it up for years, fighting my body's pleas for nutrition. It wasn't until I stopped working in the corporate world and started cooking that I actually developed a healthier relationship with food.

And my body.

Now my body conforms to its natural state: curvy, with a narrow waist but hips and boobs and upper arms that no one would ever mistake for a twelve-year-old boy's (the ideal I had aspired to for so long). Once, I would have considered this body hideously fat. I would have been horrified at the prospect of "letting myself go" to this degree.

Now I'm horrified that I ever thought that way.

And I was looking at a dramatic illustration of how badly that line of thinking could potentially go.

"Do you know what this feels like?" she asked suddenly. "It's like being trapped inside a tiny, claustrophobic place." She looked at me, and I saw she was crying openly.

But I was careful not to invade her space. This felt like an important revelation, and I didn't want to interrupt it. "What do you mean?"

"This body, which must look so enormous to you from the outside, feels like something wrapped tightly around my real body, keeping me from moving, from running, from swimming. From driving a car, from flying in an airplane, from even leaving the house." Her voice trailed off. "People look at me, I know this, they look at me and imagine me to be some lazy pig who derives enormous pleasure from consuming disgusting amounts of unhealthy food. That's just not true. I can think of no greater pleasure than"—she thought for a moment—"to be able to take the steps to the top of the Washington Monument as fast as a child. And not die."

"There's not a reason in the world you can't get there," I said. "How much weight have you lost in the past two weeks, since you first started being vigilant about the diet?"

"Twelve pounds."

I gasped. "Are you *kidding*? That's *great*!"

She snorted. "It's like throwing two deck chairs off the *Queen Mary*. Statistically insignificant."

"It's fantastic," I said firmly. "And you're doing it in a healthy, *permanent* way."

"As long as I can afford you!"

"Well, I'm not looking to lose any more work, but the truth is, you could do what I'm doing. Easily."

"I doubt that!"

"No, really. I'll teach you. Come on."

"Nooo, no. I'm the one who can't be trusted to have ingredients in the house, remember?"

"That's why you need to learn to buy the *right* ingredients."

"I don't know. . . ."

"I do." I went to her and put a hand out to help her off the sofa. "We'll start now."

And thus, I began my first cooking lesson.

I had to be mindful of the fact that there would come a time, in about seven months, when I would have to take some time off, and I didn't want to leave Willa—who by then I hoped would have made tremendous progress—alone to fend for herself.

I didn't want to make myself obsolete, of course. That was the danger of teaching a person to fish, so to speak, instead of just preparing a nice thick swordfish steak with tropical salsa and rice pilaf.

But it was a chance I had to take.

Chapter 17

"I don't care what Angela's saying or doing," Penny said, "you can't afford to be worrying about this right now."

And there it was.

No, it wasn't just me I had to think about. I had run into this *exact* problem when I was a teenager and too young to reasonably have an answer to it, but I never, ever thought I'd come up against it again. And I had spent an adult lifetime being *really* vigilant in order *not* to run into this again.

Yet here I was.

A more woo-woo person than I might have called it fate.

I, on the other hand, just called it bad luck. I had stolen condoms from my friend's bedside table drawer without checking the label, the expiration date, or even to see if they were novelty items made from chewing gum. In short, I'd told myself I was being responsible when, in fact, I was masquerading for my own sexual convenience.

Not that I thought I "deserved" the result as a consequence for being irresponsible or something. I had been completely confident I was being responsible. At the time, additional vigilance hadn't seemed necessary.

Hindsight, of course, was 20/20.

Now I had to keep my eyes open.

"I think you need to expand your horizons," Penny said. "Think about working new places so that when one goes down, it doesn't mean the end of your career."

I nodded and reached for a cookie. She started buying those Danish butter cookies from Costco right when they started selling them around Halloween, and I'd probably already put on two pounds from them in the past three weeks.

Or from something.

"I have been," I told her. "It's not so easy, though. I'm a luxury in a bad economy."

She smiled. "Oh, honey, you're a luxury in *any* economy!"

"Right. This has always been my problem."

"It's always been your *choice*! You took a huge chance leaving the corporate world, and it paid off! You have a wonderful job, you work for yourself, and all of that took courage most people don't have! Yes, it's hard sometimes, like now, but you're living your dream."

As was so often the case lately, my eyes teared up. "You're right. I shouldn't be complaining."

She shrugged and took a cookie. "I don't know, you've got plenty to complain about, too!"

I had to laugh. "Great."

A moment passed, and then Penny grew serious and said, "Have you thought about finding him?"

Mack. "Not much."

"*Not much* because you don't intend to or because you don't think you can or what?"

Another cookie. "*Not much,* meaning I've thought about it a ton and have seriously wondered if there's karmic significance to the fact that it was a big clusterfuck when I ran into him at the grocery store."

"Karmic significance?"

"Like, maybe I'm not supposed to be with him. He was physically significant, obviously, but maybe not spiritually."

She looked at me, aghast. "Are you joking? That is the dumbest thing I ever heard!"

"I would think you, of all people, with your belief in psychics and signs and fate and all of that, would be on board with this."

"Okay, you want signs and fate? You met a stranger in a bar, had an instant attraction to him, took *more than reasonable* precautions to stay safe, yet ended up pregnant anyway. Tell me that's not meant to be!"

"Of course, I could argue with some of that."

"Of course you could, but it wouldn't ring as true as what I just said. This was meant to be. There is no question."

"Then what about the other pregnancy? Was that *meant to be* as well?"

"Of course."

"Then fate isn't always very nice." Tears filled my eyes and burned down my cheeks.

"No," she agreed, handing me a box of Kleenex from the table next to her. "It isn't." She rested her hand on her belly and moved her thumb along it thoughtfully. "But most of the time, I think fate just isn't always very *clear*. So far, it's not clear for you, but it will be."

I wanted that to be true. I really, really wanted it to be true. But I was deeply afraid that it wasn't. That this was all a mistake or a glitch that would become the exact nightmare for the child I was carrying now that I had worried the last time would be for the child I gave up.

Just the thought made me cringe. I had gotten pregnant by accident not once but *twice* in my life. From the outside, that made me look like an absolute idiot.

What business did someone like me have raising a child?

"I'm afraid," I said.

"Of what?"

"Of not being good enough."

"We all are." She looked down and gave a dry spike of a laugh, but I saw her swipe a tear from her eye. "Every single day. You just have to do your best."

Charlotte came into the living room then, wearing bright little pajamas that had cartoon cowgirls and horses all over them. Life looked so easy for those cowgirls. "Mommy?"

"Yes, honey?" Penny put out her hand, and I gave her the box of Kleenex back. She dabbed at her eyes. "What are you still doing up, Char?"

"I thought I heard Gemma." She looked at me shyly through the thick glasses she wore.

I held out my arms, and she threw herself into them, sitting on my lap. The fabric was warm, and just a little pilled, and I remembered *exactly* what those kinds of pajamas felt like to wear.

It was unexpectedly poignant.

I gave her a squeeze. "I'm sorry I didn't go in and say hi, but I thought you were asleep."

"As you're *supposed* to be," Penny said, falsely stern. I'd seen this before. She and Charlotte were pals, and many, many times Penny had kept Charlotte up watching old movies or playing board games.

A small hope surged in me. I'd spent a lot of time thinking about the potential negatives here, but I hadn't really allowed myself the luxury of looking at the potential positives. The snuggle time, the cookie baking, the arts and crafts, the bedtime stories, the thrill of watching a person I already loved grow from wordless infant into whatever he or she would eventually be.

These thoughts didn't come without melancholy, of course, and they never came without thoughts of the last pregnancy. Hopefully, that would change when this baby was born and the reality superseded the memory and imagination, and sadness if not regret, that had been brewing all these years.

"Good night, Gemma." Charlotte threw her pipe cleaner arms around my neck and hugged me.

"Good night, baby."

My eyes met Penny's, and she nodded.

She knew.

Mother-to-mother, she knew I was struggling with the past I'd let go and the future I was facing now.

Absentmindedness. That was another thing I remembered from being pregnant. I had gone all the way to Mr. Tuesday's to make his dinner, and I'd forgotten the key.

I stood at the door and rang the bell. No answer. Of course. So instead I sat down on the hall floor with my back against the wall and took out my phone to call him and find out if one of the neighbors might have a key, or the doorman, or someone.

As soon as I'd dialed, a man got off the elevator, his cell phone ringing.

A very familiar man.

"Mack!" His name exploded from my mouth before I could stop it. Then suddenly everything hit me. What was he doing here? He had lived here all along? Had I been strolling past his door this whole time, oblivious of the fact that he was right there behind it?

Then the heavier stuff set in. I was pregnant. My heart sank. I was pregnant.

There was a child here now, someone who would grow to adulthood, be a force in this world for far longer than I would. As hard as it was to fathom now—since *now*, pregnancy simply felt like a medical condition—I was responsible for a new human being coming into the world.

And so was Mack.

This man I was looking at, whom I didn't know. My God, what did I know about him beyond that he was charming and hot in bed? Was he *married,* for instance? I didn't even know that for sure. Was he a good person or not? Was he the kind of guy countless women had sobbed over, gently patted by their best friend's hands amidst reassurances of *He's not worth it!*

Who *was* the father of this baby?

And how would I ever know? Now any chance of normal interaction or playful coyness was out the window.

I pushed END on my phone.

At the same time, he glanced at his phone and pushed the DECLINE button. "Applesauce," he said, tilting his head and smiling. "What the hell are you doing here?"

"I'm here to meet one of my clients." I slid up the wall and straightened out my clothes. I pulled in my stomach a little. I knew I wasn't showing yet, but still. "What are *you* doing here?"

"I live here." He gestured vaguely at the door behind me.

No way.

But yes way. Of course.

The phones.

I hung up on him, he declined me, all so we could talk to each other. It was too much—too coincidental to be true.

"You live . . . *where?*" I asked, already knowing the answer.

Then something washed over his face and he took a deep breath. He glanced to the door behind me. "Gemma?"

Despite the obviousness of what was currently happening, I had to stifle the urge to ask how he knew my name, since I remembered distinctly that it had somehow been overlooked by both of us on that fateful night.

But the answer was obvious.

"Are you . . . Paul's brother? Mack—McMann—it makes perfect sense." I shook my head and stared at him.

He looked at me curiously. "Wh—? No. I *am* Paul."

Chapter 18

The floor seemed to fall away beneath my feet. This made no sense. It was impossible to comprehend. *"What?"*

He pointed at himself a little self-consciously. "Paul McMann."

"G-Gemma Craig."

"Why would you think—?" He tilted his head. "Okay, this is too weird."

"But you said your name—"

"Mack." He nodded. "I was with a couple of buddies from college that night." He gave a crooked smile. "I didn't want to tell you I was Paul and then have them call me Mack all night and make me look like some creepy liar."

We both stood there in silence for a few moments. Finally, he snapped out of it and walked hazily toward his door. "Come . . . come in." He paused and gave a dry laugh. "You have a key. You could have let yourself in."

"Yeah . . . um . . . I forgot it. There's . . . stuff . . . on my mind." Too much. Too too much.

He nodded and unlocked the door.

I walked through and then turned. "But if *you're* Paul, who was that the other day?" The guy I'd chatted away at as if he knew exactly who I was and I knew exactly who he was and we'd known each other—at least on some level—for more than a year.

"Who?"

"The guy who got here when I was leaving the other day."

"My brother." Then, with a small raise of his eyebrow, he said, "Oh, *that's* why you thought I was him."

"Well." I shrugged. "Yeah."

"He told me you were beautiful."

"Oh, did he?" I responded automatically.

"Yeah. I had no idea how right he was."

"Ha." My legs felt a little weak. I sat down in the chair I knew well to be behind me.

He started to take off his coat, then froze. "But you must have known it was me—you had my number." He looked like he was trying to figure out a puzzle.

I remembered his instructions to listen for the phone the other day, and felt a little hot. "I knocked over a bottle of water the morning . . . um . . . after we . . ." I looked sheepishly at him and he nodded. "And I didn't even notice the note until it was ruined. I couldn't read it." I shook my head. "God, it's just unbelievable."

"I know. The grocery store—"

"Right, and you were on the phone and it was obviously important and I couldn't just stand there, waiting like an idiot. . . ."

"Right."

I felt an uncomfortable cramp in my stomach as I thought of everything. The notes, the banter, the sex—it was all him. The baby . . .

He cleared his throat. "So . . . how've you been?"

I laughed. "Well, you pretty much know that, don't you?" Except for the baby. "We talk every week."

He shook his head and raked his hand through his hair, his gesture perfectly reflecting the confusion I was also feeling. "We do. It's true. You've been in my house every week."

Yes, his baby and I, walking around, doing domestic stuff in his place, never realizing. I didn't know what to say. In fact, there was so damn much to say that I couldn't say anything.

He broke the silence. "We could probably stumble over how strange this coincidence is all night."

I laughed. "I'm ready to."

"Or we could skip that and pour some wine and get to know each other." He smiled. "I don't know how to make those drinks you were having at No Plans."

"Yeah, I'm really not that big a drinker," I said, the words heavy with meaning now. "Particularly when I'm on duty."

"Gemma." He smiled and my heart skipped. There he

was, the guy who had caught my attention that night, and who had monopolized my imagination ever since then.

The guy Penny would call my fate.

"As of now," he said, "you are officially off duty for the night."

"Oh." I wasn't sure what to do with that. On the one hand, I was used to being his employee, so it was hard to break that habit, but on the other hand, we had a whole new relationship going here.

"I think we have a lot of catching up to do," he said. "So start at the beginning. Tell me who Gemma Craig really is."

It was a long, leisurely evening of talk. Everything just flowed *so easily*. We talked, we laughed, we agreed, several times we said the same thing at the same time.

It was like the silliest old romantic movie come to life, with every piece falling into place like a stack of blocks in Tetris.

For a couple of glorious hours, I thought maybe It was finally happening. Fate had taken a strange course, baby in the baby carriage coming first, but maybe fate thought I was just so thickheaded that I wouldn't get it otherwise.

Mack, I thought, might be the One.

Then he sprang it on me.

"The timing of this all just couldn't be worse," he said right after we had marveled, again, at the coincidence of me having been in his home every week for so long with neither of us knowing what we could be together.

For a crazy moment, I thought he was referring to the pregnancy, but of course he wasn't. He had no idea.

"What do you mean?" I asked, foolishly expecting a simple answer along the lines of, *We could have been having so much fun together this past year.*

But no.

"I've taken a new job," he said. "I'm going to be a partner in a huge firm in Seattle."

"Seattle," I repeated. Was there a Seattle, Maryland? Seattle, Virginia? Was Seattle the name of some small enclave of D.C. I didn't know about?

Please please please let it be anything other than Seattle, Washington.

No hope springs as aggressively eternal as desperate hope.

"Ironic, huh?" He looked grim. "I couldn't get much farther away in the States without actually going to Hawaii or Alaska."

My stomach tightened. "So . . . it's definite? This move?"

"As of today, yes. I was going to call and let you know, anyway. So you could get more work."

Work. I wasn't even thinking about work. But if he had called, if we had had this conversation without knowing who each other was, it would have been a devastating blow.

This was even worse.

"When do you leave?" I asked, and my voice sounded thin and limp.

"Next month. Four and a half weeks, actually. I spent the afternoon on the phone, getting a broker to sell this place and arranging for a moving company to come haul it all away." He looked into my eyes, and my stomach flipped.

"I would love to keep seeing you, to get to know you better, but the long-distance thing . . . that's not fair for me to ask."

Ask, I thought. *Please ask.* But what could I say, really? How could I do that? I had maybe two months before I would be showing obviously. Six months before travel would become prohibitively uncomfortable.

This could never work.

I had to take the moments I had right now, get to know as much about him as I could so that someday, I don't know, I'd have at least a *little* background for this child if he or she had questions about his or her father.

That was the best I could do.

"So you didn't tell him you were having his kid, then?"

Penny had been listening enraptured to my story over the phone, but it was obvious I hadn't given her the ending she wanted.

I moved the phone from one ear to the other. "No. I couldn't find an easy way to tell my client-slash-one-night-stand that I'm carrying his child. It didn't seem the right time."

"But you'll have to tell him! There's never going to be a *right time.*"

The guilty knob in my throat hardened. "Actually, you're right. I don't think there is. He's moving. To Seattle."

"*What?*"

"I know. He's got some great job lined up out there, it's

all official, and if I tell him about the baby . . . I don't know . . . I think it would make him feel conflicted. For all the wrong reasons."

"Wrong reasons? Give me a better reason than a baby!"

"Oh, Penny, come *on*. There are scores of people out there who stayed together as long as they could—right up to the moments their relationships got threadbare and horrible—because they thought they needed to keep it together because of the kids. I know far more people who were fucked up by terrible marriages than by single parents."

"You're right. But he has the right to know."

I sighed. "I just don't know how to reconcile that. What I *do* know is that he's leaving in a month, and that gives us a month to get to know each other a little better without the additional weight of this responsibility on the relationship. Then—" I paused. Then what? "—then we'll see."

"You're going to tell him eventually, right?" she asked.

"Yes," I said, but did I mean it? What if things fizzled three weeks from now and he moved and, under normal circumstances, it was one of those things where we'd move on and never see each other again?

Did we really need to be in the awkward position of co-parenting then?

How many single women had gone to great lengths for artificial insemination in order to have babies by themselves when they reached a certain age and didn't want to compromise? Couldn't this just be, basically, the same thing?

"You want to keep seeing him, though, right?" Penny

asked. "Maybe do the long-distance thing until one of you moves to the other if things work out?"

I took a bite of the brownies I'd swung by Giant for, then went and flumped down on my sofa. "I don't know."

"Oh, come *on*! I can hear it in your voice right now! You're totally into the guy. You were when you met him, or when you *thought* you met him, *and* you've been really fond of him as your boss, too. You've been into him two different ways, and you didn't even know it! If that's not fate, I don't know what is!"

It was a compelling argument. But. "All I can say is that I'll play it by ear. This is a huge element to add to a small relationship."

I could practically hear her raise her eyebrows. "Well, it seems clear to me that it was meant to be. I mean, for all intents and purposes, you're already practically his wi—"

"Don't"—I actually held my finger up in the air even though she couldn't see me—"even say it."

"All right, but I'm just saying that you have a foundation most people don't have at this point in a relationship."

I knew very well what Penny was saying. It was like being a wife. A very June Cleavery wife. There was a small, crazy part of me that thought it didn't seem that bad an idea. It was like standing on top of the high diving board and thinking, *I could just . . . I could just do it. Just jump in.*

But this was different. It wasn't just a dive for me. It would be a big one for him, too. If only I could press PAUSE on my whole baby situation.

"Gemma?"

I'd been quiet for too long. "Yes, sorry. Um. What were we saying?"

"I'm saying—"

My phone beeped. I glanced at the screen. MR. TUESDAY was still his designation in my phone book. "Oh my God!"

"No way! See? It's a *sign!*"

"I'll call you back, Penny." I switched over. "Hell—hello?"

"Gemma. It's . . . Paul."

"Hi, Paul."

"Hey. So, I know earlier was sort of awkward and I wanted to make sure you felt okay with everything."

"Yeah, I'm sorry." For what? Turning out to be me?

"No, no, it's no one's fault. I mean, it's a *good* thing. I was just very surprised."

"Me, too."

"Well, I just wanted to apologize. I feel like I should have known or figured it out or tried harder to find you or something."

"No, don't worry about it. We *couldn't* have known." Or could we? Should we somehow have known?

He paused. "This is *bizarre,* right? I mean, what are the odds?"

"I was always bad at math."

"Maybe you don't need to be that good at math to put two and two together."

I paused, thinking, then just went ahead and said it. "I'm sorry, I don't know which four you're referring to."

He laughed. "I'm not sure I do, either."

Call me a crazy romantic, but hearing him say it made my heart pound. "Do you think we might ever—?" How could I finish that without sounding needy and grasping?

This was such a strange position to be in, not knowing if we knew each other or not. Not knowing if we were already halfway there or, in some ways, further apart than strangers.

"Arguably, we have a head start," he said, as if reading my mind. "I mean, I already know your worst qualities."

I recognized the humor in his voice. "Uh-huh—do you, now?"

"Yup. Your weapon of choice is a pepper grinder, and you don't know when to stop with the garlic."

"Right. Good thing I know yours, too."

"I have no bad qualities."

"*A*, you don't write in waterproof ink," I said, as if he hadn't spoken, "and *B*, you have trust issues."

"Trust?"

"As in, trust me, you like all that garlic."

"Right," he said, and I imagined that smile.

"And *C*," I went on. "You're moving across the country."

He hesitated, but I could imagine him shaking his head in resignation. "That's the truth."

"No way around that."

"I guess not."

A moment of silence passed, so long that I almost laughed at my complete inability to come up with something clever to say.

242 / Beth Harbison

Finally he spoke, "But it's late. We can't figure everything out right now. My primary concern was that you weren't feeling too uncomfortable with . . . things."

I had to smile to myself. "No, I'm not too uncomfortable with things. Are you?"

"No. They could have gone smoother, of course, but I'm kind of liking things."

"Good. Me, too."

"Moving thousands of miles away seems like something of a hindrance."

"It does," I agreed. "So we'll have to fake our way through that until it makes sense."

"Is that your usual MO?"

"When I don't know what else to do, yes. Better that than forcing an issue into something unrecognizable."

"You're a pretty cool chick, you know that?" He laughed.

"You have no idea," I said. "So sleep on that."

"Yes, ma'am."

And we hung up. In some ways, I couldn't wait until I next talked to him. But also, saying *Oh, this banter is fun and all, but let's get serious about our child* was not a thrilling prospect.

Was it even possible that I might never have to say it?

Chapter 19

O kay, so tell me what a diet meal is to you," I said to
Willa.

She was sitting at her computer at the kitchen
counter, having just finished—and won—a five-thousand-
dollar hand at poker. It was incredible, really. I had to wonder what her yearly gross was.

And what on earth she could write off on her taxes,
since her overhead pretty much consisted of her computer
and Internet connection. There was no way to get a deduc-
tion for the brain you were born with.

"When I was really dieting hard, I'd have a plain yogurt
and a banana for dinner."

"Typical. I can see why that *seemed* reasonable." I nodded
at the computer. "Look up the nutritional content of that."

She started clicking away, and it was clear she was ace

on the computer. "Got it. An average banana has a hundred and twenty-one calories."

"Write that down. We're going to do a comparison."

She switched screens and clicked, then switched back. "What now?"

"How many carbs?" I knew that would be high. Frankly, that was what was so *good* about bananas. Especially if you sliced them in half, sautéed them in butter and brown sugar, then topped them with toasted cashews and vanilla ice cream. But this didn't seem like the right time to point all that out.

"Thirty-one carbs," she said. "But no fat."

"Fat is not your enemy," I said. "At least not unsaturated fat. How much protein in a banana?"

"Um." Click. "One-point-five grams."

"Okay, jot that down—now find out the same information on the yogurt."

It took her only seconds. "Eighty calories, no fat, eight grams of protein, and only fourteen carbs." She looked pleased with herself. "I bet the fruit yogurt has a lot more than that."

"I'm sure it does. So, in a way, that was a good choice. Plain versus sweetened. But how satisfying was the meal?"

"Yogurt and banana?"

I nodded. "I mean, you can't call it a *meal*, but that's what you were using it for."

"True. And *un*. Unsatisfying. Completely unsatisfying. Almost worse than having nothing at all."

"Did you tend to eat something decadent a few hours later?"

"Not always. I was really, *really* militant about my diet back then." She sighed, as if she missed those days. But clearly, those days were gone and I had to show her a better way. I had to do whatever I could to help her.

See, I really liked Willa. I didn't always particularly like the people I worked for. The Van Houghtens were a good example of that. I was always grateful for the work, and grateful to anyone who was willing to pay me good money for the thing I loved to do, but not everyone felt like a friend.

Willa was beginning to.

And the more I saw her, and the more I got to know her, the more I truly did worry that her health problems were going to take a serious toll on her.

"Add that up, would you?" I asked. "What are the totals?"

"Two hundred and one calories, forty-five grams of sugar, and nine-point-five grams of protein."

"And satisfaction, one to ten?"

"Two." She shrugged. "I do like bananas."

"Me too." I smiled. "Okay, now consider this. We're going to compare values, nutritionally and satisfaction-wise, okay?"

"What's the goal?"

"To match or beat the calories in the banana and yogurt with something that's actually *delicious*."

"Wouldn't a Three Musketeers bar do that?"

"Okay, yes." It was true. "But also something that's satisfying and gives you energy and vitality and all that stuff that makes us feel good."

"Go for it."

"All right." I reached into my bag. "Six large shrimp." It was the Costco ones, which I loved. Each was like one of Paul Bunyan's fingers, solid and meaty.

"A hundred and ten calories, no carbs, two grams of fat, and twenty-two grams of protein."

"Good stuff, right?" I turned on the water in the sink and started slipping the shells off the shrimp, putting them in a colander to dry as I went along. "All of that is good."

"I do know protein is key. Especially for me. Carbs make me want to sleep."

"They turn to sugar in your system right away." I finished the last two shrimp, then sprinkled all of them with a little bit of salt and pepper. "No caloric significance here," I said as I did it. "But flavor. *Flavor* is significant."

"I'll say. What next?"

"Butter."

"Margarine?"

"No, seriously, butter."

"Be real. I can't eat butter. There are like a million jokes built right into that one single ingredient!"

"*Moderation*," I said, then crinkled my nose. "Don't you hate that word?"

"Totally."

"But it's really true with food. A little bit of real butter or real cheddar or real Parmesan or whatever can make a huge flavor difference where you might use a lot more of something a lot less healthy. I remember there was this diet guru a few years back who said we could eat whatever we wanted as long as there was no fat in it."

Willa nodded. "I remember her."

"Do you remember how we all ballooned when we believed it? Because they added sugar and fake ingredients to everything. So"—I took out my stick of Land O' Lakes— "two teaspoons of butter in a nonstick pan. What's the nutritional value there?"

I have to admit here, I wasn't entirely sure how this was going to shake down. There was the possibility that what I concocted would end up having the calories of a Big Mac, making the yogurt and banana *seem* like the better option, but I knew that even if it did, we were talking about food that would be used nutritionally so much more that it was worth it, regardless.

Still, the butter concerned me.

"Two *teaspoons*?" she asked.

"Yes."

"That's just a sliver."

"Well, no, it's a couple of slivers. Theoretically, we could sear the shrimp without any, but we want the flavor and the moistness. So go ahead, hit me with it."

There were a few clicks, and Willa gave a low whistle. "Seventy-two calories and three grams of fat."

"Fine." I dropped the butter into the nonstick pan. "Keep the heat on medium so the butter doesn't burn, thereby making you add more. As soon as it's melted"—I paused a minute, then pointed—"like this, add the shrimp." I dropped them in and they sizzled in the heat and immediately started to curl. "This takes only a minute or two per side. The rule of thumb is that when they curl into a *C*, that means they're cooked."

"Cute."

"Completely." I turned off the heat. "Okay, this is gratuitous, but let's go for it anyway. Three cloves of garlic."

She concentrated on the screen and announced, "Four calories, one carb, no fat, no protein. But that carb surprises me."

"Statistically insignificant."

"I know."

I chopped the garlic quickly and tossed it in the pan. "Now, this stuff you don't even need to look up. A little lemon juice and some Cajun spice don't add up to anything." I tossed them in and moved the shrimp around with tongs.

"I have to admit, that smells *amazing*," Willa said.

"Better than yogurt?"

She laughed. "A little bit."

"All right. Now we have a bunch of romaine lettuce, as much as you want, really, but this is one small heart of it." I'd already washed it—there's nothing I hate more than watery salad from lettuce that was washed but not dried properly, so I tore it quickly into a bowl. "Dark leafy greens have fiber, iron, calcium, lutein, magnesium, and vitamins C, E, and B. In other words, this is worthwhile."

"Gotcha."

"Now look up two teaspoons of olive oil." I poured two teaspoons into a measuring cup with a spout.

"Forty calories, four grams of fat." She looked at me. "That seems like a lot."

"Yeah, but it's worth it. Monounsaturated fats aren't as troubling as, like, bacon fat."

"Which is awesome."

"Tell me about it." I took out another bottle. "Two teaspoons of balsamic vinegar?"

She clicked, then laughed. "Ten calories, nothing else."

"Good. And honestly, you might want to go more. Sometimes I do like three-quarters vinegar to one-quarter oil, but the oil has omega-threes for your heart and brain, and it's important for absorbing the nutrition of the greens, so don't skip it."

"And chocolate is important to mood."

"It is."

"I know."

We laughed.

"Okay, and we've got a little chopped onion, chopped carrot, salt, pepper, mustard, nothing significant." I tossed them into the measuring cup as I spoke, then took out a whisk and whisked it all together to emulsify it. "And that's it." I poured it onto the lettuce and tossed it well.

"I have to admit, it looks impressive."

I plated the salad and arranged the shrimp next to it. The plate was full, and it was a regular dinner plate, not a tricky, optical-illusion salad plate. "What's the breakdown here?"

She looked at her computer screen and raised her eyebrows. "Two hundred thirty-one calories, one carb, five grams of fat, and twenty-two grams of protein." She made a face. "Jeez, you went over by *thirty* calories."

For a moment, I thought she was serious, but then she broke into a smile.

"So try it," I said.

She took a bite of the shrimp and nodded. "That's *amazing*."

"Try the salad."

She did. "Wow."

"So on the one-to-ten scale of satisfaction?"

"Ten!"

"Come on, it's not Brie en croûte. But, seriously, one to ten."

She thought about it. "Brie en croûte being a ten?"

"Or whatever your poison of choice."

"Deep-dish pizza from Armand's." She sighed. "Okay, I'd give this an eight. For real. Maybe even a nine." She took another bite. "It's seriously amazing."

"See what we're doing here?"

She nodded. "Thinking. Calculating."

"Which is exactly what you do for a living, right?"

"Ideally." She had another bite. "Don't you want some?"

"I already ate," I lied. The truth was, I was a little queasy, and shrimp wasn't on the list of foods that appealed to me right now. "Besides, if you had only half that, you'd be hungry again in a couple of hours, and fast food would be looking all too good. Believe me, I've been there."

"Okay, so what's really going on with you?" she asked, as if she were asking where I'd gotten my shoes.

"What do you mean?"

"Something's bothering you. It's obvious. What is it?"

"Oh, nothing. I've just had a lot on my plate lately. No pun intended."

"Yeah?"

"Believe me."

She didn't meet my eyes, but I could tell there was a lot behind her next question. "You're not going to quit here, are you?"

"What? No!"

She looked at me. "Really?"

"Of course I'm not going to quit! You're not going to fire me, are you?"

"No way!"

"Good!" I smiled at her. "Then we have no problems at all."

She squinted at me, clearly assessing me and seeing right through my veneer. "Okay." Pause. "But if you want to talk about it, feel free, okay? I might not be the ideal person to give diet advice, but I'm not too bad with regular life stuff. Keep it in mind, okay?"

I believed her. And meant it when I said, "I just might take you up on that."

As great as Willa was, Angela Van Houghten was the exact opposite. Obviously, I'd learned this over and over again, but it didn't stop me from being surprised every time she did something I didn't see coming.

"I won't be here to eat tonight, so don't bother with anything for me," she said, stepping up to me in a cloud of heavy perfume and standing before me like we were gang members playing chicken. "In fact, it's just Peter tonight. The two of you will be completely alone."

She paused only briefly, but a shudder ran through me.

"So," she went on, "there is a rib-eye steak in the refrigerator for you to prepare for him."

"A rib-eye steak!"

She nodded. "It's his favorite."

"Okay." Something was off here. "But I thought you were concerned about any sort of cross-contamination, whether it's pans, utensils, or whatever. I'm not sure how to prepare a steak without using the tools I usually do."

"Don't worry about it." She waved her hand airily; then her tone changed to something, if not nice then at least *nicer*. "Just clean it well, and I'm sure it will be fine."

This just didn't sound like her. "Are you sure?"

"Of course. Why are you doubting me?"

"I'm not, it's just . . ." Just what? "Whatever you want, Angela. I just don't want you to be concerned about it later."

"I won't even be here," she said, as if that were the solution. "That's why I thought it would be nice for you to just give him what he wants for once. If I'm not here, who cares?" She shrugged broadly. "It's nothing to do with me."

It didn't make sense, but I wasn't interested in figuring

out what was behind this change of heart. Maybe she was slipping off to sleep with some boyfriend or something and wanted to assuage her guilt by letting her husband eat something she would normally deem sinful—who knew? It wasn't for me to decide.

"Okay, I'll make the steak."

"Perfect," she said without enthusiasm. "And, I hate to ask this, but perhaps you could stay with him while he eats, since Stephen and I won't be here? It can be upsetting to eat alone."

As far as I knew, he'd done that plenty, but I was pretty sure she was up to something now and whatever it was, I did *not* want to know, so I just nodded and said, "If he gets here while I'm still cleaning up, then, yeah, of course I'll keep him company."

"Good." She headed for the front door and didn't say another word.

Peter came in about fifteen minutes later.

"What is that smell?" he asked, incredulous. "Is that steak?"

"It's about to be," I said, scraping shallots out of the pan and onto a plate. "Angela got it for you."

"Angela got me a steak."

"Yup."

"Did you check to make sure there were no holes in it from the injection of poison?"

"No, I didn't. But it's right there if you want to take a look." I gestured with the spatula.

And he actually went and looked.

"She said she wasn't coming back, so she wanted you to have one of your favorites," I fudged. "I think she was trying to make a nice gesture."

He looked at me as if that were every bit as unlikely as it felt when I said it. "Nice."

"So how do you like your steak cooked?"

"Rare."

I nodded. I could have predicted the answer. Whatever I asked, the answer was bound to be the opposite of what Angela approved of. "I can have it ready in fifteen. Does that work?"

"Sure. Just give me a shout. I'll be"—he gestured—"in the den, watching TV."

"Will do."

When he'd gone, I seared the steak for two minutes on each side, and then set it aside, tented with foil, while I reduced port wine in the hot pan. I couldn't get over how incongruous it was to be doing this in Angela Van Houghten's kitchen. If she were here, smelling the delicious aroma of steak and anything from the onion family, her head probably would have blown off.

But that scent was going to linger for hours. When was she planning on coming back? Was whatever she was doing so compelling that she was willing to put up with this in order to do it?

It seemed so. She didn't have a suitcase in her hand when she left. There was no moving van out front. Presumably, she was going to come back to this tainted kitchen and her husband's steak breath, and then what?

Oh, well. It wasn't for me to figure out.

All I had to do was cook when, where, and what I was told to, and to take the money and run.

And after I called Peter to dinner, and he brought the day's *Wall Street Journal* and a clear disinterest in any sort of interaction with me, that was exactly what I did.

With tremendous relief.

Chapter 20

I was surprised to find Mr. Tuesday himself—well, okay, *Paul*—in his apartment when I got there. This *never* happened.

But I have to admit, I felt a thrill as soon as I saw him.

"Hey," I said, dropping the keys into my pocket. "I wasn't expecting you."

"Sorry." He put some papers aside and stood up. "I should have warned you so you wouldn't be alarmed."

I laughed. "Yes, from now on, you must make sure to tell me when you're going to be in your own home."

We walked into the kitchen together. "I finished early at work."

"Oh?"

He shook his head. "No, I wanted to see you." He opened the fridge. "Beer?"

"No." My hand shot instinctively to my stomach. "Thanks."

He didn't appear to think anything of that, just took one out and opened it for himself. "You know, you've been coming here for more than a year, and suddenly even the word *Tuesday* makes me nervous as a cat."

"I know what you mean." Excitement flowed through my veins and muscles like cool water. "I'm having a hard time thinking of you as Paul and not Mr. Tuesday."

"Mr. Tuesday?"

I nodded. "You were very mysterious for a long time, you know. I couldn't puzzle you out. All I knew for sure was that you were a man and I cooked for you on Tuesdays. Hence, Mr. Tuesday."

He smiled. "So if I'd introduced myself to you that way at No Plans . . ."

"I would have completely freaked out." I laughed. "But at the same time, maybe I would have recognized your voice."

"I've thought about that same thing. I wonder if that wasn't just part of what made you so comfortable to me."

"Familiarity?" I took a block of cheddar and a block of Monterey Jack out of the grocery bag and set them on the counter; then I filled a pot with water and put it on the stove over a high flame.

He nodded. "In a way."

"Doesn't that breed contempt?"

"Not in this case." He watched me work for a minute. "Macaroni and cheese," he said appreciatively.

I took out the box of elbow noodles and smiled, feeling warm at the pleasure on his face. "Sometimes you've just got to have the best of the worst."

"And you definitely make the best."

"Thanks." I pulled out the food processor and set up the shredder disk. "I bet you say that to all your cooks."

He nodded and drank his beer. "Yeah, I do."

I shredded the cheeses while he walked around me to the sink. As he passed me, he knocked lightly against my elbow.

The heat shot straight up my arm.

He stopped. "Gemma."

I turned. "Yes?"

He hesitated, then expelled a breath. "I want you to keep cooking for me."

"I am." I looked at the ingredients spread out before me.

"I mean, I don't want to ask you to resign—"

My heart filled with dread.

"—and I don't want you to work for free. But I don't want you to stop coming on Tuesdays."

Now I knew what he was getting at.

But I didn't know how to pinpoint it any better than he did.

So I leaned my back against the counter and looked up at him, waiting to see how he'd put it.

"What do you want?"

"You know what I want."

"I don't." It wasn't a question, but even I could hear the hope in it. I hoped he wanted the same thing I did.

"I want you."

Feeling as if I were watching someone other than me doing this, I reached out and he pulled me into his arms. But somehow between the impulse to reach for him and the actual connection, everything came together. The next thing I knew, we were mouth to mouth.

I don't know for sure who initiated it.

I think it was him.

All I know is that I thought I was cooking in his kitchen, just as I had done every Tuesday for more than a year, but suddenly I found myself kissing him, openmouthed, tongues touching, arms tightening around each other, and hearts pounding just inches apart. It would have been easy just to keep doing this forever.

But I drew back. "This is unprofessional."

Stupid, stupid, stupid. Unprofessional? This was . . . Well, whatever it was, the least important thing was "unprofessional." If anything, it was appropriate, right? An attraction that could—God willing—go somewhere between two people who had a lot more at stake than just dating.

Right away, he looked chagrined, though he didn't move his arms from my back. "You're right. I shouldn't put you in this position."

"No, wait." I wasn't making sense. I wasn't going to make sense. I knew that already, but I couldn't stop. "I don't mean it's unprofessional of you, I mean it's unprofessional of *me*."

"No, it's not—"

"Yes." I looked at him and bit my lip. Time to stop

thinking—thinking was too foggy for me right now—it was time to *feel*. "But." I drew him in closer. "I don't think I care." I kissed him again, and he met me with equal passion.

This time, he drew back. "Are you sure?"

"Yes." Oh, I was sure. "Aren't you?"

"Yes." He pulled me against him, and once again, his tongue was in my mouth, warm, comforting; the taste of him sweet and yet oddly familiar—or at least *right*, if not *familiar*—all at once.

"It's not too late to pretend this never happened," I pointed out, though weakly. Of course it was, but I didn't want him to do anything he didn't choose of his own free will every step of the way.

"Yes, it is. I'm not going to pretend *anything* didn't happen."

"Are you sure?" *Please say yes, please say yes, please say yes.* "Yes."

Still kissing, we moved over to the sofa together and sat down, somehow twining ever closer. I felt like I could just crawl right inside him and be safe forever.

And for hours, that's exactly what it was. Touching, kissing, talking, then touching and kissing some more. We were like teenagers, yet like adults as well, wound up inside some vortex that felt familiar and yet incredibly new to me all at the same time.

Though I really wanted to on some level, we didn't go to bed together that night.

Instead, we sat and made out on his sofa for about an hour and a half, like hormonal teenagers.

It was the best night I'd had in a long, long time.

At least when I was able to forget I was already pregnant.

Chapter 21

I 'm sorry to tell you this," Makena said, and I didn't even want to hear the rest. "Another party has canceled."

"*Who?*" This was unfathomable.

"National Theater Group."

"No!"

"I'm sorry, Gemma." I heard her sigh, but I could tell she was more irked at the extra work this was creating for her than she was worried about the effect it would have on me. Which was fine; she wasn't responsible for making me feel good. "Luckily, this time Angela was here to suggest an alternate caterer who was, thank God, available that day."

Like this was good news to me.

"Angela suggested an alternative?" I questioned.

"Yes, isn't that incredible? She's never done anything

like that before, she's usually so into her own thing, but it worked out great this time."

"How lucky for you," I said drily, but she didn't notice.

"Totally! Anyway, sorry for the bad news, but this is starting to feel like a bad trend. I don't want to be a buzz-kill, but you might want to start looking for another place to supplement your work."

"No kidding."

"Sorry?"

"I agree with you." I was struck by a sudden thought. "Makena, was Angela the one who told you the NTG wanted to cancel?"

"Yes! How did you know?"

I frowned. "Well, you said she was right there with an alternate suggestion."

"Oh yeah. That's right." Clearly, she could not have cared less. And why would she? "Anyway, I have to go. As usual, I'll let you know if anything new comes up."

When I got to Willa's on Friday night, I was surprised—no, I was *shocked*, seriously—to find her sitting on the sofa, eating from a large bag of Maui onion kettle chips.

"Hey, Willa," I said cautiously.

She looked shocked herself and dropped the bag; crumbs scattered everywhere. "You're early."

I looked at my watch. "No, I'm not." I had to approach this carefully. She looked so alarmed that I was there, that

I had "caught" her having fallen off the wagon, that I didn't want to make her feel any worse than she already did. I went to a nearby chair. "What's wrong?"

She bent down awkwardly to pick up the chips. "What do you mean?"

I chose my words carefully. "Willa, when you hired me to cook, you said it was because you didn't want to have any other food in the house except what I made. Now, I'm not judging, and I love those chips myself, but as your friend, I have to ask if something has happened to make you change your course here."

She took a breath and sat up very straight for a moment, then wilted. "I want to give up."

"But you're doing so well!"

"Things have tapered off." She paused, then dropped a handful of crumbs into the bag, folded the top over, and tossed it to the side. "To be totally honest, I'm really afraid."

"What are you afraid of?" I expected the answer to be something along the lines of the cruelty of others, but I was wrong.

"I'm afraid that dieting isn't really going to work," she said. "That all the work and deprivation are actually pointless."

I nodded and she continued.

"I'm afraid I'm going to have to haul around a body that feels like a bunch of saddlebags for the rest of my life. It's exhausting. And this isn't a problem many people can relate to or, you know, talk to me about. It seems absurd to them."

"Everyone has *something* they're insecure about."

"Come on. Not many people get like this." She swept her hand across her hips and thighs. "I'm fat, not stupid, not blind, not unaware, and not bulletproof." Her voice cracked over the word *bulletproof,* and I knew this pain must be close to the surface for her all the time, even as she struggled against the cruelty of judgment or outright mockery from strangers.

I went and put my arm on her shoulder and looked earnestly into her eyes. "But *everyone* who has a goal starts somewhere and then moves toward it incrementally. Always incrementally. No matter who you are or what your goal is."

"Do you really believe that?"

"Of course. How many people can decide on some lofty aspiration and then just jump right into it? *No one.* No one can just lose weight instantly because they decide to. You can't just *be* a great tennis player immediately because you decide to. It takes work and small steps. Don't give up now!"

There was a long silence before she said, "Sometimes that seems easier."

"It probably is," I agreed carefully. "But do you want easier or better?"

She looked at me. "I'm just not sure. This is my last-ditch effort to lose weight. Strict portioning, exercising, though that's pretty limited so far, and trying to be patient while I wait for time to pass and results to show. But like I said, I'm scared it won't work. That I'll be like this forever, and I can't endure that. I just can't. I can't live like this."

"Worst-case scenario, and I don't believe you will fail,

but *worst-case scenario*, you don't lose much weight. . . . Is that *really* unendurable? You've been this weight for some time now, haven't you?"

"A long, long time. It's a nightmare. It's hard, it's embarrassing, and maybe worst of all, it's"—she bit her lip just as I saw it start to quiver—"it's like slowly turning to stone."

"What do you mean?"

She nodded. "This isn't who I am. This isn't who I want to be. I want to walk—no, hell, I want to *run* and jump and climb and . . . *whatever*. I want to be able to move and do whatever I want, just like anyone else. Instead I feel trapped in this body like you'd feel trapped in a straitjacket."

"I don't want to be cliché, but in this case it seems like the most appropriate response: You need to look at this one day at a time. If you look at the whole, you'll go crazy. But one day at a time, you will reach a day where you find you've done it. And, yeah, sometimes you'll fall." I gestured toward the chip bag. "But you just have to get back up again."

I'd learned so much from Willa, so much about what she was going through, what an unhealthy relationship with food looked and felt like, and how unfair my own conclusions about grossly overweight people had been in the past.

Obviously, hers was not a condition that looked like *fun*, but I had a feeling it was a more hellish battle than I could even imagine.

"I'll try. That's all I can say, I will keep trying." She shook her head and stopped talking. A tear slid down her cheek.

I gave her a hug. "Listen to me. You're not in this alone.

I'm with you every step of the way. We're going to do this side by side, and we're going to do it *slowly*, okay?"

"No miracles?"

"There are a million miracles here!" I thought of the baby inside me. "We have our friendship to do this together, we have our brains to figure out how to do it, and we have our determination to get there. *Both* of us. Right?"

"You'd call me a friend?"

"Of course! Wouldn't you?"

She considered me, then nodded. "Yes."

"So would you bet on us or against us?"

"On," she said. "Definitely on."

"Excellent." I put my hand out. "We have a pact, then. We're going to get through this, even when it's hard."

"Yes." She shook my hand.

"And listen, Willa, seriously, if you ever need to talk, I don't care what time it is, you can call me."

"Thank you."

I smiled. "How *did* your weigh-in go, by the way?"

"This week I only lost two pounds."

I was surprised. Given her level of discouragement, I'd been half afraid she'd gained. "Two pounds is a lot."

"It's nothing."

"Think about a pound of butter," I pointed out. "Seriously, think about how it feels in your hand, so much bigger than your palm. You can't wrap your hand around it. Then consider one of those in each hand. If you stuck them to your hips, you'd notice a huge difference. But you didn't, you lost that much fat. That's something to consider!"

"I guess you're right." She nodded. "I wished it was more, but I guess that's not realistic."

"Listen, if the rest of the world thought it was realistic to lose five pounds in one week, I think there would be a lot more motivated dieters out there."

"You're probably right."

"I am. And that's what we're going with." I didn't ask her why she'd felt afraid it wouldn't work, because I knew very well that fears weren't always logical or reasonable. When she looked in the mirror, she didn't always see the two pounds down; she also saw the two hundred, or whatever it was, to go. "You see that this is progress, right? That this is exactly what we were just talking about."

"I guess so." She brightened a tiny bit. "Plus I do have a bit more energy as well. Not a lot. Like I said, I'm not going out to any big social events any time soon, but maybe—just *maybe*—I can imagine reaching that point in the future. The metabolism is firing up, albeit slowly."

"Wow, that's really exciting! Way to go!"

"Thanks, but so much of this relies on my willpower and"—she gestured at herself—"as we've discussed, that has been a challenge for me in the past."

I shook my head. "You're doing great. You're determined, and you're already succeeding in leaps and bounds!"

"Okay, okay." This was clearly making her uncomfortable. "I'll try, like I said. Now, tell me about you instead."

I knew the conversation was over. She'd opened up in a way she didn't usually, and now she seemed a bit self-conscious about it. I had to take small steps with her, too.

So I went ahead and regaled her with my own sob story. "I lost another party at the country club today."

Willa gasped. "How is that *possible*? You are truly an amazing cook."

"Well. Thanks. Something is going on, and I don't quite understand what it is."

She eyed me keenly. She sure could read people. "But you think it's—?"

"I don't know."

"Oh, please, Gemma. Don't kid a kidder. You just got me to spill my guts, so to speak. Now it's your turn."

She was right. "I think that woman I work for is sabotaging my business." I explained about Angela's connection to the country club.

"Could this be about her wanting to have you work for her on weekends? Something simple like that?" Willa asked.

I shook my head. "She's never asked me for any other days."

"Has she asked you to cut down on the days you work for her?"

"Never."

She frowned. "That doesn't make sense."

"I know."

"Does she have something against you personally?"

"Not as far as I know. Yes, her husband made that pass at me a few weeks ago, like I told you, but she wasn't there and you can be damn sure he didn't tell her—or she would be on the other side of the country and would have taken half his fortune with her."

"Is this that TV guy?"

No point in playing coy. "Yes."

"Why would his admitting anything give her more of an advantage over his money?"

"Adultery is frowned upon in divorce court in Maryland."

"Unlike all those other places where it's applauded?"

I laughed. "Okay, true, but especially here. If she knew he'd done something untoward, she'd have him by the balls."

"But there's probably a burden of proof."

"An admission would be proof," I said. "That's what I'm saying. I'm sure he didn't admit anything, so that can't be it."

She nodded. "Unless they have a kid and you were caught on the nanny cam."

Oh my God.

How had this not occurred to me before?

I'd been changing my shirt in Stephen's room, in front of that row of stuffed animals. That is *exactly* where a nanny cam would be hidden. Angela wouldn't even have been looking for me, so what a shock it must have been, if this was really what had happened, for her to see me waltz in and take my shirt off, followed shortly by her husband coming in and planting one on me.

"That's what it was!" I gasped.

"What?"

"Nanny cam. She saw it on the nanny cam. But it wasn't incriminating enough." I remembered the steak she wanted me to make for Peter. "Good Lord, so she started to try to set him up to make another pass at me. She got him a steak and left the house so I could prepare it."

"The way to a man's heart is through his stomach?"

"Exactly. Especially since he'd already made a pass at me, so she might have felt his interest was established."

Willa nodded. "That makes sense. So she wanted to catch him in the act, preferably on film, so she could skewer him in court."

"*But* she didn't get anything incriminating on him, because he hasn't tried anything since."

"Which means you have job security as long as she's trying to nail you and her husband."

I had to laugh. "Except for the fact that she's blacklisting me at the club and who knows where else."

"From a sociological standpoint, it's really pretty interesting."

"Maybe, but from a practical standpoint, I'm panicked." Instinctively my hand went to my stomach.

She noticed. "Are you sick?"

"Not exactly," I said. "Pregnant."

She gave a low whistle. "Wow. How far along?"

"A couple of months. I'm not even sure. I have my first doctor's appointment next week."

"Do you have money saved?"

"I hate that question."

She nodded, understanding. "I used to as well. If you need help—"

"Oh, thanks. No, I'll be okay." My voice didn't hold the conviction I wished it did. But how could it? I wasn't convinced at all. "I just need more work, that's all. If you hear of anyone looking, let me know. Especially for events."

"Absolutely. But Gemma?"

"Yes?"

"I mean it," she said.

And even though I would never, ever take her up on it—I would never put a friend in a position to feel like our relationship was anything other than 50–50 equitable—her offer was so heartfelt that it almost made me burst into tears.

She said, "Not just now or never, but if you find yourself in a bind and need a loan, please don't hesitate to let me know."

Chapter 22

I had to confront Angela.

Didn't I?

I went to the Van Houghten house two hours earlier than usual with the idea that I could get all the cooking done and be ready to talk to her without distraction when she got home. That way I could leave afterwards, rather than having the potentially awkward problem of a tense conversation followed by an even more tense silence while I cooked her dinner.

But there was no question that it had to be done.

If she was blacklisting me with potential clients in the relatively small D.C. social scene, I had to stop her if at all possible.

So why wasn't I more relieved when I pulled up to the house and saw her car out front?

Better still, Peter's wasn't there. We could, theoretically, have this out without added complications.

I walked in with my bags from Whole Foods and called out, "Hello?"

No answer.

Good. That gave me a little time to investigate.

I went into the kitchen and looked around. There had to be a camera in here somewhere. That would prove my theory was correct. Or at least it would go some way toward proving my theory was correct. There was no way she would expect her husband to have a dalliance in her son's room or in the playroom—that he had made a pass at me in Stephen's room was just a strange coincidence—so if she really wanted to catch him at it, she'd have to put the camera where she thought he'd make his move.

And if she thought he'd make it on me, that would be the kitchen.

The kitchen was so sparse and clean that there weren't very many hiding places. The drawers were smooth and solid, as well as the cabinets, and the countertops had nothing on them at all until I opened my bag of tricks and started cooking.

That left décor.

If she expected me to be by the counter where I usually worked, that meant the west wall was probably the best place to get a good view. I went over to three framed black-and-white family photos on the wall, and found the small camera strategically placed so the lens was in the iris of Angela's own eye.

It was a nice touch.

"What the hell are you doing?"

I whirled around to find Angela standing there, scrutinizing me, her hands on her hips.

I've never been fast on my feet when it comes to lying. Especially when there wasn't even a semi-reasonable lie to come up with, as in this case.

"I have a question for you," I countered.

Interestingly, that seemed to take her off guard. "Do you?"

I made an effort not to sound combative. I'd seen enough horror movies where incensing the bad guy only led to worse things. If Angela was my Bad Guy, I had to play this as smart as possible.

"I've learned from several sources that you are recommending people replace me as their events caterer at the club," I said, trying to keep my voice strong and even. "Why is that?"

She raised her chin. "I can't control who people choose to cater their parties."

"But you can influence them."

"Why would I?"

Now, if I had been 100 percent sure that she had seen the nanny cam video of Peter making a pass at me, I might have called her on the carpet right there, but I was aware that there was still a small chance that my theory was wrong—kitchen cam notwithstanding—and telling her about Peter would have just incensed her and made her fire me on the spot.

And I didn't want that.

Did I?

Well, actually, I wasn't sure. I didn't love working for her, that was for sure—particularly now that I knew she was trying to harm my career elsewhere—but I had the baby to think about now, so I just couldn't risk it without some sort of net to fall on, if at all possible.

So all I said to her was, "I don't know! But I *want* to. Do you have a problem with what I've been cooking for you?"

The front door opened. She looked startled for a moment until Stephen came running in.

As soon as he saw his mother, he stopped running.

"Hello, Stephen," she said.

"Hi." His voice was quiet, as if he'd been told too many times to hush up.

I hated to see that.

Kim, the nanny, came in behind him, and like Stephen, she slowed her gait when she saw Angela.

"I thought you . . . weren't going to be here this afternoon—?" she said to Angela, looking confused.

"Did you?"

"Well, you *said* . . ."

"Run upstairs and put your indoor clothes on," Angela said to Stephen.

I looked at him—he was wearing the same uniform of khaki pants and a T-shirt that he usually wore—and wondered what on earth *indoor clothes* could even mean. But this was Angela I was speculating about, so there was no telling.

"I'll get him cleaned up," Kim said.

"No!" Angela barked the word, startling both Kim and me. "No, you'll stay here. I need to talk to you. *Both* of you."

We stood in silence, like guilty children, listening as Stephen's footsteps disappeared up the stairs and into the muffled distance of the hallway and his bedroom.

"Is something wrong?" Kim asked, biting her lower lip and darting her eyes from me to Angela and back again.

"Very interesting question," Angela said. "And perhaps it depends on how you define right and wrong."

Clearly, we were being led into a lecture of some sort, but she wasn't doing it very smoothly. It struck me that she seemed to have something on her mind but no planned way to articulate it.

In the end, she simply threw it right at us.

"Which one of you is sleeping with my husband?" Angela demanded. Then, to me, "Is it you?"

"No! Why would you—?"

"I saw that he kissed you! It was on the security video."

Kim gasped.

Oh, great, now everyone was going to think I was this home-wrecker. "What you saw," I said in as controlled a voice as I could muster, "was, yes, your husband had a few drinks and then made an advance on me."

"Oh my God," Kim muttered.

Stupid little suck-up, trying to keep her job by agreeing about how awful I was.

I wanted to slap her.

Hormones, of course. My temper was very short, given

the wrong set of circumstances. And this was *definitely* the wrong set of circumstances.

"But," I said pointedly, "if you watched the whole exchange, you know that he didn't get anywhere with it. I rebuffed him, he apologized, and that was all there was to it."

I could *feel* Kim's judgmental energy pulsing at me from three feet away. And there was no question but that the same was coming from Angela, but then again, there was *always* negative energy coming from Angela.

"That is not all there was to it," Angela countered.

I tried to remember if there was anything else after that, any moment that might have been caught on the video and misinterpreted by someone with a vested interest in what happened next.

"Several times when I have come home at night, the sheets have been made up incorrectly on my bed."

It was perfect. Exactly the sort of detail she would notice.

"That doesn't prove anything about *us!*" I said. "Maybe he came home and had a midday nap or something. Did you ask him?"

"Of course I asked him! He said he was never home! He's a liar. That's how I know it's one of you!"

"Angela, this is just crazy. Honestly." I shot a look at Kim, hoping she could read my sincerity, but she couldn't, because her head was down.

But even so, I could see that her face was red.

Clearly, at that moment, Angela saw it, too.

No wonder Kim had been so shocked at Angela's accusations toward me! She thought *she* was Peter's one and only.

"Well, that answers that," she said. "I should have known that was your cheap makeup smudged on the pillowcase and not Gemma's. Or at least"—she looked me up and down—"not *just* Gemma's."

"Look," I said, "I don't know what's going on here, or what the truth is, but I have not had *any* physical contact with your husband, and frankly, I resent the accusation."

"Good." She raised her chin, but I could tell her confidence was faltering. "Then you may leave."

I paused, wondering if she meant she was firing me and wondering if I should be quitting, but she caught that fatal hesitation and swooped in for the kill herself.

"And I mean for good. You signed a confidentiality agreement when you started work here. I expect you understand that all of this"—she gestured—"*all* of it falls under that agreement."

"Of course," I said crisply, collecting my things. Including the food, by the way, which was a huge pain in the ass. It was very hard to gather it all together again, quickly and neatly enough to make a tidy escape with my dignity.

But I did it.

As I left, it occurred to me that what Vlad Oleksei had predicted about me being on film was actually 100 percent correct. If I'd been a little less skeptical, I might have seen it.

What else had he said? Now I wished I had a tape of it. Or the kind of memory that would let me recall it word for word. Wasn't there something about the man I was with now? Could that have meant Paul? Or was I just getting carried away now, hoping the good stuff was true since one bad thing seemed to be?

It was easy to see how people got hooked on psychics. If you could really believe—wholeheartedly believe—that everything was going to work out, what a relief that would be.

No regular therapist could give you that much peace of mind, that fast!

Peter was getting out of his car just as I reached the end of the sidewalk.

Which was odd, as he wasn't usually home this early.

But wait—maybe it really wasn't odd, now that I knew what I did about him and Kim. They probably had a tryst planned. That explained her surprise at running into Angela and me in the kitchen.

And it explained the jaunt in his step as he passed me, giving me a quick wave and nod.

For just a moment, I thought about warning him what was inside waiting for him. But if I did, then I would be involving myself in something I wanted—no, I *needed*—to distance myself from as much as possible.

It wasn't my problem.

None of the Van Houghten drama was my problem anymore.

But even in its death throes, it had managed to create a whole host of new trouble for me.

Chapter 23

The next few days passed slowly and were filled with fears and trepidation about the future. What had begun as a niggling worry had become a full-out emergency.

How could I be here again?

Seriously, how?

It wasn't just the pregnancy part. I had come to terms with that. I mean, I wasn't *proud* of getting into this spot twice in my life, but the first time I was just a kid and the second time . . . Well, you know already. Granted, I didn't know Paul—or at least I didn't know I knew him at the time—but the unexpected and complete failure of birth control was different from the failure to take personal responsibility.

Now was the time I needed to take responsibility.

I had lost more than half my income over the past few weeks. I was not very different from the teenager I'd been once, as far as prospects for taking care of my child went. How could I keep this child after letting the last one go when, essentially, nothing had changed?

I had to figure it out. Because there was no question as to whether I would keep the baby this time—no question at all. I was keeping him or her, no matter what.

The problem was that, even though there was no question, *still* there was no easy answer.

Only hard ones.

Only increasingly hard ones.

Including—and this was a big one—finding a way to talk to Paul about this.

And a time to do that.

I had learned enough about people in my lifetime to trust my instincts about them. And I just couldn't see Paul opting for indignant accusations about traps and tricks. Not only was he logical enough to remember that I was the one to take the extra step of trying to protect us that night, but even if I hadn't, even if he thought I'd been careless, he would have known that he was equally responsible and he would react accordingly.

In short, he was no Cal. I was sure of it.

And that was the problem—he was so *not* Cal that I knew he would take responsibility for the pregnancy, and I didn't want that. He was obviously excited about his new job. Evidently, it was a great opportunity, the kind of thing people work years toward.

There was *no way* I was going to blow that for him.

The phone rang at 2 A.M. on Tuesday morning. I'd half expected it the whole time, but still I was disoriented and alarmed when it came.

"Hello?" The receiver was upside down, just like on a bad sitcom. I fixed it. "Hello?"

". . . water broke sometime in the last three hours, we're not sure when because she was asleep," came the frantic voice of Dell. "How soon can you get there? God, I've called you like four times!"

I was already up, shoving on the sweats I'd been wearing before bed. I wouldn't remember the chocolate brownie ice cream stains on them until later. "I'm a heavy sleeper. Okay, I'm leaving now," I said, moving the phone from one ear to the other while I pulled on a cardigan sweater, one arm at a time. "Ten minutes. Get her into the car, and I'll be there when you're ready to leave."

And here we were. The moment when Penny's baby was going to be born and all of this would, inevitably, become more real to me. I knew it was coming, I'd been waiting for it—in many ways like a kid waiting for Christmas—and yet somehow, the reality of *Penny's* baby coming now just made the inevitability of mine that much more clear and obvious.

I grabbed some old Uggs from a pile of shoes as I passed

the front door and grabbed my keys and purse from the foyer table. Times like this it was a good thing to have a tiny apartment—everything was within reach. I ran down the stairs, vaguely noting the fact that the stairwell smelled like urine again, and out into the parking lot. I'd forgotten a bunch of guys had been out there drinking green bottles of beer earlier, and that I'd heard at least two smashing bottles, but the memory came back to me sharply as I stepped, hard, onto a shard.

"Shit!" I yelled, because I'm a firm believer that prompt and loud exclamations help alleviate pain in this kind of situation.

I hopped the last couple of yards to my car and threw the door open, leaping in. If there was ever a time for multi-tasking, this was it, and I started the ignition with my right hand and pulled the glass out of my foot with my left. Ahh. Done. Success.

I threw the car in gear and jerked out of the parking lot. It was about three miles to Penny's house, and at this hour all the lights should be blinking yellow. A quick glance at the clock on my dash showed 2:16. Good. That meant it was 2:06—don't ask me why keeping it ten minutes fast always fooled me, it did—so I should be there just about when I said I would.

When I got to the intersection of Fernwood Lane and Democracy Boulevard, the light that should have been blinking was solid red. Impatiently, I pressed my foot to the brake (alerting me to the fact that there was still glass in my foot and that I'd just pushed it deeper) and waited.

And waited.

And waited.

The numbers on the digital clock advanced—2:18, 2:19 . . . When it hit 2:20, I lost hope that the light was going to change. It had to be broken. Since no one else was on the road, I advanced slowly through the intersection, feeling a strange glee when I made it to the other side and no emergency lights flickered to life in the bushes or behind a bunch of trees.

By 2:22—2:12, real time—I was pulling up in front of Penny's house and she was yelling at Dell to "Stop acting like I'm made of eggshells!"

"At the moment, you might as well be," I said, smiling at her full, round belly for the last time. "Now, get in the car and go to the hospital. Charlotte will be fine with me."

"I know you have to work in the morning, and I think my neighbor, Sheila, can take over for you, but I didn't want to call her right now. But if she can't do it, I can call LeeLee, whose daughter plays with Charlotte sometimes after school. I can't remember their last name at the moment, but—"

"It's *fine*," I interrupted as Dell shot me an exasperated look. "I can take the day off. It'll be fun!"

Penny looked relieved, but then suddenly, her expression shifted and she looked really concerned.

"What's wrong?" I asked, immediately hurt that she didn't want me to stay with Charlotte for the day.

"I'm in labor," Penny snapped. Even under the pale

streetlamp, I could see the subtle shift from pain to impatience. "Jeez, don't take everything personally!" she said on a long exhale. "Charlotte will be thrilled to stay with you."

There was no point in asking how she knew I'd taken it personally; she'd been freaky like that since we were kids. "Go! Have a baby, would you?"

"Baby, linebacker . . . whatever it is, I want it out of here." She moved her awkward form into the passenger seat. "You want me to drive myself?" she asked Dell, still standing by her door.

"I'm just trying to help you in."

"I'm in!"

"I'm coming!" He hurried to the driver's side, and I thought I heard her say something like, "That's how all this started," as he turned the key in the ignition. Thirty seconds later, he was jerking out of the driveway and gunning it down the street.

I watched the taillights disappear into the darkness, then stood another moment on the driveway, still warm from the day's sun, enjoying the quiet that hushed over the neighborhood. Overhead, stars dotted the black sky and a tiny sliver of moon hung like a light on a string.

It was a great night to be born.

And the lucky kid was being born to great parents.

All kids should be so lucky.

I breathed in the cool, wet air and realized with a startling thought that that would be me. In a little over six months.

Holy cow.

Where would I be in six months? Would Penny be driving me to the hospital? Would it happen for me in the middle of the night? Would . . . Paul be there? I'd have to move. Have to have an actual room for my son or daughter. There was a small thrill in me as I realized it would *be* one of those two. I'd be a mother.

But panic followed and took over the thrill quickly.

I was suddenly startled by a small voice just a few feet before me.

"Where are my parents?" Charlotte's question quivered with fear and false bravado. "Who are you?"

"It's me, Char." I moved forward and knelt in front of her so she could see me more clearly. "Gemma."

Her face crumpled. "I don't have my glasses!"

That's right, her glasses. Honestly, she should never venture out of the house without them; it was dangerous. "It's okay, let's go inside and find your glasses so you can get a good look. In the meantime, we can talk about that girl you were telling me about in your class a few weeks ago. . . ."

It wasn't great, but it was the first detail that came to mind that might prove to her who I was in the dark as I took her small hand and led her into the house, where we could get her glasses. She pulled reluctantly against my hand, but I was afraid to let go for fear she'd run away, dodging into the dark slices of land between houses, where it would be hard to find her. "What was her name? Pamela? The one with the black cat clock?"

Charlotte nodded. "I saw it at her birthday party."

"That's *right*, and it sounds really cool. Maybe I can find one for you for your birthday."

I dropped my purse and keys on the table next to Penny's door—it was the same place I had mine—closed the door, and locked it. Charlotte, several feet ahead, had found her glasses. She turned wary eyes back to me, and I saw the recognition come into them.

Just before she burst into tears.

"Charlotte, what's wrong?" I rushed to her, completely unsure how to handle this. Obviously, the one thing I couldn't do was call her parents, and it was too late to call anyone else I knew who might have even an iota of experience with kids, so I was on my own.

"I . . . want . . . my . . . mom," she sobbed, lifting her glasses and swiping a hand across her teary eyes.

"Your mom and dad went to the hospital—"

The horror in her eyes nearly made my heart stop.

"—because it's time to have the baby," I added quickly. Good Lord, hadn't Penny and Dell warned her that the baby was due soon and that it would require a trip to the *hospital*?

Charlotte's face crumpled again.

I was in way over my head.

"Don't cry," I said, as if that had ever helped any anguished person in the history of the world. I put my hand on her thin shoulder and felt it shaking with her sobs. This was awful. "Charlotte?" I tried the name her mother called her sometimes, "Char Char?"

She glanced at me.

I tried to think of what made me feel better in a situation where I felt like crying. "Do you want some ice cream?"

She sniffled and nodded.

Score! "Let's go find some," I said excitedly, and together we rushed to the freezer.

I shouldn't have started patting myself on the back so soon. The freezer was filled with foil-wrapped items and a few plastic containers with unknown contents—all of which looked just like my mother's freezer had when I was growing up—but no ice cream. Which was also like my mother's freezer when I was growing up.

"Uh . . . Charlotte?"

She looked at me with wide eyes. Something about them seemed much older than her six years. "My mom doesn't get ice cream," she said solemnly.

"She doesn't?"

"She's bacteria intolerant."

I bit my lower lip. "Okay." I wasn't sure what to do. It was only a little after two thirty in the morning, but both Charlotte and I were wide awake, and I'd promised her ice cream. "Is there anything else here you can think of that you want?"

She wrinkled her nose and shook her head. "I don't think so." She took a deep breath that wavered with the aftershocks of her tears.

In that moment, I made a decision that Penny would never have approved of, but I didn't care. I was the Adult in Charge, and I was going to do whatever I could to make sure poor Charlotte's memories of the night her brother or sister was born weren't imbued with negativity and a Mean Cousin Gemma.

"Then we'll go get some ice cream."

"What?"

"Come on. We're going to Seven-Eleven to get ice cream."

She looked hesitant. "My mom might get mad. It's after my bedtime." I could tell she really, really wanted to get the ice cream, though. What a good girl, I thought. She deserved a prize.

"Well, tonight is a *very* special night for you, Miss Charlotte. By tomorrow, you'll have a little brother or sister. And if that doesn't need a celebration, I don't know what does."

Her smile was wide, and I saw now that her two front teeth were growing in slightly crooked. "A *celebration*? Like a party?"

"Sort of." I didn't want her to get a big Chuck E. Cheese's extravaganza in her head. "But just the two of us, while we wait at home to hear from your mom and dad about the baby."

"I can't wait to find out if I'm going to be a big brother or a big sister."

I knew what she meant. "Me neither," I agreed, and took her out to the car for a field trip to 7-Eleven.

That night ended up being one of the best of my life. Charlotte was such a great little companion, I couldn't believe Penny ever went anywhere without her. Everything she said was cute, and when I spoke, she really seemed to listen, although that could be because I mostly talked about ice cream and the movie she'd chosen for us to watch when we got back, *Finding Nemo*.

Around four thirty, as we were searching around for the copy of *The Aristocats* that she was *sure* they had, I decided she wasn't going to school in the morning. At this point, I'd already made executive decisions that stood to make her school day unsuccessful—why send her in for that misery?

Besides, I was sure Penny was going to call any minute, and I didn't want to waste precious time going to school to sign Charlotte out before getting over to the hospital to meet her new sibling.

She held up well, I've got to say. The kid hung in there until the first light of dawn started edging up on the horizon. To tell the truth, I was kind of disappointed to see it. There had been something so magical about the night, about us perusing the freezer section of the brightly lit convenience store and then driving home on empty streets with three pints of Häagen-Dazs, since we couldn't decide which one we wanted most.

And sitting on the sofa, eating ice cream from the container, watching Nemo swim the seas while the evening wound down, exhaustion took over.

We fell asleep on the sofa, watching an infomercial for Total Gym. Chuck Norris had always bored me. I made a mental note to tape this particular infomercial on my DVR for the next time I had insomnia.

Anyway, we woke to the sound of the phone ringing. By now, Kelly Ripa was interviewing Russell Brand at a volume I don't know how we'd slept through, so I hurriedly found the remote and pressed MUTE before answering the call.

It was Dell. "We're having some trouble. Looks like it's going to be a while."

"Trouble?" I was instantly on alert. "What kind of trouble?"

"Labor started, then stopped. It's pretty normal." There was a catch in his voice that told me he either didn't believe what he was saying or he didn't know if there was any real truth to it. "They just gave Penny some Pitocin. That should get things moving again. How was Charlotte this morning?"

There was no point in telling him about Charlotte's and my Excellent Adventure right now; he had enough to think about. "Perfect," I said. "Not a problem at all, everything's fine."

"Good. Are you going to go in to work tonight?"

"Yes, but it's pretty much a drop-off night, so I can take Char with me if you're not back."

"Thank you so much." He sounded relieved. "That's a load off my mind."

"Don't give it another thought. Just take care of your wife; she needs you right now."

He gave a single hard laugh. "You'd be hard-pressed to convince *her* of that."

"Aw, she adores you and you know it. It won't kill you to just take it silently for the moment."

"I guess not." There was a loud announcement over the speaker on his end of the line, and then I heard him say, "I'd better go. They're bringing the doctor in to consult about an emergency C-section."

"Oh-oh. She's not a fan of knives." I know, stupid to talk like that with a kid a few feet away, right? All I can say in my own defense was that I was *never* around children and was therefore very stupid about them. "Give her my best, and call me as soon as you know anything."

I ended the call and sat quietly for a moment, thinking about everything he'd said, but then I heard the sound of soft crying and looked to see Charlotte weeping quietly on the sofa.

"What's the matter?" I asked. I shouldn't have kept her up, I thought. She was a Craig as well as a Neiman, and we were all just useless piles of tears and complaints when we didn't get enough sleep.

"Is someone getting hurt?" she asked tentatively.

"No, why?"

"You said something about killing," she said, blinking behind the glasses that were still crooked from falling asleep with them on. "And knives."

"Oh, *that*." I went over to her and pulled her into the crook of my arm. "I was talking to your dad, but it was just an expression. You know, like, 'Would it kill you to do the dishes sometimes?'" I'd deliberately chosen something I could totally picture Penny saying. "Do you know what I mean?"

She looked up at me and nodded. "But what about knives?"

This was tricky. I could tell her the truth—that they might have to have a routine operation to get the baby out, but that seemed unnecessarily honest. And I didn't know how much Penny and Dell had told her about this whole *giving birth* thing, so there was no way I wanted to take a chance on freaking her out further.

I needed a lie, and I needed it fast.

"They took pancakes in for your mom to have breakfast, but she didn't want to use a knife to put the butter on them."

Miraculously, this seemed to satisfy her. "At McDonald's, when I get hotcakes, I always put the butter on with a fork."

"I do, too!" It wasn't great—but, hey, whatever worked.

"We should have breakfast at McDonald's today!" she declared.

Again, this was probably the sort of thing one would normally consult with the parents about, but while I was in charge, if she wanted to drink syrup through a straw for breakfast, that was fine with me.

"Let's go!" I said, and we were off on another junk food–hunting expedition.

When we came back, a very sleepy Charlotte fell asleep on the couch. I picked out a book from the shelf by the TV and fell asleep only a little while after her.

I woke up to my phone ringing. I grabbed and answered before looking at the screen. "Dell?"

"No, this is the king of Sweden, who is this?"

Paul! I was so glad to hear his voice. "Queen of the Sweet Potato Festival."

"Sounds like a match made in heaven."

"If only sweet potatoes were big in Sweden."

He laughed. "Aren't they?"

"I don't know."

"So where are you?"

I looked at the time on my phone with a wrench in my stomach. "Am I late?"

He laughed. "I don't mean to be all, 'Where's my dinner, woman?' but . . ."

"I know! I'm sorry! How did it get to be—? My cousin Penny went into labor! I was up all night, I must have fallen asleep. I don't know how—I'm so sorry!"

I hadn't had this feeling since a summer job when I was a teenager when I was supposed to work the brunch shift—yes, brunch, not even breakfast—and I'd overslept. Only to wake up to an irate call from my boss.

Who fired me.

"Really? Wow, that's big news! Don't even worry about it. I'll just um . . . I'll throw something together. I really just wanted to make sure you were okay."

"No, no, I have your stuff here and it's ready, except for tonight's . . . Hold on." I put my hand over the receiver. "Charlotte? Do you mind if I have a friend over to eat dinner with us?"

She looked as confused as I felt. "Is it already dinnertime?"

"Yep. Almost. So *do* you mind if a friend comes and joins us?

"No," she said, her eyes still on the TV screen.

Paul heard me over the phone. "Oh, no, don't worry—," he started to say.

"I want you to."

He paused. "Text me the address."

We hung up, and I stepped outside to look at the house number. No, it's not something I should already know. I knew *where* it was. That was enough.

One episode of *The Jetsons* later, the doorbell rang. I got that teenager-y surge in my chest and stomach, and ran to get it. It was only then that I realized I must look like I'd been up all night and eating at McDonald's.

I pulled open the door to see him standing in the glow of the porch light and holding two bags.

He smiled and held them up. "You like sweet and sour chicken, right?"

I smiled back. "You didn't have to—"

"Let me in."

"Sorry." I held open the door.

Charlotte came bounding around the corner and then immediately got shy. She stood behind me, peeking at him, and twirled her hair around a finger.

"Hey, you," he said. He set down the bags and crouched down to her level. "I'm Paul."

She stepped out a little bit. Even she seemed charmed by him. "I'm Charlotte."

"That's a nice name. Do you like Chinese food?"

She nodded.

Of course she did. My cousin, who ate nothing but chicken fried rice in college *and* throughout her pregnancy with Charlotte, would have stood for nothing less.

"What do you like?" he asked her.

"Rice," Charlotte said. "And honey chicken." She fiddled

around, like kids always do when being asked about themselves.

Paul opened his mouth. "Well, isn't that lucky? I picked some up!"

"Really?" It was me who asked. How could he have known?

"Yep. My niece likes honey chicken, too, and she's about your age."

"What's her name?"

"Susannah."

"Cool," said Charlotte. She immediately started to giggle and then ran back to the couch to watch *The Flintstones*.

I eyed Paul. "So you got me sweet and sour, and you got her honey chicken. What are you, some kind of Chinese food whisperer?"

"Maybe." He reached around my waist. "Or maybe you told me once on the phone that I had better like the sweet and sour chicken you were making me because it was your favorite, and so you *knew* it was good. And then maybe you said that if I was going to be a big baby about it, then I could just go out and get myself some honey chicken, because that's what the child in *your* life liked."

"Very clever, Detective."

He smiled and tapped his temple.

"What else you got going on up in that brain of yours? Anything I need to know about?"

"Shh! Guys!" Charlotte had turned to us and held a finger to her mouth.

"Let's go in the kitchen," I said, and led the way.

I took the bags and prepared a little plate for Charlotte. I cut the pieces into bite-sized ones, and gave it to her. "Thanks!" she said.

I went back into the kitchen, which had a full view of Charlotte and the living room.

I sat down at the island, and Paul sat across from me. We both opted to eat straight out of the cartons.

I took a bite, and I swear it may have been the most delicious thing I'd ever eaten. "God, this is awesome. I can't believe you're willing to leave this town and go to Seattle, when you have *no idea* how good the Chinese takeout will be!"

He laughed. "Chinese takeout is the least of what I'll miss."

"So what's the most?"

His eyes met mine. "Until a few weeks ago, I would have said your cooking." He smiled. "Even your chicken with five million cloves of garlic."

"You *love* my chicken with five million cloves of garlic."

"I do. But I think it's possible there might be something I love even more."

My heart flipped. I knew what he was going to say. I knew it, and I couldn't wait to hear it. I could barely find my voice. "What's that?"

"You know what it is." He touched my nose. "You. I almost wish I hadn't gotten that job." But before I could question if he was wobbly on taking it, he went on, "Professionally, it's the best thing that's ever happened in my career."

A petty little voice in me wanted to say, *Seattle's rainy*

and depressing, even though I'd never been and had no idea if the stories were exaggerated. Instead I just said, "Do you think you'll come back to this area to visit sometimes?"

He considered me. "I do now. As often as I can. And maybe you'd like to get a change of scenery every now and then yourself?"

Oh, yes. Under normal circumstances, I would have, of course. But I was well aware of what the year ahead looked like for me. A lot of changes, and not the ones that could be overlooked on visits spaced weeks or months apart.

"We'll see," I said to him.

And it was clear: Somehow I was going to have to tell him the truth.

Chapter 24

About a half hour later, my phone rang.

"Hello?"

"It's a boy!" Dell shrieked, barely giving me time to get the *o* out on my *hello*.

"Congratulations!" I smiled and felt the most curious surge of feeling. It was as if the full impact of this miracle was finally hitting me. "Ten fingers, ten toes, one nose?"

"He's perfect," Dell said, and I could hear the beaming smile in his voice. "Just perfect."

I was thrilled for them. "And Penny?"

"Hungry."

"That's a good sign!" The only time I'd ever seen Penny *not* hungry was when she was in a lot of pain—like when she'd fallen off a horse and broken her arm at Potomac Stables—or completely depressed. That she wanted food now was a good sign that labor had gone well, despite the problems at first. "Let me get Charlotte together, and we'll come right over."

"Third floor, room 321."

"We'll be there!"

I hung up and found that my eyes were welling with tears.

Paul smiled. "Congratulations on the new first cousin once removed."

I laughed and wiped away the tears. "I have no idea why I'm crying."

He raised an eyebrow. "You don't?"

"Okay, maybe I do." I went into the other room. "Charlotte! You have a brother!"

She started jumping up and down. "Yay yay yay yay!"

"Let's go to the hospital!" I said jovially. It's about the only time you can say that in a positive way. "Go get a coat on, and some shoes, okay?"

She darted off for her room.

I turned to see Paul packing up the Chinese. "I'm sorry—"

"No problem. Obviously."

"I mean, I missed work and—"

He laughed. "Like that's what I'm thinking about right now." He must have seen something in my expression, because he walked over to me and kissed me. "You go. I'll take care of this and lock the door behind me when I leave."

"Let's *go!*" Charlotte said, going to the door.

"Charlotte, wait a sec!"

"No, go, it's fine," Paul said. "Come over after if you

want. I'll have the Chinese in the fridge. It's always better after a little time in there, anyway."

"That's because of the onions," I said. "They sweeten overnight. That's why everything oniony is better the next day."

He touched my cheek and said, "You're a nut. But I like it."

Half an hour later, Charlotte and I were getting off the elevator onto the third floor of the hospital, flowers in hand and excitement in our hearts. The nursery was the first room on the left, and we stopped in front of the wide band of windows to look at the little wiggling bodies in their Lucite bassinets, each with a pink or blue label announcing a last name.

"Look for your last name," I told Charlotte, pointing at the babies. "It'll be a blue label."

She pressed her face to the window. "There he is!"

Sure enough, there was the bassinet marked BABY BOY HOFFMEYER.

I barely got a glimpse of him when a nurse came in and started fussing with him and rolling him out of the room.

"Where are they taking him?" Charlotte wanted to know. She was already being protective of her little brother. That was a good sign.

"Probably to your mom's room," I said. "Let's go there."

We went down the hall, took a wrong turn, then back-tracked until we found ourselves behind the nurse and the baby. We all entered the room together.

"Look who's here!" Penny said, holding her arms out for Charlotte, who went running to her. "Did you come to see me or Alexander?"

Alexander! He was named after our grandfather. Penny's eyes met mine, and all of them filled with tears.

"Do I have to call him *Alexander,* or can I call him Alex?" Charlotte asked.

Penny gave her a hug. "You can call him whatever you want, baby. Now, come over here so you can get your first good look. You, too, Gem. Get over here."

I laughed and went to the side of the bed where the nurse had wheeled the bassinet. I stepped over some wires and tried to stay out of everyone's way, but as soon as I saw little Alexander's eyes, I lost interest in all else.

His eyes were a milky blue, and even though he was only a few hours old and I knew—absolutely *knew*—he couldn't really see me, I was positive he looked right into my soul.

Funny how that moment of connection with a newborn can have a more profound effect on you than the same sense of recognition in an adult. Maybe it was because there was no weight to this connection at all—the baby didn't want anything from me, and the guilelessness in his eyes clearly wasn't the practiced move of a manipulative adult.

It was pure honesty.

And at that moment, for the second time in as many weeks, I felt jealous of Penny.

Then that jealousy morphed into something more like excitement. For the first time in a long time, I wasn't just happy about where I was in life. I was completely excited for the years ahead of me.

Chapter 25

I called Paul later that night. "I want to see you," I said, "but I should sleep, shouldn't I?"

"Are you tired?"

"Not really." Which was weird because I usually was lately.

"You want me to go there or you to come here?"

I thought of the delicious comfort of his dark, cool apartment. Nothing could have suited me more. "I'll be there in ten."

And I was. I pulled up and parked in my usual parking spot and walked up the stairs like I usually do. Then I knocked on the door, arms unburdened by groceries for once.

"Hey," he said, and gave me a kiss on the cheek. "Are you hungry?"

For the first time, I realized I was. Starving. "Yeah, I'll heat something up."

"Just because you're *used* to cooking in my kitchen doesn't mean you have to. I may have hired you to cook, but that doesn't mean I'm completely helpless in here."

"Good." I laughed and melted onto the sofa.

"So how's your cousin?"

"It's so strange. Penny was just a stick figure with a beach ball in her stomach yesterday, and now there's just this . . . small person that looks like her and Dell. It's so *amazing!*"

I heard him shut the silverware drawer and press some buttons on the microwave. He came back into sight and leaned on the doorframe.

"That's pretty much how it works, you know. Pregnant, then not pregnant, and there's a baby."

"Well, yes." This was it, this was it, this was the perfect time to introduce the subject. "Actually—"

The microwave beeped. "Hang on."

He returned a minute later with a plate of hot leftover meat loaf and mashed potatoes and handed it to me.

"Thanks," I said. And opened my mouth to *try* to come up with the words, but his phone beeped.

He looked at it and frowned, then looked at me. "I hate like hell to say this," he said. "But there's been a mix-up with some of my paperwork, and I need to redo it and get it faxed over to the new office as soon as possible. Can you give me a half hour, forty-five minutes?"

"Of course," I said reflexively. "Yes, go! Don't worry about me."

"I won't be long," he reassured me.

But the moment, at least *that* moment, was gone. "Don't give it another thought," I told him. Suddenly I was very tired. "I'll just lie down here and watch some TV."

"You're the best." He kissed my forehead. "Absolutely the best."

The next morning, I awoke in his bed. He must have guided an embarrassingly zombielike me to his room at some point the night before. He was gone already for work, I was sure.

I blinked around blearily. I'd never seen his room before. It was dark and sleek, like the rest of his apartment, and smelled good. Like men's shampoo and clean laundry.

I sat up and noticed a note on the nightstand. The familiarity of his handwriting made me smile.

G—

First, you look beautiful. Second, you are impossible to wake up in the middle of the night, even to be directed toward a bed. Third, I can't wait to see you again.
—P

P.S. Left the water bottle on the floor so you wouldn't knock it over onto this note.

I smiled and looked down. Sure enough, there was a bottle there. Adorable and wise. Good combination in a man.

I got dressed and went home, wishing I could stay there forever.

I went to the Olekseis' on Thursday night, feeling like I could just scream at any moment.

I walked into the dark house and could already hear the distant shouts of Cindy and Viktor in another room. I set my bags down on the counter and got to work.

My mind was reeling as I boiled noodles and browned ground beef for dinner. I couldn't stop thinking. All I *wanted* was to stop *thinking*.

Suddenly my old fallback thought was creeping up on me.

I was about to be broke.

Broke.

I needed more work at a time when I was becoming rapidly less able to handle it.

I couldn't have a *baby*. I was good at only one thing— cooking. That was as multitasking as I could be. And count- less times, I'd burned a sauce because I got tangled up in a problem with frying or something. How could I cope with a baby? I pictured myself turning my back on it for just a second, and it falling off the couch. What was he doing on the couch alone to begin with? I imagined it screaming in the night and me not hearing anything because of how deeply I slept.

What would I do with him or her when I was at work? Day care? In the late evening? Would I bring him with me? Surely not. Would I make enough money? I remembered a

poster in my high school that said something like: A BABY
COSTS $750 A MONTH. CAN YOU AFFORD THAT?

And that was *years* ago!

Good scare tactic for teenagers, but unfortunately, it also
seems to work pretty well on thirty-seven-year-olds. I mentally kicked myself again for not having savings.

It wouldn't always be a baby, either. Someday, it'd be a
teenager. It'd have a boyfriend or a girlfriend. And I'd be . . .
Mom. Then suddenly I'm old, and making way for the next
generation—my *kid*.

Then I remembered Charlotte the other night. Yes, that
had been one day and it had been filled with things that
weren't strictly *the norm*. But still. I'd handled it. Kids weren't
so bad at that age. Just like overemotional adults that have
comprehension issues.

God knew I could handle a lot of those.

"Jenna!"

Look, here comes one now.

Cindy Oleksei came wheeling around the corner.

"Yes?" I said, turning on the oven.

"That divorce lawyer you knew. I need him now."

Any time my head was about to float into the clouds
about possible marriage, I could always count on the Olekseis to bring me crashing back down without a parachute.

"Oh," I said, suddenly feeling nervous. I took a knife out
and started chopping an onion. "I don't—I didn't say I knew
one."

"Of course you did, you remember the other week
when—"

"No, I mean, I remember the conversation, but I never said I actually knew one."

"Well, do you?"

I was starting to say no for the hundredth time when her husband followed her.

"Come away with me." His words were sudden and firm.

"Come—where?" she asked, tilting her head and narrowing her heavily lined eyes.

"To Paris. To Rome. I do not care where." He took her hand. "I love you, Cindy."

What?

There was no figuring these people out.

Her face softened. "I love you, too, Viktor!"

"So we go. Where is it you want?"

"You really mean it? This isn't something where you say it and then change your mind about it later?"

"No, no, no. I do that too often. This is time for change. Time for me to change."

I wasn't even chopping anymore. I was just watching them.

She threw her arms around him, and he carried her off. And I just stood there, blinking at where they'd been.

That was the kind of thing Penny always told me marriage was really about. She said it was *about* the problems, and that what shows real love is not just kissing and laughing. It's getting *through* the hardest times. Together.

I started back at the onions.

Not that anyone was proposing. Hell, Paul might not even be the marrying kind. I had no idea.

Who knew if I even wanted a relationship with him at all?

But on that thought, my confidence and assuredness wavered slightly. I'd been thinking about him for months now. Longer, if you counted the time I'd worked for him and we'd passed bratty notes back and forth. Even the thought made me smile.

"You!" Vlad's voice barked from behind me.

Funny enough, there was so much yelling and cacophony in the Oleksei household that I wasn't usually startled, even when it was directed at me.

"Chicken Kiev tonight," I said to him. Chicken Kiev is so common now, it felt unimaginative, but Vlad *loved* this recipe, so I made it at least a couple of times a month.

"Mmmmm." He actually rubbed his belly. "Good for me."

I smiled and took out the butter. "I know you love it."

"I want to talk to you," he said. His voice sounded serious, and a thrum of fear rushed through me. Not another job loss. Please not another job loss. I'd had days where everything went so wrong, it started to feel almost comical, but not whole weeks. That couldn't happen, surely. How much bad news could one person take?

I turned to him. "What is it?"

"Why are you scared?"

"I'm not scared."

"It's not good for"—he gestured at my stomach—"you know. . . ."

Yes, I knew. Did he?

"Your appetite," he finished.

But I wasn't totally sure that was what he'd initially meant.

"My appetite," I hedged, "is fine."

He nodded. "I know it. Just take it easy, as they say."

"All right."

"Love," he said, "is a great blessing. No matter what it looks like. My son and his wife"—he gestured at the door and rolled his eyes—"they are not such a pretty picture of love, and yet"—he shrugged—"they have it. They are not alone."

I nodded, though I wasn't sure what he was getting at.

"What they give, they give to each other, no? Even when it is arguments and yelling, they both give it to each other, and then they go sleep in the same bed together. They are not lonely. Does that make sense?"

"Yes. Yes, it does." Their definition of love didn't have to be mine, nor the other way around.

"Love is good. Love is always good. And you have love, I think. Do you not?"

I thought about it. My feelings for Paul were strong. I realized they'd always been strong. I'd always enjoyed working for him and interacting, even on paper when we were just passing notes. So it was kind of like he was saying: It didn't matter so much *what* our interaction looked like to the outside world; what mattered was that we were on the same page.

And we were.

We had been for a long time.

"I think so," I said cautiously. Maybe I loved Paul. I wasn't sure how he felt. "I'm not sure."

Vlad nodded, like *he*, at least, was sure. "Then it's good. Is all good."

I smiled. "I believe you."

"What else I wanted to tell you is this. You're going to have a lot more work if you want it."

I have to admit it—given everything he'd said that seemed to have come true, I felt a surge of hope. "Lucrative work?"

He nodded sagely.

"Can you tell where?" Here I was again, buying it hook, line, and sinker. "What it has to do with?"

He frowned slightly. "Of course. I have friends at the embassy who took dinner with me, here, two nights ago. Your stroganoff was very popular with them. They would like to hire you to . . . what do you say?" He tapped his temple. "*Cater.* To cater events at the embassy sometimes."

It had never occurred to me that this could happen.

"So this isn't a psychic premonition," I confirmed.

He splayed his arms. "What premonition? They want to hire you. They said it!"

"Did you give them my number?"

"Of course! They are not psychic like Vlad!"

I laughed. "Thank you!"

He shrugged, and his face broke into one of his rare smiles. "I know you worried about the work. Especially now." He didn't move his eyes from mine, but it was as if he'd looked right at my abdomen. I knew he knew.

And as crazy as it might sound, that fact alone—believing in something that seemed impossible yet also seemed true—made me feel a whole lot better.

Chapter 26

An invitation arrived both by e-mail and in the mail for me to attend a gathering at Filigree, one of D.C.'s oldest and poshest restaurants, hosted by Lex and the mysterious Terry. There was to be some sort of grand announcement, it said.

Well, there was no way I could possibly miss that.

But I almost did. Traffic was a mess, parking was worse, and everyone on the road *and* sidewalk seemed to be in a foul mood.

By the time I found a parking place in Georgetown and got into Filigree, Lex was standing on a platform under a spotlight, talking into a microphone. "... so *very* pleased to announce that Filigree and Simon's Department Store will be partnering." He smiled at a tall blond several feet away. I wasn't sure if it was a man or a woman, as the person's

316 / Beth Harbison

hair was medium length, and his or her facial features were fine from the side, but the figure left no clue.

Terry, obviously.

Just like Pat from that *SNL* sketch that went on way too long.

"Filigree Café will be opening in both Simon's locations in the early spring," he finished triumphantly.

Everyone burst into applause, and Lex beamed.

This really was a huge deal. Filigree had been an institution in D.C. for nearly a century. Presidents had dined there. Royalty had proposed there. A political mistress had even *died* there, though the gruesome details of the murder were usually ignored in favor of the more romantic notion that she now haunted the place.

An unusually good-looking waiter stopped before me and offered me a mini crab cake.

I took four.

When I wasn't experiencing morning sickness, I was experiencing a completely piggish appetite. Hopefully things evened out. What I told myself was that I needed to get as much nourishment in, as often as I could, since I never knew when I'd feel ill.

It was the famine theory of eating.

"Gemma!" Lex swooped over me just as I popped a second crab cake into my mouth.

I hadn't quite finished the first.

"Hey, Lex." I put my hand in front of my mouth. "Wow, these are really good."

"Aren't they, though? Not as good as *your* cooking, though."

Not true. "Aw, thanks, Lex."

"Have you talked to Willa? I was hoping she might make it out tonight."

I shook my head. "I don't think she's ready yet. But she really wanted to. She's dying to know what the announcement is. In fact, I should call her and tell her—she's probably waiting on the edge of her seat." I started to reach for my phone, but Lex laid a hand on my forearm.

"Not yet," he said. "I have someone I want you to meet."

Suddenly, illogically, I had a fear that he was trying to set me up with someone. Paul came to mind, and I felt a pang of longing like I'd never felt before. A tender warmth spread in my chest and, inexplicably, I almost felt like crying.

Was this love?

Real love?

I wanted to call Paul. To run to him. To spend the night in his arms and never, ever leave.

Maybe it was the hormones talking. They'd done a lot of chattering lately, heaven knew. Telling me I was depressed when everything was fine, telling me I wanted sex when I needed to work, telling me I was hungry when I'd just eaten almost an entire box of Cap'n Crunch, and telling me I was sick when they were just swimming around in my stomach after a long, dull night of inactivity.

No, my hormones definitely couldn't be believed.

But my heart? That was another story. These feelings I had for Paul were different. I wanted him.

And I definitely didn't want anyone else.

Fortunately, it turned out Lex wasn't trying to set me up with anyone. "Terry!" He looked over my head and waved. "Come over here! This is her!"

The moment had finally come! I was finally going to meet Terry and figure out the mystery.

It was solved the moment he spoke. "So this is the famous Gemma," he said, his voice surprisingly deep and rich. Kind of like the shock of hearing Jim Nabors sing for the first time.

Even without that, though, the face, though definitely androgynous, tipped toward masculine up close.

I put my hand out. "Nice to meet you."

"I know I was cagy with you, but I didn't want to let the cat out of the bag until it was official."

His excitement was contagious. "Yeah? What's going on?" I was sure we were all about to witness some sort of commitment ceremony or something, but I was wrong.

"Terry is the *owner* of Filigree," Lex said pointedly. "As of, what, two months ago?"

"Three." Terry nodded. "It's very exciting."

Lex clapped his hands together. "I'll say! Tell her what you plan to do."

"We'd like to make the menu a little more modern," Terry said to me. He reached for a menu off a local table.

I couldn't help noticing that the logo for Filigree was a peacock feather.

A slight tremor of premonition ran through me. My recent drama had begun with a peacock. . . . Was that all about to reach some big, horrible crescendo?

"If you look," Terry said, "you'll see that there's room for perhaps twenty percent more fare and the menu would still be specialized and seasonal."

I took a quick look. It was true, the menu was, arguably, a little limited. "I see what you mean."

"We don't want it to look like a Chinese food menu, of course," he went on. "And we *cannot* get rid of any of the few remaining Filigree iconic specialties, but as you can see, it's all rather . . . heavy."

Prime rib, shrimp Louie, sautéed filet of sole. Yes, it was old-fashioned and a little heavy. Looked delicious to me right now, but I could see what he was getting at. "But you're not looking to lighten *these* dishes up, right?"

"Oh no, no, no. Those must stay or the public will object."

"I can imagine."

"This is where you come in," Lex said excitedly.

"Me?" I asked.

He nodded. "I told Terry that if there was anyone in the world who could beef up the menu, pardon the pun, and add dishes that were in keeping with the spirit of the original, it would be you."

"He was quite adamant about that, actually," Terry said with a smile. "I've been wanting to meet you for weeks."

Likewise. "So you want the menu rewritten?"

"Yes," Lex said. "Reconceived. We want you to be the

executive chef, primarily in charge of concept and execu-
tion, what do you think?"

"Executive chef," I breathed. It was an *incredible* offer. A
dream come true. "But, honestly, I'm not sure I'm quali-
fied," I admitted. "You must have the crème de la crème in
this town begging for the job."

Terry gave a shrug. "I've spoken with several people already," he said. "Naturally, everyone wants to make it their
own, but no one offered to do so in a way that respected the
Filigree history in the way I wanted. Of course, we will
have to speak more in depth about this, but Lex feels quite
sure you're the person for the job."

"I do," Lex confirmed.

Terry regarded me. "And I have a good feeling about it,
too. If you're interested."

"I am *definitely* interested." This was incredible. A few
weeks ago, I was afraid I was going to end up in whatever
the modern-day equivalent of debtors' prison was. Now,
with the potential jobs for the Russian Embassy and this, it
looked like things might actually be all right.

I had been right about the peacock feather bringing a
premonition, but it was a wonderful one.

I didn't realize I had unconsciously put my hand to
my stomach until I caught Lex's scrutinizing eye looking
at me.

He cocked his head. "Is there something you haven't
told me?"

"Yes."

"Care to elaborate?"

"There isn't time now," I said. "Suffice it to say, I'm pregnant."

There was a moment of stunned silence. Then he smiled broadly, his face going red with excitement. "I see we need to have a nice long chat. Soon."

"Yes. I'd like that."

"Is this for real?" he asked.

I nodded.

"My goodness, we are going to have one *hell* of a trip to the baby department at Simon's. And this time, I'm not taking no for an answer, missy. We're going to outfit your nursery so completely that it's going to look like Martha Stewart herself is going to sleep in the crib."

I laughed.

"Okay." He clapped his hands together. "Meanwhile, you haven't heard the most exciting part about Filigree's news. And I'm starting to think this might be *quite* timely."

It was like Bob Barker was telling me there was still more in the "Showcase Showdown." A new car. A boat. A cruise around the world. Financial security. An IRA. "What is it?"

"Simon's is going to be producing and selling, exclusively—"

"At least at first," Terry interjected. "Then we go national."

"Yes, that's right, after a brief, exclusive period, we *will* go national."

"With what?" I asked.

"The *Filigree D.C. Cookbook*." Lex beamed. "Can you

even imagine a better time to do a project like that?" He looked me up and down. It was clear he knew what was going on, and it was also clear this was going to drive me crazy for some time to come. He was going to be like the doting old aunt, always asking after the pregnancy.

And I loved him for it.

"You want *me* to write a cookbook?" I asked him. Then looked to Terry. "Are you sure?"

"Unless you're not interested," Terry said. "I realize we'll have to discuss terms, but I'm sure we can reach an agreement."

"I'm *sure* of it," Lex repeated. "What do you say?"

I almost couldn't breathe with the excitement of it all. "I say I'm on board with whatever you want. Absolutely all of it. I'm just afraid at midnight you're going to change your mind and this delicious pumpkin is going to turn back into a coach."

Both Terry and Lex laughed heartily at that.

"Not going to happen," Lex said, stopping a waiter whose platter held Filigree's signature chocolate truffles. He took three off the tray and handed one to each of us.

"To our new alliance," he said, raising his chocolate in the air like a flute of champagne.

"To us," Terry agreed.

"Amen," I said.

And we touched our chocolates together to toast what wasn't just a new job for me, but also, quite possibly, my salvation.

. . .

For the next few weeks, I continued to disprove the "morning" part of morning sickness repeatedly—as well as the notion that it ebbed by the end of the first trimester—but thankfully, I never had a problem with it while cooking food. On Tuesday, I made Paul an unfortunate meal that tasted *delicious* to me, but which didn't quite translate to unpregnant mouths.

"I just don't know that mint *goes* with pesto and pineapple," he said when he took a bite. I had just popped them out of the oven, and presented them proudly.

"Are you sure?" I said, and took a bite myself. "I think that's delicious!"

He looked at me like I was crazy, and then said, "Please. Have some more."

"Don't mind if I—" There was a sudden cramp in my stomach.

"What's wrong?" he asked, quick as a whip. He lay a hand on my back and arm, and looked concerned.

"Nothing. It's gone." I shook my head as if trying to forget a nasty memory. "I have no idea where that came from."

"What was it?"

"Just a cramp— *Oh!*" I bent over as another one gripped me.

"Come here," Paul said, guiding me strongly to one of the chairs in the living room.

I breathed deeply. "I think the cramps are gone," I assured him. Then: *"Ouch."*

Somehow, I had stopped expecting them. Maybe because I had spent most of my life *not* being pregnant and not thinking about pregnancy. It's like that first morning you look in the mirror after a dramatic haircut. It kind of takes a second before you remember.

Only, you know, this was way worse.

Paul must have seen that in my face. "I don't like this. We should get you to an emergency room."

"I don't . . ." That was foolish. This was no time for stoicism. "You may be right. Let me just rest for a minute."

"Something else is going on." It was a statement, not a question. He was putting the pieces together, whether he realized it or not.

And this was my chance.

"Yes." I took a breath and closed my eyes, concentrating on my abdomen for a moment. There was no pain. But I felt like all my insides had turned to Jell-O. Which incidentally, sounded just awful right now. "I'm pregnant."

He said, "Should I ask—?"

"You're the only one I've"—I dropped my voice—"slept with in months." I couldn't meet his eyes.

When he said nothing, however, I had to. He was looking at me. I couldn't read his expression.

Finally, he spoke. "That's . . . wow. I just . . . I don't know what to say."

"Yeah. Believe me, I was . . . shocked, too. To say the least."

"Do you—" He stopped, and a muscle twitched in his jaw. "Are you planning to keep it?"

Interesting that he regarded this as my choice, even now that he knew how intrinsically involved he was in it. I took the tension in his jaw to mean he was wrestling with that.

I bit my lower lip. "I am. I'm sorry, I know I should have talked to you about this, or found you, or"—I shook my head—"I don't know, done *something*, or maybe *everything*, differently before this was some big fait accompli that I'm telling you about like this, but . . ."

He nodded and looked down at his lap.

"Look," I said, "I'm not asking for anything from you. I mean, we haven't really even dated. You're a one-night stand, and so am—"

He looked up with raised eyebrows. "That's not exactly true, though, is it?"

I met his eyes. "I don't know. I don't know *how* to define this. Any of it."

"If you think about it," he said with a slight and unexpected smile, "we have known each other for a while."

I smiled back. I couldn't help it. "Yeah . . . but we don't know enough about each other to . . ."

To what? Become a family? Interesting how you could commit the act with just about anyone—have sex, make love, do the deed, whatever you wanted to call it—it meant as much or as little as you wanted it to until the sex became decidedly *un*sexy and became, instead, a medical condition.

And then a person.

"Right," he said. "We don't know each other that well. But I like you."

My face grew hot. "Well, I like you, too." Such a small thing in the face of such a big reality.

"I *really* do. And there's no way I'm not going to be part of that kid's life." He still looked shocked, but I could tell he was adjusting. "So here we are. Wherever *here* is."

Questions came to me now. The kinds of questions a person should ask a potential mate long, long before they reached this point. "Did you ever envision yourself, like, even having kids?"

He furrowed his brow in earnest. "Absolutely."

"Really?"

"Yes. I wasn't desperate for it. Just kind of figured it'd land in my lap if it was meant to be. The whole thing, wife, kids . . . kind of a lot of pressure to put on fate, I know."

"No, I"—I ignored the skip in my heartbeat—"I have always said the same thing."

We made eye contact.

His eyes dropped to my belly. "Kind of hard to imagine at a time like this, though, right?"

I sucked air in through my teeth. "Yes. Seriously. I mean, how freaked are you, really?"

He furrowed his brow again, this time in thought. "Strangely, not that much."

I wanted to believe it, but it was hard. "Really?"

"Really." He nodded. "I don't know why, but really."

I shifted my position, and another pain stabbed through my abdomen.

He didn't have to be told; he saw it. And he didn't hesitate. "We need to go to the ER now. If there's *any* possibility this is something more than food poisoning or a virus, we need to get you checked out."

Now, I was never one to make a big deal out of things unless the need to do so was overwhelming. But in this case, I agreed—I didn't want to take a chance.

This baby felt like a second chance in so many ways; I had to protect it at all costs.

The emergency room was surprisingly busy for a Tuesday night, but as soon as they learned I was pregnant, they took me straight back to triage.

It was strange having Paul there with me as they went through the series of questions that were normally routine and done alone. Health history and so on. The answers were so different now than the last time I'd been to the doctor.

What would they be next time?

Would I still be pregnant?

Or would I have to answer the medical questionnaire differently from now on when it came to the questions of live births and miscarriages?

I knew these were maudlin thoughts, of no use whatsoever to anyone, and certainly not to me in that position, but they still plagued me. The longer I sat there, wondering what was happening and how the night would end, the more nervous I became.

Part of me wanted to run away, to not get tests or diag-noses, or anything, as if Not Knowing would protect me. Logic and intelligence have no power over fear, and the impulse to basically put my head in the sand was so over-whelming that a couple of times I looked at Paul and actu-ally began to suggest we leave, but I knew—of course I knew—that I couldn't really protect myself or the baby by remaining ignorant of what was really happening.

So I sat there, on the cold, hard chair in the ER, breath-ing shallowly as the blood pressure gauge tightened around my biceps, and trying not to look at the man sitting next to me, who was growing more important to me by the mo-ment.

When I looked back on it, I realized that the moment I saw him at the bar, something about him had struck me. I'd never gone in much for the ideas of fate and soul mates and things like that, yet as soon as I'd laid eyes on him, something inside me said this was the One.

Then, of course, he'd disappeared and I thought I might never see him again, but maybe, on some deeper level, I knew even then that that wasn't true. That he would be part of my life, in my head and in front of my eyes, for a long, long time to come. I felt I'd know that face forever.

I still feel that.

And sitting in that sterile, impersonal ER, something about his quiet, strong presence both reassured *and* disqui-eted me. I was glad he was there. Profoundly glad.

As if reading my mind, he reached over and took my hand in his.

I looked at him.

"This will all be okay," he said. "I can't explain it, but I'm sure of it. It will be okay."

I tried to smile. Yes, deep down I thought he was right. But my brain always questioned my gut. "I hope you're right," I said, and twined my fingers in his.

The triage nurse declared my blood pressure fine and went off to find a room they could install me in for the next—if past history was any indicator—four or five endless hours.

When she'd left, Paul leaned closer to me. "Look, this is too right for everything to go wrong now. It's like when I showed up at my door that day, and it was you. All along it had been you. And somehow, it wasn't an outright shock. It was more like spending an hour on a math problem, and then getting the answer. And then the answer is really obvious, and you feel like kicking yourself." He shrugged. "It was more like that."

It was the perfect analogy. "I know what you mean." The electronic doors to triage swung open, and a woman in scrubs walked past. "That's kind of how I felt, too."

"So the baby . . . I should have been shocked or maybe felt like my whole world was being shaken like an Etch A Sketch. But instead, it felt like . . . it feels right somehow. Something about a birth control failure, versus failure to use any birth control, makes this feel more"—again, he shrugged—"meant to be, I guess."

"I hope so." I started to cry. I couldn't help it. It felt like so much was at stake.

"Hey, come on." He pulled me closer to him and kissed the top of my head. "Don't cry. Too much stuff had to happen just right to get us here. It isn't all going to break now."

I closed my eyes against an onslaught of burning tears. "I hope you're right. Please be right."

"Miss Craig?"

I looked up. The nurse was back.

"We're ready to take you to your room."

Six hours later, I was home, resting on the couch with the uncomfortable knowledge that I had an "incompetent cervix."

I mean, seriously, of all the insulting terms, *incompetent*?

But the good news was that the doctor was going to be able to do a procedure to fix it. Everything was going to be fine, though I'd have to take it a bit easier than I'd planned to, and I had had the last wake-up call I needed in order to realize just how much I wanted this baby.

Just how determined I was to have him or her, no matter what.

I was going to make it work.

No, *we* were going to make it work. One way or the other.

I didn't even really know Paul. But having him there, holding me and looking strong but worried—nothing could have soothed me more.

"Thanks for bringing me in and waiting with me."

"I wouldn't have had it any other way." He swept a

strand of hair from my forehead and looked very seriously at me.

I nodded and looked at him, letting his presence comfort me. I took a deep breath and let it out carefully. It wasn't until then that I realized there were tears in my eyes.

I *was* in love.

Paul gave a small squeeze to my hand and stroked my hair. "So," he said. "How are you feeling now?"

"Fine, I think." I bit my lower lip. "But that really scared me. At the same time, it made me realize, even more, just how much I want this baby. And that's no command for you to perform," I amended quickly. "You can be as involved or as uninvolved as you're comfortable being. But I want you to know that, no matter what, this child is loved."

He looked at me for a long time in silence. Finally, he gave a small shake of his head and said, "I want this, too. We're going to have to figure out the logistics, of course. We can't have an entire country between us, that's clear."

"But—"

He put a finger to my lips. "Don't worry about that now. We'll figure it out. I'm not going to let you go."

A tear went down my cheek, and I could feel them welling in both eyes now. "I'm glad."

I don't know if I'd ever felt so genuine or honest.

Or, honestly, so good.

"So we'll give it a go?" Paul asked. "You and me?"

"Yes." I tightened my grip on his hand. "You and me."

And baby makes three.

Epilogue

One Year Later

Her name is Grace.

She weighed eight pounds seven ounces at birth, and she was—and is—absolutely perfect. Barely cries, smiles and laughs all the time, and sleeps straight through the night. She has the light blond hair I had throughout my childhood, and she has her father's eyes, a fact that makes my heart sing every time I look at her.

Or at him.

Which is every day, on both counts, because after two months of "trying to figure out what to do" while commuting between Seattle and D.C., we finally just decided life is too short not to take chances—especially on things that are so big and so wonderful.

So I resigned from the jobs I had left and moved on out to Seattle.

I haven't regretted it for a moment.

I do miss my weekly visits with Lex and Willa, of course, but I still see Paul on Tuesdays (and Wednesdays and Thursdays and you get the point), but I don't spend too much time missing the weird energies of the Olekseis' or the Van Houghtens' households.

Though it has to be pointed out, the Oleksei energy is coming, at least in part, from a pretty legit mental force. About a month after I left, Vlad made all the papers by predicting—and preventing, with the help of his burly sons—an assassination attempt on the Russian ambassador during a reception in D.C. You probably heard about it; it was all over the place. PSYCHIC SAVES AMBASSADOR with all the details of police who were too skeptical to believe it.

By that time, I wasn't surprised. Vlad's accuracy in his predictions with me was pretty startling. Enough so that, as tempted as I am at times to consult with him about my future, I'm mostly nervous about knowing too much.

Willa, on the other hand, has become a big fan of his. No, he can't predict lottery numbers or the hand someone will play in poker—there are no crazy financial advantages to seeing a psychic—but his guidance has actually really helped her move toward her goals, though whether that's because he's right or because she believes it and moves forward on her own, I can't say. Nevertheless, I stayed in town long enough to get her cooking her own meals, and it seems she really excelled at it. She is now within twenty pounds of her weight goal.

On top of which, she convinced Lex to give more space

and publicity to the plus-size department at Simon's. He jokes that it brings in more people who want to nosh at the store's satellite Filigree eatery, though I think he's right.

The best part of that is that it got Willa out from behind her computer and into the real world, dealing with people as the store's unofficial buyer for that department. When I first moved, she and I played Scrabble online quite a bit, as she was still homebound and I was bedbound. But I noticed that, as her ideas took root, she was on less and less, which I took as a good sign.

When I saw her at a cookbook signing at Filigree—one of Simon' Department Store's bestselling items of all time, and they had the Bop It back when that was *the* Christmas gift of the year way back when—I might not have known it was her if she hadn't been updating me with pictures all along.

"You know," she confided, "your recipe for Cajun Chicken Pasta? On page twenty-eight?" She nodded toward the book I'd just signed for her.

"Yes?"

"Totally works with skim milk instead of heavy cream." She nodded proudly. "Not that I tried the cream version. I'm sure in a blind taste test that's the one I'd prefer, but skim *works!*"

I imagined the dish, using milk in the pan with the chicken fond, sun-dried tomatoes, oregano, and blackening spice, and could see where the milk would reduce into a nice thick sauce. "I'm going to have to try that," I told her. "I've still got a few stubborn pounds to lose." More like ten, but I knew I'd be doing a lot of running around as soon as Grace started to walk.

"You look *great*," Willa said. "Really! God, don't think for a moment you need to lose any weight."

"It's true," a woman said behind her. "You *do* look great."

I smiled at the woman. "Thanks. I appreciate it." I turned my attention back to Willa.

"Maybe you were too thin before," the woman said.

Before? Before when? Who the hell was this woman? She had dirty blond hair (the color, not the quality of hygiene), a broad, lineless face, and she was wearing a patterned wrap dress and eating a small bag of Simon's organic potato chips.

Barbecue flavor.

Willa stepped aside, casting me a puzzled look, and the woman moved forward and took a book out from under her arm. "You can just sign this to me. I'm not with Peter anymore, as you might imagine."

Oh my God.

It was *Angela*.

Angela plus forty pounds. Which made her approximately normal, by the way. She looked fantastic, if unrecognizable.

I was grateful I didn't have to ask her name. "I didn't know," I told her honestly, though I could imagine all kinds of reasons she might have left Peter. "What happened?"

She looked surprised. But surprise registering in now bright blue eyes instead of the hollowed sockets she'd once had looked good on her. "You didn't hear?"

336 / Beth Harbison

"I didn't tell you?" Willa added, then glanced self-consciously at Angela.

"No, what happened?"

"My husband"—Angela straightened her back—"was caught with an underage prostitute in Georgetown."

"On the Exorcist Stairs," Willa said with a nod.

"Appropriately enough, yes," Angela confirmed.

The Exorcist Stairs are on M Street next to a gas station. The key scene where the priest falls down them in the movie *The Exorcist* both freaked us all out as kids *and* compelled us to go visit the steps at night.

"I don't know what to say," I said, gaping at Angela. "I'm sorry."

She waved the notion away. "I should have seen it coming a mile away. My marriage wasn't working. My *life* wasn't working." She gave a dry laugh. "God knows my *diet* wasn't working." She ate a chip and raised the bag to me. "I'm a lot happier now, I can tell you that."

"There's onion powder in those, you know," I said with a smile.

She shook her head. "I checked." Then she gave a self-effacing shrug. "Some old habits die hard."

"How is Stephen?" I asked.

"Incredible," she said. "He's doing great, despite the circumstances. I put him in the public school down the road, so now he has tons of friends in the neighborhood and he seems really happy." She hesitated, then said, "Listen, I owe you an apology. When I saw that video of Peter and you, I . . . I don't know, I went a little crazy. I couldn't stand the idea of you being perfect to him, doing everything right, looking great, and outdoing me in every conceivable way. It was my fault you didn't get more work at the club. I did everything I could to stop people from hiring you."

She looked so shamed that it was hard to be angry. I'd known it was her, and I'd long since realized my life ended up a million times better than it was before or would have been, even with triple the country club jobs. "I know," I said to her. "It's okay."

"I really want to make it up to you. Can I recommend you now?" She looked at the book, then at me. "I guess that's a dumb question. You've gone way beyond the club now."

I smiled. "But thanks for offering."

"Tell me, where's your little one? I heard you had a baby girl."

"She's—" I looked across the room and saw Paul heading toward us with Grace in the football hold. He'd read a book called *Hold It Like a Football . . . Just Remember Not to Spike It* in preparation for the birth and now prided himself on his ways with the baby. "Here she comes now."

Willa and Angela turned to look, and I heard them both take in a breath.

"She's beautiful," Angela said, and looked into my eyes for perhaps the first time ever in all the time I'd known her. "That's the most important thing right there. That baby. The hot man with her is just icing."

Which she probably eats now, by the way.

So everyone turned out okay, whether because they

needed me (as in Paul and Grace's case) or because they needed to take care of themselves (Willa and Angela) or their countrymen (Vlad). But the bottom line is that we all still had each other, for better or worse, if we wanted each other.

Speaking of *for better or worse*, now I have a wedding to plan. Not my own—Paul and I got married in a civil ceremony the week I moved to Seattle—but Willa's. See, as soon as she started going in to Simon's most days, Lex and Terry (whose relationship remains unclear to me) decided to fix her up with Sam Frost, a guy who'd been working in the suit department since he was eighteen. He never goes near the computer, and the only thing he'll watch on TV is the five o'clock news on Channel 4. But they make it work.

Sometimes in life, all you need is a little hope, a lot of courage, and—oh yes—butter.

Turn the page for a sneak peek at
Beth Harbison's new novel

Chose the Wrong Guy,
Gave Him the Wrong Finger

Available July 2013

Chapter 1

June, Ten Years Ago

There are five stages of heartbreak.

The first is Denial (He didn't! He wouldn't!), followed by Fear (What if he did? What will happen to me if I dump him?), a variable period of Rationalization (He didn't even have *time*! I would *know* if he'd been with someone else!), and eventually Acceptance (Okay, he did it, I have to move on, he doesn't deserve me).

Then comes Revenge.

Unfortunately, all too often these stages mix themselves up or repeat, repeat, repeat like a film on a loop, and sometimes another person gets thrown into the mix.

Once upon a time, that was what happened to Quinn Barton.

. . .

"Quinn, Frank's at the door. He says he needs to talk to you. He says it's urgent."

Quinn Barton turned to her bridesmaid, Karen Ramsey, and lifted her veil, an act that was soon to seem very prophetic. "He needs to talk to me *now*?"

Karen nodded. "He's *insisting*."

This was weird.

Something was wrong. Had something happened to Burke? Had he been hit by a car? Killed minutes before their wedding?

Heart pounding, Quinn pushed past Karen and hurried to the door, holding her skirt up enough so that she didn't trip, but otherwise unconcerned about what she might knock over on her way past.

"What's wrong?" she asked Frank as soon as she saw his face.

His eyes darted left and right. "I need to talk to you privately."

"Is Burke dead?"

"What? *No!* No one's dead, there's just something I need to tell you about."

All of Quinn's anxiety immediately melted into disproportionate irritation. "Really? Hm. I'd love to chat, but maybe now isn't the best time. I'm about to get married."

His expression hardened. "That's exactly why it has to be now."

Something about the way he said it, or maybe that granite set of his jaw, gave her pause. "Fine. We'll go out the back door. There's probably no one out there. I don't want Burke to see me in my dress before the wedding, it's bad luck."

Frank made a derisive noise.

They stopped on the sidewalk a few yards outside the church and Frank said, "I think you need to consider stopping the wedding. Or at least postponing it."

"You think I should stop the wedding now?" she asked, vaguely aware of a hint of feeling, deep inside, that she'd been waiting for something like this. Then, numb, afraid to hear the answer yet looking for it like a rubbernecker in traffic looks for severed limbs and disembodied heads at the scene of an accident even though those details could never be forgotten or less horrifying, she added, "Why?"

"Come on, Quinn, you *know* why. Surely you know why."

"No, I don't! Tell me, specifically, *why*."

"Because he's *cheating* on you, that's why!" Like she was stupid for asking. Like she already knew it, like *everyone* knew it, and he was just tired of watching her silly game.

She felt her hand go reflexively to her chest. What is that gesture? Why do people do it when they get a shock? To make sure they're still alive, that there's a heart beating under there, that they haven't died and gone to hell?

Because this revelation certainly made Quinn feel like she was in hell. Quite suddenly and unexpectedly.

"No, he's not!"

Denial.

"He wouldn't do that," she went on. Her voice was small. Childlike. But that didn't make him any gentler on her.

There was no compassion in his voice. "He would and he did."

"I don't believe it."

"You want proof?"

Fear.

What kind of proof? If it existed, would she want to see it? Or would that just be the kind of thing that, once seen, could never be forgotten and would gnaw at her forever?

"I don't believe it." She swallowed and leveled her gaze on Frank. "When did this supposedly happen?"

"Are you kidding, Quinn? You know he did. *Repeatedly!* Probably different girls. Probably even last night. Definitely in the last month. Does that answer your question enough?"

It felt like she'd been punched, hard, right in the gut. That's the cliché, there's a reason for it. Felt like she'd been punched in the gut. Shorthand for the myriad emotional, intellectual, and physical ramifications of being stunned.

Punched in the gut.

Except that was *exactly* how it felt—the unexpected blow connecting to the solar plexus, forcing the air from her lungs, tripping her heartbeat, curving her shoulders over in the time-immemorial position of, *Stop! I give up! I can't take it!*

Uncle!

No mas.

In short, his words immobilized her. It was like crazy sci-fi technology in action—he said it and she was instantly frozen into complete inaction at the very moment the church bells began to ring their call *to* action.

It's true, her most fearful inner voice said. *You know it's true*. But fear is such a liar, isn't it? Always there for you, louder than anything else inside, always pretending to be on your side. It's just looking out for you, right?

"When *exactly*?" she challenged, but she knew she wasn't going to like the answer. This wasn't fear she was talking to, or at least it wasn't fear who was going to answer, this was a real-life person who would *know*. Her hands tingled and she balled them into and out of fists as she paced on the sidewalk in front of him.

Frank. Francis Albert Morrison. Named, by his mother, after Frank Sinatra, despite his distinctly English ancestry and complete lack of creative talent, musical or otherwise. He wasn't a romantic either, or at least he'd never demonstrated anything resembling that in the six years she had known him. Why he was suddenly Dustin Hoffman yelling, "*Elaine!*" at her would-be wedding, she didn't know.

Well, that wasn't quite fair. He wasn't yelling, *Elaine*, he was yelling, *Cheater*, not *to* her but *at* her, and actually he wasn't even yelling it so much as he was *condescending* it, and he was talking about someone who, right up to that moment, had been her fiancé.

Someone who, at that very moment, was waiting for her at the altar of the Middleburg United Methodist Church to become her husband.

Unless, of course, he was fucking her maid of honor behind the pulpit, which perhaps Frank would have her believe was equally likely.

Or which, God forbid, *was* equally likely.

"Give me the details." Her knees went weak. She sank down onto the curb next to Frank and took off her wedding shoes. Her grandmother's wedding shoes. Something old. It took some effort. Her feet were dented and grooved where the material of the slightly small shoes had cut into her flesh, which had swollen in the heat and stress.

Later she realized that "Give me the details" are some of the most ill-advised words anyone can ever utter. Details *never* make anything better.

"I don't want to say . . . I can't do that to him . . ."

"*Him?*" she raged. As if he could just go this far and let her handle the rest on her own?

"I wouldn't do it to *you* either. Maybe even *mostly* you." Like that made it better. "It's none of my business at all, I'm just trying to help you before you make the biggest mistake of your life."

"Then *help* me! You cannot make this implication *while I'm supposed to be walking down the aisle,* and not tell me exactly what you're talking about."

He looked pained, it had to be said. A good actor, or just a guy with a conscience? She didn't know. She realized, all in that one moment, that she'd *never* known. Because she'd actually always thought he was a good guy. Solid. Not one to whip up some sort of dangerous passion inside his soul and use it to potentially destroy someone else.

"*Frank.*" She stood and continued pacing in front of him even though her bare feet were killing her. Her feet always swelled when she got really stressed out. It was weird, but it was her *thing.* Maybe weirder since she wasn't really into shoes like her mom was. She'd spent a lot of time barefoot as a teenager, pacing her feet into a size that, as her father always said, was better suited for the box than for the shoes that came in it. At this moment, every tiny pebble of the street pavement felt like it was cutting into her feet like glass, but she couldn't stop and try to wedge her Jurassic feet into her wedding pumps now. "I don't believe you."

He looked surprised. Hurt? Maybe insulted, maybe just worried that she'd dismiss something important. Ego or altruism, she didn't know. But he went forward boldly. "I saw her," he said. "I saw them. Together."

"You saw her," she repeated dully. A foreign student learning the language by repeating.

He nodded. "Yes. I saw her."

"*And . . . ?*" She didn't want to know. She really, really didn't want to know. But she *had* to. She wanted every single awful detail. She was ready to hear it all and slice herself with each tiny detail again and again for the rest of her life, regretting it each and every time. "Where? How? Elaborate!"

"A few times, she was at the farm," he began.

Her throat went so tight she nearly gagged.

Eight words that held so much. The shortest longest story ever told, at least to her.

A few times = there were too many to count. Not one single betrayal, possibly drunken, possibly mistaken, possibly— somehow—forgivable.

A few times . . .

But, worse, *the farm* = *her* place. The place she loved more than any other. His family's farm went back generations. But she'd been going since she was fifteen, so it was part of *her* as well. She grew up in town, but Burke's family had a farm—actually, it was a huge horse farm to her, ninety acres of the most beautiful rolling green hills you can imagine, with stables so pristine Thurston and Lovey Howell could move right in. It was a place she'd always loved. Middleburg was horse country, and, as a girl growing up, she'd loved horses and always wanted one of her own. Her family wasn't particularly wealthy, despite their zip code, so that dream remained an impossibility for her.

But when she'd begun dating Burke at age fifteen—which was still young enough to cling, if only in some vaguely subconscious way, to those childhood dreams and wishes—the place might as well have been Disney World to her.

There was a five-page entry in her high school diary describing the farm from the first time he took her there. Every detail was still correct, from the ebony bookcases in the den to the crocheted bedspread in the guest room. And everything she wanted to change, on the day she was certain she would eventually move in, was also still in line with who she was and what she wanted. It seemed so much like fate.

It wasn't just a place to live out her childhood fantasies of horses and stables and whatever old *Spin and Marty* episodes were shown on *The Mickey Mouse Club* reruns they played on Channel Five. When Burke and she started to date and fall in love, that became *their place*. Burke and his grandfather, and often his brother as well, would work around the place while Quinn would sit on the patio with his grandmother, Dottie, drinking iced tea and hearing tales of the old days while the wind hushed across the long stretches of green nothingness that were increasingly rare in the D.C. suburbs.

The farm was sacred space.

Surely Frank knew how much it would hurt her to bring this up this way. Surely he wouldn't do it if he didn't think he *had* to . . . would he?

"He took her *there*?" she said. Her voice sounded so much stronger than she felt. Her throat was so tight she felt like someone was strangling her, yet it sounded like she had the conviction and anger appropriate to a woman who has found out, *just in the nick of time,* that she's been betrayed. She'd ask the questions she had to ask, even though she didn't want the answers. She *needed* the answers, and she'd get them. She was a detective, she was fucking Columbo or something, with a pretend pad and pen in her hand, saying, *And what, exactly, do you know about that?*

"I really don't want to say more. You know enough. Ask him now. How could he deny it?"

"Apparently he has for some time!"

Frank shook his head. "I can't betray him any more, it goes against Guy Code."

"*Fuck Guy Code!*" How could anyone look at a woman in the pain she knew was contorting her face and burning in her eyes, and think it was sufficient to give a small, yet powerful, detail without follow-up? "What. Else. Do. You. Know. About. Her?"

Long pause.

"She's a stoner," he finally said with a shrug, though his tone was one of disgust.

Ah.

That should make her feel better.

She was lesser than Quinn, because Quinn wasn't a stoner. Quinn was the opposite. How comforting. She was totally anti-stoner. But so was Burke! Burke was as straight and narrow as they came! She'd never seen him have anything stronger than a beer, and he usually opted for milk at that.

Yet he'd taken some stoner chick to the farm and banged her there? This was either a huge flaw in Frank's story or it was the detail that dropped the *Price Is Right* Plinko chip into the $5,000 slot of her lingering doubt about Burke's truthfulness.

Her throat tingled and she thought she might pass out, a big white unidentifiable splash in the street gutter that people wouldn't even slow down before running over.

What was that? A sack of sweet feed?

She straightened, with some effort in the now-ridiculous dress, and tried to breathe and walk off the shaking that emanated from a spot in the center of her being.

Her heart.

Then Frank went on with his final blow, which she'd never have time to figure out if it was an incredibly clever manipulation via lies-so-weird-they-had-to-sound-true or just truth-is-stranger-than-fiction.

"Actually, she got stoned there with Rob." He looked at her earnestly, his wavy dark hair short and controlled just like his demeanor, versus Burke's wild mane. And Frank's eyes were a serious amber brown, in contrast to Burke's hearthrobby blue.

It made Frank easier to believe somehow.

He considered for a moment before adding—as redemption for Burke?—a lame, "That did piss Burke off."

"But . . ." Her mind couldn't compute. Couldn't make sense of this. Couldn't do the math. Yet couldn't stop trying. Rain Man trying to add every single number in the phone book. Rob was a hired hand who'd moved out, what, a year ago? *Ages* ago. It was weird enough to say that Burke had somehow condoned this, but adding the detail—Rob—that conceivably had credibility *and* the vague insinuation of a time frame . . . well, honestly, she just would never have given Frank credit for being that creative. He was *very* smart, but in a left-brain, numbers sort of way.

Weaving these perfect, weird details for her just seemed out of his league.

Hell, it was even out of *her* league, and she was what she would normally consider a fairly wily woman.

"But he hates . . . ," she tried, then lost her voice. Or her point.

Or her soul.

This just sounded too true, if only in its very falseness. It didn't matter what Burke hated or approved of, maybe there had even been some perverse fetishish pleasure in going for someone deliberately opposite her. Still, it was the timing that stung like lashes from a whip. "It's been going on *that* long?"

Frank gave a half shrug. In cynical retrospect, she would

believe it was meant to look sympathetic. Or maybe *commiserative* was the better word. *Hey, I know, it sucks,* that shrug implied. *I'm so sorry you're going through this, but give the jerk what he deserves.* Because he *clearly* expected her to be outraged by this news.

As pretty much any self-respecting woman would be.

But all she could think about were weird little clues, tiny things that she'd ignored—though consciously—time and again. There had been scratch marks on Burke's shoulder once when she was massaging his back. She'd noticed them, thought the curve of them seemed pretty distinct and specific, yet she didn't even *question* him about them because she *completely* trusted him. She just figured there had to be a reasonable explanation.

Because there's *always* a reasonable explanation for things, right? How many times had she been worried about something and been 100 percent sure the only possible outcome was that something awful had happened, when, in fact, a little series of innocuous things had happened?

She didn't enjoy being angsty and upset. She didn't want to be Jealous Girl. Jealous Girl is just so uncool. She's Walter Mitty's wife, the harpy nag who gains power with a wedding ring, then demands an accounting of every moment her man isn't with her. The fat actress in every old movie who lost her guy to Marilyn Monroe or Myrna Loy or Katharine Hepburn. Jealous Girl was Insecure Girl, and she did all kinds of ugly things that turned life into drudgery for everyone around her.

Quinn wasn't Jealous Girl! She honestly thought she was

a good catch *because* she didn't freak out about every little thing! Once upon a time, she would have been all, *"Ugh, I hate those girls!"*

But here she was, pacing on hot, rough pavement in what was once a beautiful wedding gown, her mind racing with angry, suspicious, painful thoughts.

A couple of times he's told me the same story more than once, without remembering he'd already told me. Is that because he thought he'd told her?

Those times he said he wanted to stay in because he was "tired," even though he obviously *would have had hot sex with me if he'd seen me—was he having hot sex with her instead?*

Oh, *my God, hott*er *sex with her?*

Was that even possible?

The pain of imagining it was awful. Him touching her, stripping her, her hands on him, her *mouth* on him—that was *Quinn's* man, that was *Quinn's* body to love, he reserved it for *her.* She knew every single millimeter of it, knew which muscles hurt just by touching him, he never even had to say a word. No one else would know, or care proba- bly, that he held his tension in his shoulder blades; that the arch of his foot tightened when he ran, and that that turned his calves to tight painful ropes; that for some reason his left upper body was usually tighter than the right but his right lower body was tighter than his left. . . . All those meticulous little details that Quinn had so proudly believed proved she loved him better than anyone else ever could.

Had he cupped this other girl's face and kissed her while he was on top of her, moving inside her? God, that was the worst of all. Him *kissing* her. Kissing was so much more intimate than the rest. Emotional.

Not that *the rest* didn't matter. Not that the rest didn't exist. Apparently it did. This puzzle had so many more pieces than she'd anticipated. Had he ever been with her the same day he was with Quinn? Had her kisses still been on his lips when *she*, Quinn, kissed him?

She felt like she was going to puke.

"Why would he do that to me?" she asked Frank, though she wasn't really looking to him for an answer. How could he have it?

"You know him. He did it because he *could*. He did it because he always wants more. More money, more attention, more pizza, whatever, he's like a six-year-old who thinks of no one but himself."

And she did know Burke. She knew he was completely capable of being a child. Wild, irresponsible. His sense of humor was sometimes raunchy, his timing sometimes inappropriate. Sometimes he laughed too loud, drove too fast, pushed too hard. But in spite of that—perhaps even *because* of some of it—he was wildly charismatic.

And *she* had won his heart. *She*—Quinn Morgan Barton—whose Awkward Phase had gone on longer than many other girls' in junior high, who had always thought just a little too much about things, and tried just a little too hard to do everything right—maybe sometimes erring on the side of being too dull for a guy like Burke—*she* had won his heart in tenth grade and had been with him ever since, almost six years.

Yes, they'd had their challenges now and then. There *was* that time they'd broken up because he refused to go to the homecoming dance, and then, while they were broken up, he went with Tammy Thomas, whose stupid name made her sound like a brand of shoes and whose stupid face could probably model for the ads. That had sucked. But he'd done it to spite her for dumping him and, in some weird way, that was better than him doing it without regard for her at all.

At least he was thinking of her.

But for the most part everything had been good between them. No, they'd been *great*. The two of them were the best of friends, they had a long history, God knew they had amazing chemistry.

They *loved* each other.

He'd loved her enough to propose. She hadn't even seen it coming, but he'd done it, he'd proposed, and here it was, their wedding day.

Or was it?

"Why are you telling me all this now, Frank? Why now?"

"Because you need to know before you go in there and marry the wrong guy."

She sank down next to the curb again, her own private rise and fall of service, and hugged her knees closer to her, her feet stinging against the hot pavement of the gutter.

There was a steady drumbeat of, *This isn't true, this isn't true, this isn't true, this isn't true,* thrumming in her head.

But she didn't buy it.

"But why now? Why at the last possible minute?" She met his eyes. "Why not, I don't know, yesterday? Last week? Last month? Just how long have you known all this was going on?"

"I've known it all along. I thought you knew—I mean, how could you *miss* it?—but I guess you didn't want to know. It wasn't until today that I realized maybe you really didn't get it. You missed every hint."

"Hint?"

"There were a million of them. Hell, *I* gave you a million of them!"

"Jesus, Frank, you might have a million thoughts in your head, but if you throw me a balloon, all I'm going to catch is the balloon!" She threw her hands in the air and came perilously close to hitting him in the face. Which she wouldn't have been sorry for at all. "Who wants to leap to conclusions only to have their heart broken?"

"I understand," he said, in an infuriatingly calm voice. "But sometimes you need to be realistic."

"I thought I was, *Frank*." She practically spit his name. "Right up until this moment, I thought I was. Because no one gave me the benefit of, apparently, the facts."

"But you knew them, Quinn. Come on. Deep down, you must have known."

Had she? Her stomach tightened at the thought. Had the occasional worry or mistrust been significant, or just paranoia? Didn't everyone have doubts in a relationship now and then? Didn't *everyone* occasionally think the person they loved might be . . . attracted to other people?

"I think you're mad at the wrong person," Frank concluded.

"No, I'm not! I'm mad at all the *right* people. I'm mad at you, I'm mad at that sonofabitch in there"—she gestured toward the church—"and I'm mad at myself most of all. Myself and you. And him." God, she hated everyone.

He gave a soft laugh. "I guess that about covers it." He looked as if he wanted to reach for her, to comfort her, but thought better of it. "I've known you a long time, Quinn. In fact . . ." He held a breath for a moment, pent-up, then expelled it. "I . . . well, I kept hoping you'd see what was going on. The truth. I would never treat you like this."

She looked at him incredulously. "You are not seriously making a pass at me."

"Quinn, I've known you for years. I care about you. I love you. I want you to be treated the way you should be treated. You know me, you know who I am. There's no need to sell myself to you, I'm not right either, I'm sure, or you would have seen it a long time ago. That's not what this is about. I told you what my conscience said I had to tell you. What you do with it is up to you." He stood up and dusted off his pants. "I'm going in now. I'll let them know you're on your way, no matter what you decide to do once you're in there." He shrugged. "And, Quinn, I'm really sorry to have done this . . . this way. Or at all. I just didn't know what else to do at this point. I couldn't sit on it without giving you a straight shot."

Then he went into the church, his gait certain, if not confident. And why wouldn't it be? *He* wasn't the one whose life was just shattered. *He'd* be okay no matter what. Obviously he'd made something of a confession to her, but it was equally obvious that his life—his heart, his sanity, his well-being—didn't *depend* on what *she* did.

She didn't know how long she stood there, staring at the carved wooden door after he'd gone through it. It felt like forever. She was completely numb. Part of her wanted to never move again. To never have to do anything again. Her world had been shattered, and she wanted to just collapse into a million little pieces on the ground, the million little puzzle pieces she would otherwise have to put together in order to make sense of this.

Then she heard her mother's voice calling to her. "Quinn! Come on! Come in here! Everyone's waiting!"

And that was duty's call.

Mechanically, she got up and started to walk toward the door, aware that her veil was askew, that she'd sweated her makeup into something of a blur, and unaware of the gum she'd sat on, and marched to the internal beat in her head, morbidly in tempo with the "Wedding March."

It can't be true, it can't be true, it can't be truuuue, it can't be true.

That beat carried her all the way up to the altar. She was aware of eyes on her, but she met no one's gaze. Not even Burke's, though she knew—she could just *feel*—it was questioning.

What's wrong? What's going on?

No clear answer formed in her head. She didn't know what was going on, exactly. She was dazed, being carried on a rickety raft by an ocean of adrenaline.

She didn't know what she was going to do until she was right there by his side.

That's when it all came clear.

She drew her hand back and slapped him with all the power of every unacknowledged hurt he'd ever inflicted on her.

Then she turned and ran back down the aisle, out of the church, followed, not by the undoubtedly stunned Burke, but by his best man. His brother.

Frank.

Five hours later, as the night crept over town, Quinn sat alone in her shop—she had refused her friends' well-intended offers of help and support, half ready to strangle the next person who offered either—opening presents, writing awkward *thank you anyway*'s for them, and repackaging them to ship back to the sender.

And all the while, her anger grew stronger and stronger, like hoofbeats from an oncoming calvary.

She couldn't believe she'd put so much trust in Burke. Couldn't believe it. Everything seemed so clear now.

Yet, as clear as it was, she still worried about how she'd struggle when her current anger dissolved tomorrow, or the next day, into sadness.

She put her pen down and cracked her knuckles. Her hand was *killing* her from all this writing. If it were thanks for wedding gifts it would have been a lot more fun. But this? Explaining. Apologizing. Wondering which recipients would understand and which would be angrily tucking into their returned gifts, wondering if she'd opened them and made toast with them first.

And why did *she* need to do the explaining anyway? Apart from the million things he should have done to prevent this catastrophe to begin with, *he* should have gone straight to the pulpit and done the one gentlemanly thing there was left for him to do: tell the guests that the wedding was off, it was entirely his fault, and . . . whatever. Offered them cake to go or something. Gotten Ziploc bags and plastic forks and let everyone have at it at one of the many traffic lights along Route 7 on the way home.

And maybe assured them right then and there that their gifts would be returned *by him*, so she wouldn't have to be sitting here wondering which guests thought she was the kind of inconsiderate runaway bride who thought the damn Vitamix was her right just for letting them sit their butts on the pew for an uncomfortable forty-five minutes while she dithered about whether or not she actually *wanted* to have the party she had invited them all to.

How many of them thought she was a flake who just had second thoughts for no good reason?

Now she'd have to spend the whole damn night packing stuff up for UPS to get the next day.

When she was *supposed* to be in Jamaica!

Middleburg, Virginia, was most definitely not Jamaica. It was just the same old scenery she'd been looking past for twenty-one years.

She'd *wanted* more. She'd wanted to broaden her horizons, open her world, grow with him. With Burke. The man she'd loved since he was a boy of seventeen and she was a girl of fifteen.

That was laughable now, given the truth.

How many other people had known the truth before she'd even put on the blue silk garter?

What were they thinking about her now?

What would *she* be thinking about her now?

An uncharitable part of her saw that she would be shaking her head and clucking her tongue at the dumb girl who'd ignored every sign that had been offered to her on a silver platter because she was so damn eager to wear a gorgeous dress and saunter down the aisle to a gorgeous man who was waiting there to take her hand in marriage.

Oh, the sucker, she'd think to herself, *she sold her soul to the devil, then tried to marry him in God's house.* Actually, no, she wasn't that religious. Or that kind. *Stupid bitch,* she'd more likely scoff. *Um, hello! It's not just about the* hand *in marriage on the* one *party day, it's about a whole lot of stuff, a* lifetime *of stuff, including "keep thee only unto her." Look at her crying like she's really surprised by all this! She wanted the nice sheep so badly she didn't care that she could see his wolf fangs behind the mask.*

Well. Maybe Metaphorical Mean Quinn was right.

She looked around at the wedding announcements— *Joanne and Bernard Barton proudly announce the loving union of their daughter, Quinn Morgan Barton . . .* —and the clouds of white satin and tulle that filled Talk of the Gown, her family's bridal shop, where she had spent the past *six months* lovingly sewing her dream wedding gown, which now had dried mascara tears down the front of it and fucking *gum* on the back from when she was sitting on the curb outside the church, trying to figure out her life.

That's how all great decisions are made, right? Winston Churchill probably ground his coattails into three hundred years' worth of grime on a Downing Street corner and questioned, *Should we just give up and have some bratwurst? Ja or nein?*

But, actually, she didn't even have her own last-minute thoughts and hesitations. She couldn't even hang her hat on that small an accomplishment.

Her decision was handed to her by someone else instead. Well, not her *decision*—even though she was essentially left with only the one possibility, it was her own. But her options were certainly presented to her by the wrong person, in the wrong way, at the worst possible time. There she was, *literally* on her way to the altar, and her options were practically hand-engraved and sealed in an envelope that read *Pride*—clearly marked so she could take it or leave it forever.

As long as she lived, she would never forget the way it felt when Frank said she should stop while she still could. She'd thought it was a joke at first, yet she'd known—in that horrible gut way you sometimes know things—that it wasn't.

And now here she was, writing note after note after note, the same nine words; her only explanation to the two hundred guests who had come to see the fairy-tale wedding she'd dreamed about for years:

Chose the wrong guy, gave him the wrong finger.

She stopped. With maybe twelve more notes to go, she just stopped. And she went to the phone and dialed the number that was more familiar than her own.

It rang twice before there was an answer.

"Hi," she said, out of habit more than salutation. "It's me. I hate how everything happened today. And I totally hate how I feel now. I don't think I can get through this going back to my house and going to sleep and picking up my life like . . ." Her voice wavered and faded. She closed her eyes tight for a moment before taking a steadying breath. "Can you come to the shop and pick me up? I need to get out of here. Just get in the car and drive as far away as possible. Let's go to Vegas."

She only had to wait a moment for his answer.

Yes.

"Good," she said, and swallowed hard over the lump in her throat, looking at the work she'd done and knowing she was going to just pick up and go and leave it for her mother to clean up. Right now she just didn't care. She couldn't. "I'll see you out front."

She hung up the phone and picked up a few pieces of silvery wedding gift wrapping and tossed them in the general direction of the trash can. Some fell by the side, but she didn't pick them up.

Instead, she took a length of receipt paper from the cash register, pulled it out, and wrote a note to her mother on the back:

*Gone away for a few days. Don't worry, seriously. I'm
okay. I'll be back. Sorry to leave the paper all over.*

Then she set it down on the counter and went out front
to wait for Frank.

"Harbison continues to wow readers with charm and genuine characters."
—*Booklist*

"Touching, truthful, and profoundly satisfying."
— *Jen Lancaster, New York Times bestselling author*

"Will strike a chord with any woman who has ever looked in the mirror, or the bank account, and said, 'if only.'"
— *The Province (Vancouver)*

"As slick and enjoyable as a brand-new tube of lip gloss."
— *People*

"Zingy and funny."
— *Publishers Weekly*

"Like the designer shoes that pepper its pages, this book is pleasing and stylish."
— *Booklist*

 St. Martin's Griffin

Enjoy Beth Harbison in audio!
Narrated by Orlagh Cassidy.

Audiobooks available on CD and for digital download:

Shoe Addicts Anonymous
Secrets of a Shoe Addict
Hope in a Jar
Thin, Rich, Pretty
Always Something There to Remind Me
When in Doubt, Add Butter

Don't miss the next
Beth Harbison audiobook:

**Chose the Wrong Guy,
Gave Him the Wrong Finger**

Available July 2013

Visit www.macmillanaudio.com for audio samples and more!
Follow us on Facebook and Twitter.

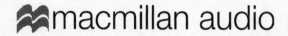